BEST LAID PLANS

A Cozy Mystery

Jo Lauer

www.jolauer.com

For Donna, who couldn't wait.

Acknowledgements

A writer's journey is not for the faint of heart. Without the support and encouragement from the following people, my best laid plans would have gone astray. Thank you to Kemari Howell for her brilliant editing and guidance, who refused to let me stop short the mark; Ronni Sanlo for publishing support; Trudy Vandell and Sue Spight, my second and third pair of eyes and truth-tellers; Marsh Rose for virtual hand-holding and life support; sister Sue Spight, brother Bill Bidwell, and daughter Sara Frampton who believe in me unconditionally; Andy Bauer, cover artist, for bringing into form the weird ideas in my mind; Kathryn Marcellino for her back cover and layout assistance; my writers group: Anne Marie, Dmitri, Nancy, Gayle and Kimberly who listened tirelessly to endless revisions; The Redwood Writers chapter of California Writers who are a font of inspiration, resources, and guidance. It takes a village.

BOOK ONE
THE FIRST STEP

Chapter 1

Jenny Pond hadn't planned to kill anyone, but fate has a lousy sense of humor.

"It was one of those sensual autumn days that just makes you want to hug a tree, you know?" Jenny said to Shalese. They sat by the window in Jenny's kitchen, a pot of tea and a plate of English muffins between them. The June sun sifted through the Venetian blinds and landed in soft stripes on the oak table.

"Cloudless, blue sky, warm breeze, that mulchy smell of the earth at the end of a long summer . . ." Jenny ran her hands slowly through her honey blonde hair, and it cascaded breeze-like through her fingers as she told her story for the first time since her release from prison a month ago.

She had met Shalese—a thirtyish, earnest, blue-collar social worker from Detroit—at a meeting of professional women at the local junior college last week.

"I was just walking along, minding my own business . . ." Jenny's voice trailed off. Her career had been derailed when she inadvertently murdered a man. Having served her time in prison, Jenny struggled to get her life back on track.

"Sorry Jen, you know we can't have a felon working in an investment firm," her former boss had said just last week. The tone of his voice made her feel stupid for even asking.

"Gee, sweetie, I'm just plain booked-up for the month, but maybe I'll see you at Marcie's party?" Kate said when Jenny called to let her know she was back. "Oh, I'm sorry," Kate said. "I guess you didn't get an invitation. None of us knew you'd be, uh . . ." Awkward couldn't begin to describe Jenny's attempts at reaching out.

1

Shalese DuBois was singly-focused on establishing a halfway house for female ex-felons. Jenny's story and desire to improve her life would be a perfect example of how a halfway house could benefit the community. In Shalese's more cynical mind, the fact that Jenny—white, twenty-nine, and a trust-fund baby from the Midwest—was not black, poor, or drug-addicted would be a plus.

The sun on the table was softening the stick of butter, and Shalese moved it to a shaded spot. A hummingbird stopped to admire its reflection in the window then zipped away. Jenny seemed lost in thought.

"So there you were, walking along," Shalese prompted. "Where were you headed?"

Jenny blinked. "Oh," she said, and continued. "My plan was to grab a latte and croissant at Starbucks on my way to the office where I worked as executive assistant to a trio of investment managers. I had a corner office with windows on the fifteenth floor of the Leblanc Tower," Jenny explained with a hint of pride.

"Impressive," Shalese said, jotting some details in her spiral-bound notebook. "You were on quite a career track before you . . ." Shalese faltered. In social work school, they'd taught her to do informational interviews of course, but never with a stunning blonde felon dressed in capris and a cute little tee with go-ahead-and-kill-me-now red toenail polish blinking up from barely sandaled feet. Shalese squirmed in her chair.

Jenny seemed not to have noticed. She focused on her hands, now folded on the table in front of her, and continued. "I was supposed to get married, you know—his name was Lawrence, and he was a law student, a perfectly nice guy—but I wanted more from life than cocktails at the club, Bridge, and a boatload of money that I didn't earn to spend on things I didn't need, which is pretty much the definition of my mother's life. When I came here, I left Ohio and Lawrence behind." She glanced up at Shalese and noticed a glazed look in her eyes. "I'm talking too much, right?" she asked.

"No. Go on," Shalese encouraged with a smile. "You were on your way to work . . ."

Jenny closed her eyes and tilted her head back, reliving the details as they unfolded. "I stopped under a cedar tree to retie my running shoes—which were easier to walk in than the three-inch Manolo knock-offs in my tote bag . . ." She opened one eye and squinted at

2

Shalese, whose eyebrow twitched slightly. "I needed those, really, I did. For work," Jenny justified. Eyes closed again, she resumed her story. "Nearby, I heard a dog bark—the friendly kind, not the scary kind."

From across the street, a little silver-blonde spaniel came running toward Jenny, wagging its stub like a metronome on high and making those happy barky sounds that make one feel they're the most special person in the world. Jenny had one of those when she was a kid. The dog, named Duchess, was her only friend and saved her from a life of solitude.

Feeling nostalgic, Jenny bent down to pet the spaniel when she heard a sharp crack behind her. The dog dropped with a thwump *on the ground next to her. Blood trickled from its ear. "Duchess!" she cried. Her stomach clenched in horror. She turned and saw a young man step from behind a tree. His jeans were undone and hung at an odd angle off one hip. He grinned stupidly and pointed his handgun at her. "Damned dog was gonna attack me," he babbled. He was missing one of his two front teeth, and he looked totally crazed. "I was just tryin' to take a piss," he said, waving his gun in the air.*

"You killed my dog!" Jenny screamed. Adrenaline replaced common sense as she grabbed a high heel from her tote bag, held it high over her head, and charged at him, wanting nothing more than to scare that smirk off his face. Without planning, she swung at his temple with all her strength and drove the point of the heel into the side of his head.

Jenny's hand flew to her mouth. Her eyes, already closed, squeezed more tightly shut. A tremor passed through her body. After a moment, she opened her eyes and looked at Shalese, who was grimacing.

Jenny paused in her story, placed one hand on her stomach, and the other on the tabletop as if to steady herself. She looked at the plate of muffins and her now-cold cup of tea and wrinkled her nose.

Shalese stopped writing in her notebook. "Do you need a break?" she offered, feeling guilty for having Jenny relive this nightmare for the sake of her grant proposal research. Jenny shook her head, took a slow, deep breath, glanced out the window for a moment, and then continued her story. "You know how they say you 'see red'? I wasn't trying to kill him. I just wanted him to stop . . ."

The young man fell over, crumpled on the sidewalk. Jenny clamped her hand over her mouth so she wouldn't throw up. He was still hanging on to his gun. If he'd twitched, it could have gone off. Someone screamed and screamed. It wasn't until an older woman from the house across the street came running over, grabbed Jenny's arm, and pulled her back, that Jenny realized she was the one screaming.

The woman nudged the man's leg with the toe of her house slipper. There was no movement. A shudder passed through her like the ghost of a memory. "Some murders are justifiable," she said, barely audibly.

The only dead people Jenny had ever seen had been in coffins, in situations where she wasn't responsible for their condition. This man was definitely dead, and she was definitely guilty. What kind of a person would do that—just kill a man, she wondered. He was probably someone's son, or brother, or boyfriend even. She turned and threw up on the woman's house slippers.

"My name is Florence Wilson, dear," the woman said. "Is there someone I could call for you? Family, perhaps?"

"I'm Jenny—Jenny Pond," Jenny managed. Florence tilted her head, lifted an eyebrow at the name. "Thank you, Florence, but my family is back in Ohio. My grandparents used to live here, but they're dead now," she said. "Oh, gosh, I'm babbling," she said.

"Shock, dear," Florence commented as she patted Jenny's arm.

"I guess it would be helpful if you called my folks." With a shaky hand, Jenny extricated a pen and scrap of paper from her tote, wrote down her father's name and number, and handed it to Florence.

Florence glanced at the note and attempted to hide a gasp behind the pretense of a cough.

Florence told Jenny she and her husband, Herb, were dog-sitting the little spaniel, Mica, for her sister-in-law, who was vacationing in Hawaii after her last chemo treatment. Florence seemed really upset and kept fingering her strand of pearls as if it were a rosary. She stayed until the police came and arrested Jenny.

Jenny's lashes fluttered for a long moment after she finished her story, and then her eyes opened wide.

Chapter 2

"I need air," Jenny said, rising suddenly. She opened the kitchen door, stepped out onto the balcony, and inhaled deeply. Shalese followed her. She watched Jenny stretch cat-like in the warmth of the sun.

"You okay?" Shalese asked. Jenny nodded.

"Was that the last you saw of Florence?" Shalese asked, ready to tie up the interview.

"Oh, no. Not at all. She visited me weekly in jail. I don't know what I would have done without her."

Florence followed the cruiser to the county jail, where Jenny was booked and led to a cell. Florence told the detective everything she knew, which wasn't much, so she embellished ever-so-slightly. "It was self-defense," she said. "That horrible man killed my dog in plain daylight with what I'm sure was an illegal gun, then threatened poor Jenny—an innocent bystander who had just been horribly traumatized." Florence worked her beads. "How very terrible," she added.

At Jenny's request, Florence phoned the Ponds in Ohio. What are the chances, she wondered. The age could be about right for a granddaughter of Gloria's. "Pond rezdence," answered a voice on the other end of the line.

"May I speak with Victor Pond," Florence requested. For the briefest moment, the years melted away replaced by the image of a young towhead, dressed in a miniature sailor suit, clinging to his mother. Could it really be, Florence wondered.

"Who's callin' please?"

"This is Fl . . . Just tell him Mrs. Wilson is calling from California regarding his daughter, Jenny."

"Yes ma'am," the woman answered and laid the phone down with a clunk loud enough to make Florence flinch. "Mr. Pond," she heard the woman screech in the background, "someone callin' you 'bout Jenny."

5

"This is Victor Pond," said a distinguished voice.

Florence introduced herself and relayed the recent event that had landed his daughter in jail.

"I'm catching the first flight out," Victor said. "Please tell Jenny I'll be there by tomorrow morning at the latest. Thank you, Mrs. Wilson. I look forward to meeting you soon."

The wheels of justice that you often hear move so slowly spun along as if in four-wheel drive, and a trial date was set. Florence was there daily for the two weeks, but kept a low profile in the back of the courtroom and made sure to be 'unavailable' when Victor suggested they meet—not that he would have recognized her, but why take unnecessary chances.

Filled with the twists and turns of the trial, Florence came home after a particularly long day at court. "The parents of the punk hired a shark of a lawyer, who made a case for the kid being off his meds, and pleaded he was the mentally and pharmaceutically challenged victim here," she reported to her husband who refused to set foot inside a courtroom. He referred to the Hall of Justice as the Hell of Injustice. Herb was having a hard time giving up his ex-pat status since returning to the states. The American systems of governance left him cold. Had his only living relative not been diagnosed with cancer last year, they would never have returned.

"Seems the pharmacy inadvertently substituted a diuretic for his Abilify," Florence said with a tsk at the stupidity of human error. Herb gave a dismissive nod and went back to reading his paper.

The day the trail ended and Jenny was sentenced to prison, Florence was flushed with an excitement that Herb could never understand and could only barely tolerate. It was akin to watching the lions at the zoo at feeding hour.

The following day, assured that Victor had returned to Ohio as soon as Jenny was 'situated,' Florence began her weekly ritual of driving the two hours to the prison and waiting in the visitor's reception room with a sea of poorly dressed, smelly, noisy humanity, and women with long, bright red acrylic nails and way too much hair spray. Red plastic chairs were bolted to the floor. Who would want to steal such revolting pieces of plastic, she wondered. She was required to place her possessions in a filthy, metal locker and deposit a quarter, which would release the key from the lock. Florence would only retrieve the key by wrapping a tissue around it. Who knows what you could catch in a place like this.

If anyone had asked her why she continued her visits—which no one had—she would have been hard-pressed to come up with an answer. Something had been awakened in her, a sense of power and control, a knowledge that she could have a hand in moving the wheels of justice at a pace that suited her.

On her third visit, Florence spoke into the disc in the glass partition between them. "How is it going, dear? You look pale," she observed. The disc distorted her voice, making her feel like she was speaking into the wrong end of a megaphone.

"There's not much sunlight in the courtyard, and we only get half an hour a day outside," Jenny said without much enthusiasm. "Oh, and thank you again for watering my plants and garden. That's so much to ask of you."

"Not a problem, dear. Thank you for trusting me with the key to your apartment. Are you eating well?" Florence asked. Conversation with a prisoner was strained, something akin to sitting by the bedside of the dying.

"We had turkey something-or-other last night and taco salad today. It's food. I'd give it half a star on a generous day."

"Did you get the book, notebook, and calendar from Amazon?" Florence asked.

"Yes, thanks. I've been marking off the days. They all sort of run together," she answered. "Oh, and thanks for sending the tee shirt for sleep. One of the other girls said if you save up a couple days pee without flushing, you can tie-dye fabric in the toilet." With a slight smile, she added, "It works."

"God forbid," muttered Florence. "Not much longer now, dear," she promised at the end of each visit.

Jenny had no other visitors. The investment managers avoided prison as if it were a contagion. Lawrence was no doubt nursing the pain of a broken ego after Jenny called off the engagement. Jenny realized, after the fact, that she really didn't have a social network, or friends for that matter—nor did she suppose she deserved that sort of support.

On the first Tuesday of Jenny's eighth month of incarceration, she waited in her cell to be notified of Florence's arrival. To pass the time, she looked around her cell, noted the décor—a toilet, a sink, a *sleeping shelf that was bolted to the wall with metal straps—and prepared to play another mental round of Flip This House. She leaned back in her white plastic lawn chair, propped her feet on the sleeping shelf, and gazed up at the only source of natural light—a small rectangular window several feet above her head.*

Metal doors slid back and forth in the hallway, always closing with that cold clang that set Jenny's teeth on edge. Guards with firm grips accompanied the women to and from the visitors' area. Jenny waited. She thumbed through a magazine, seeing nothing. Still no Florence. Just as Jenny was giving up hope and settling into a good funk, a guard opened her door and led her from her cell to a special hearing where she was told the charges against her were dismissed. She was released. Jenny was dazed and greatly relieved to find Florence waiting outside the chambers to drive her home.

"I can't believe I was released so early on involuntary manslaughter charges," she said, as they put away the groceries they'd stopped for on the way home.

When they were done, Jenny settled on the couch and looked around the room. She noted how well her plants had survived under Florence's care in her absence. "I could have been in prison for years," she said with a shudder.

"Life is full of mysteries, dear. At my age, one learns not to question them too much." Florence sat opposite Jenny on an overstuffed chair and smiled at her own reflection in the beveled mirror over Jenny's couch. She reached over and pinched off a dying bloom from the cymbidium that sat on a three-legged table near the window. "You'll need some support, I imagine, now that you're free." She moved the orchid to a spot on the windowsill with more direct light.

"Support? I still have my trust fund to hold me over. And I have all my friends from work . . ."

"Well, dear, things may be a bit challenging socially, now that you're officially an ex-felon." She heard Jenny suck in a quick breath. I guess that little fact hadn't occurred to her, Florence thought. "I know, dear, it's unjust, but it's the way it is," she offered with just the right amount of wisdom and sympathy. "I have an idea," she said as she readied to leave. "Let me work on it; it may take a while. You know you can count on me, don't you, Jenny?"

"*Florence, you've done so much for me already. I'm so grateful. I don't know what I'd do without you,*" *Jenny said as she walked Florence to the door.*

"*My pleasure, dear.*" *Florence stepped through the door and called back over her shoulder,* "*You're like the granddaughter I never had.*" *Florence rolled her eyes skyward as she walked down the sidewalk.*

More like you're my Gloria's granddaughter. I suppose it's the least I could do to keep some sort of eye on her grandchild. Something that could pass for a moment of nostalgia flickered in Florence's eyes, then extinguished.

Later that week, Florence met with her old comrade, Sidney, at a café near the JC campus. She and Sidney were the sole survivors of a group of tightly knit and well-connected friends dating back to the 1940s. Over the years of Florence's absence, friends moved, changed positions, died. It had been difficult rebuilding the group ever since Florence's return a year ago—the younger generation had such a different set of ethics. However, greed and power still existed within the human heart, and rebuild they had.

"*Sidney, dear,*" *Florence said as she bussed his cheek,* "*you're looking dapper today.*" *They settled into their seats and gave the waitress their drink orders* "*This young Jenny I've been telling you about—I'm quite sure she's Gloria's grandchild.*" *It was good to say this to someone who knew what that meant. Herb, who she'd met and married five years ago in England, had no clue about her life that preceded him. It was a mixed blessing—he was a wonderful cover for her safe return.*

"*That's remarkable,*" *Sidney said.* "*I remember how hard you took the news of Gloria's death.*"

"*I loved her,*" *Florence said with an unfamiliar, quiet vulnerability.*

"*Perhaps this will be some solace for you.*"

"*Perhaps,*" *Florence echoed. She jutted out her chin like a period ending that train of thought.*

Sidney—a wealthy octogenarian with a twinkle in his eye that came from the knowledge he still had full control of his faculties, his choices, and the lives of others—reached across the table, took Florence's hand, and placed a kiss on her fingers, brushing her

9

knuckles with his full silver moustache. *Still lovely after all these years,* he thought, and smiled warmly.

"And how goes your project, Sidney?" Florence asked in a quiet voice once the waitress stopped hovering about their table.

"This one was unspeakably easy," he said. He released her hand with a gentle pat, lifted his gin and tonic, and said, "To the past, present, and future." They clinked glasses. With great animation, Sidney shared his findings.

"There've been a number of inquiries about criminal justice grant money by a Shalese DuBois. Seems she's interested in rehabilitating women ex-felons. Our sources say she's ripe for the kind of funding our group has available. If we can find a way around her blue-collar pride, she could provide just the kind of access we could use." Sidney swirled his drink and took another sip.

"And what do you see as our next step?" Florence asked.

"We have to find some way to get to her," Sidney said. "That may be difficult—apparently, the woman is gay. Our usual 'dashing young man sweeps fair young maiden off her feet' routine isn't going to cut it," he scoffed.

"Well," Florence said, finishing her martini, "let me think about this. I just might have an idea." She dabbed at her lips with her napkin. *Manipulating resources—that's what made Florence's heart race.* In that way, she and Sidney were gleefully similar.

Sidney nodded. He reached down, removed his shoe, and rubbed his foot, noting he really should have that bunion looked at as soon as time allowed. "It's good to be back in business, my dear."

Chapter 3

Shalese sat quietly, waiting for Jenny to continue. She could sit and look at this woman for a long time, she realized.

Jenny took a deep breath and leaned back in her chair. She rubbed her neck, stretched her shoulders back, and rolled her head from side to side after recounting the story that led to her new identity as an ex-felon. "Ever since I got out, I've felt sort of lost and confused about what I'm doing. Thank goodness for the trust fund. I don't think I could concentrate enough to hold down a job. Prison sort of takes away all sense of who you are. So does taking someone's life," she confided.

Shalese nodded. She could only imagine. A twang of compassion plucked at her heart.

"So, tell me more about this halfway house idea. That's what you're looking for money to fund, right?" Jenny asked. "What is it that you want to do, exactly?" She got up, dumped the cold cups of tea in the sink, refilled their cups, sat back down, and took a bite out of a muffin. Her movements were fluid, like a choreographed dance.

What I want, Shalese thought, *is to know what happened to Lawrence, and whether there's anyone else.* "What I want," Shalese said aloud, "is to fund a halfway house to rehabilitate female felons after their release from prison. Especially those who served time for defending themselves against abuse," she amended. "I believe women are more amenable to rehab than men." Shalese held the teacup between her palms and breathed in the aroma of jasmine.

"Why is that?" Jenny was fascinated by the contrast of Shalese's strong, dark fingers against the fragile white cup.

"Women learn from cause and effect. The lower recidivism rate suggests that. Also, the trauma of having committed a crime of felony proportion is more life impairing for women who, due to their gender alone, already start out a rung down on the socio-economic ladder."

Jenny grinned. "You sound like a doctoral thesis." Shalese blushed and took a sip of her tea. "No," Jenny backtracked, "that's a good thing. I mean, you really know your stuff."

"So, what is it that you want?" Shalese asked.

"I just want to get my life back on track. Being one of those ex-felon types, I'm having trouble finding work. Do you really think anyone is going to be interested in rehabbing a woman who commits murder by shoe?" Jenny asked, trying to lighten the conversation for both their sakes. "What?" she said, noticing that Shalese looked puzzled.

"I'm wondering why you would even want to work. I mean, you have a trust fund and all . . ." Shalese shifted uncomfortably in her chair, unable to meet Jenny's eyes. She'd never understood the ways of the wealthy.

Jenny took a moment to compose herself. She could feel her jaw clench and her eyes narrow. "How presumptuous of you," she said, hands fisted on hips. "Do you ask welfare mothers why they'd want to go back to work when they've got the government supporting them?" She leaned forward aggressively.

Shalese's eyes widened in surprise. She opened her mouth to speak but Jenny beat her to the punch.

"It's a matter of self-esteem, of pride in doing a job well, of accomplishing something, of making a difference," she ranted on, her voice rising. Shalese looked at her with a mixture of admiration and astonishment. "I don't want to be dependent upon my parents' money, for God's sake, I'm an adult. I want to provide for myself because I can, because I'm intelligent, and skilled." As if someone had pulled her plug, she withered back into her seat, drained, spent.

Shalese's eyes crinkled, her lips turned up slightly at the corners, and she shrugged. "Okay, then. Good to know." She felt pressured to finish the interview, but that tirade had gotten under her skin—not in a bad way. She'd rather just hang out with Jenny—curl up on the couch, watch a movie, eat popcorn. The girl intrigued her.

Jenny slathered partially melted butter on half an English muffin and munched it thoughtfully. "I feel pretty passionate about that, I guess." Shalese raised her eyebrows. "That said, I do have money, and I'm in a position to help with the funding, if you'd let me."

"No. Absolutely not," Shalese said, putting an end to further discussion of the matter.

With arched eyebrows at the quick rebuff, Jenny passed the plate of muffins to Shalese, who fumbled it. Muffins tumbled onto the table. Rattled, Shalese gathered them up, put them back on the plate. She wiped her hands quickly on her pants.

"A few more questions," Shalese said, regaining control. "How did that whole experience change you? I mean, prison is life altering, I'd think." Shalese dunked her muffin in the tea, leaving little golden crumbs floating on the surface.

"Well, I don't pack stilettos anymore." Jenny grimaced at the memory. She paused and stared at the teapot. "You know, I hadn't really thought about that until just this minute." She offered to refresh Shalese's tea.

Shalese covered her cup with her left hand and made a note on her pad. That Jenny no longer wore stylish shoes was not a big selling point. "Got anything else?" She glanced at Jenny.

"Brandy?" Jenny offered.

"No, I mean, what else did you learn from your time in prison?"

"I had a lot of time to think. I learned that money can't solve all problems, that for every behavior there is a consequence, and that being young in prison is not an advantage." Her hands, clutched in her lap, twisted against each other. "Oh, and I learned a craft while I was incarcerated."

"Yes?" Shalese's eyebrows rose a quarter-inch above those soft brown eyes that took in everything.

"I learned how to tie-dye," Jenny said. Shalese squinted at her like she was out of focus.

Jenny sighed. "Not exactly a cottage industry, but it passed the time."

Shalese leaned forward. "Let me get down to the real question," she said. Jenny leaned forward, elbows on the table, her chin cupped in her hands. "What would keep you from killing again?"

Jenny thought for a moment. "A ban on handguns."

"You didn't kill him with a gun, you killed him with a . . ."

"Yeah, I know—a stiletto. What I mean is if he hadn't shot that poor little dog, he'd be alive today. Or at least, I wouldn't have been the one who killed him. I may have ruined my life." Jenny stared at the table. "All the wealth and privilege, the advantages I've had growing up in my family couldn't even save me from this one. I really screwed up," she said softly and wiped a renegade tear from her cheek with her knuckle. "Can you help me?"

Shalese's heart melted like the butter in the dish on the table. She looked into Jenny's eyes and said, "If I can get funding for this halfway house, I think I can help you and a lot of other women get their lives back on track." She was rewarded with a smile that made more than her heart melt.

Shalese clicked the top of her pen rhythmically. "One last question. What became of you and Lawrence? I mean, Florence?" she quickly corrected herself. Shalese cleared her throat, flipped to a new page in her notebook, and wrote 'Support System' at the top.

After a beat, Jenny said, "Florence calls me weekly, just to stay in touch. As it turns out, some guy shot a friend of hers a long time ago. Seeing swastika-head lying there dead was some sort of closure for her, I guess. That's an odd basis for a friendship, don't you think? Trauma bonding, I think they call it."

Shalese made a noncommittal sound.

"And she gave my name to Janelle at Women's Studies, who invited me to that networking mixer," Jenny added. "Funny what life brings you. If it hadn't been for Florence, you and I would have never met."

Chapter 4

In a small office in the Women's Studies department, a young woman with brown hair severely pulled back and pinned in a tight bun, removed a diamond stud earring and held the receiver to her ear. "Hello, is this Jenny Pond?" she inquired. Her British accent made "Jenny" sound like "Janey."

"Yes, it is," Jenny said, relieved to have a reason to stop working on the crossword puzzle that had her wrinkling her brow and chewing her pencil eraser.

"Jenny, my name is Janelle Anderson. I believe we have a friend in common, Florence Wilson. She suggested I give you a call."

"Oh, well, Florence—yes, of course. What can I do for you, Janelle?" How odd, Jenny thought. Florence hadn't mentioned she'd spoken to anyone about her.

"It may be more like what I can do for you," Janelle said pleasantly. "I'd like to invite you to an end of year soiree we're hosting here at the junior college. Just a gathering of young women professionals—drinks, networking, you know. Florence thought that might appeal to you, and I'd love to meet you. What do you say?"

"Oh, I don't know, Janelle; I've had sort of an interruption in my career . . ."

"An even better reason to come and get to know some people; you never know who you'll meet. Truthfully, Jenny, this wonderful woman named Shalese will be there—she's a social worker, I believe—who is just driven by the idea of starting a halfway house for women ex-felons."

"Oh!" Jenny let out a little gasp. "Did Florence talk to you about . . ."

"I'm so sorry," Janelle apologized. "I guess I should have mentioned that right off. Anyway, Shalese is hoping to do some research for a grant proposal. I think you'd find it interesting."

"Uh . . ." Jenny, taken off guard, was speechless.

"Really, it would be perfect," Janelle continued, *"you could network with others about job possibilities in your field, and help Shalese with her research at the same time. Oh, she would be so grateful. It's a win-win,"* she said cheerfully.

"I, ah . . ."

"This Friday, May thirtieth —we'll meet for cocktails at six at the Women's Studies office on campus and have a more formal gathering around seven. I'm so excited to meet you, Jenny. I know you'll enjoy yourself. I'll see you then, right?" Janelle said.

"Uh, okay, I guess. Bye." Jenny hung up the phone and sat down heavily on a kitchen chair. She felt like she'd just been shaken about by an English bulldog. As the information filtered into her mind, she had to admit, it wasn't a bad idea after all. She picked up her pencil and filled in V-E-L-L-U-M in the spaces across. *"If I were playing Scrabble, I'd have just scored big,"* she said aloud.

Across town, Janelle dialed the next number on her list. *"Is this Shalese DuBois?"* she asked of the woman with the soft voice and slight southern twang who answered the phone.

"It is. Who's calling?" Shalese lowered herself into the rocking chair next to the phone table in her living room.

"Shalese, we haven't met; my name is Janelle Anderson. I'm a research specialist with the Women's Studies department at the junior college."

"Yes," Shalese said, her voice brittle, hard, and sharp like thick, broken glass. She didn't like being called by people she didn't know, it reminded her of childhood—bill collectors, angry landlords, and all that. She especially didn't trust people with English accents, irrational as she knew that to be.

Undaunted, Janelle continued. *"Part of what I do is data collection on research hits for various grant sites. Your name came up as a regular on the Department of Justice site . . ."*

"My name came up?" Shalese interrupted, aghast.

"Oh you know, the Internet—nothing is sacred anymore," Janelle brushed off Shalese's concern about privacy and quickly refocused. *"I'm calling you to invite you to a soiree here at Women's Studies, a networking/cocktails sort of thing—casual, you know—where you will meet other young professional women who might be useful contacts or who might know someone who knows someone. There's one woman in particular I'm sure you'd like to speak with. Her name is Jenny Pond*

and she was just released from prison for involuntary manslaughter—having a hard time readjusting to life, don't you know."

Shalese, still wondering how her name came up in connection with her grant research, was only half listening to Janelle. She did, however, hear the "just released from prison" part and the "hard time readjusting to life." Right down her alley. A woman who might need her help.

"I'll have to check my calendar, but when did you say the 'soiree' was?" Shalese rolled her eyes—a soiree? Really? Sounds like one of those white-women things, she thought. She'd rather take a hot poker to the eye.

Janelle gave her the information, said she was looking forward to meeting her, and hung up.

* * *

Friday morning, Shalese stood scowling at her closet. "What the hell do you wear to a soiree?" she asked of the shirts, slacks, coats, vests, and shoes assembled there. She pulled out something that she hoped looked enough like urban professional to pass, dressed quickly, and left for her office.

At four o'clock, Jenny sank into a bathtub full of lavender-scented bubbles. At four-thirty, she touched up her toenails with opalescent white polish. At five, she rummaged through her closet and extracted a simple black dress and a pair of low pumps. She Googled a map of campus and located Women's Studies. By five-thirty, her hair and make-up were done, and she was on her way to the networking event.

"Excuse me . . ." A rather imposing black woman approached Jenny as she stepped out of her car in the JC parking lot. Jenny startled. It was summer session and there were few cars and fewer people in sight. She cast a furtive glance toward the Quad.

"Do you happen to know where the Women's Studies building is? I'm completely turned around," the woman said. The expression on her face was as if she were about to hand someone a trunk load of bad news. She was perhaps five-eight, one-hundred-eighty pounds, and walked with determination. She wore her Afro close to her head, sported a jagged scar that ran from the corner of her left eye down her cheek in a lightning bolt pattern, and her right front tooth was capped in gold. She was dressed in khakis, a blue button-down shirt, and a

casual suede leather jacket with what could only be described as practical shoes. By comparison, Jenny felt insubstantial and overdressed.

"Are you going to the networking function, by any chance?" Jenny asked. On closer inspection, she kind of liked this woman's style—not masculine exactly, but certainly strong, no nonsense.

"Uh, yeah—I mean, yes," Shalese stammered. This beautiful, green-eyed, blonde woman, all sleeked out, was making her tongue-tied. That dress. Shit, next to her, I look like a ragamuffin, she groaned inwardly.

"Jenny Pond," Jenny said and extended her hand. "I Google-mapped it right before I left." She smiled.

"Shalese DuBois," she said, taking Jenny's hand. Soft. Nail polish. Not a crooked tooth in that mouth, Shalese surmised. Braces probably. No one in my neighborhood ever had braces.

"Shalese?" Jenny said, studying her. "You must be the social worker Janelle mentioned," she said as they walked toward a vine-covered building across the Quad.

Shalese grinned—she tried not to, felt foolish doing it—but couldn't seem to help herself. The woman had an effect on her. "You must be the . . ." Shalese trailed off, mortified. Dumb, dumb, dumb, she kicked herself mentally.

"Yeah, ex-felon," Jenny supplied, with a mirthful chuckle. She looked sideways through long blonde lashes at Shalese. The glint of the gold-capping on Shalese's front tooth caught Jenny's attention; she stumbled on the flagstone pathway and let out a yelp.

Shalese grabbed her arm, swayed to maintain her balance, and wound up with Jenny plastered to the front of her.

"Gosh, and we hardly know each other," Jenny giggled. Shalese blushed.

The rest of the evening, a gathering of young, professional women to network and share resources, passed in a blur for Shalese. She was never very good at the socializing thing, and this was way out of her comfort zone.

"I'm Ann," a young Asian woman cornered her. "I'm an Anthropology major."

Shalese clamped her teeth to keep from saying, Whoa, dig that. "Shalese, Social Work," she said instead. What's with this introducing yourself by your major thing, she wondered. Ann nodded and moved on. This must be what speed-dating is like, Shalese thought.

"Dr. Jessie Biggs," *a buxom redhead said, pumping Shalese's hand,* "Psychology."

How unfortunate, on so many levels, Shalese thought. "Nice to meet you," *she said.* "Shalese DuBois." *The woman looked at her expectantly.* "Social Work," *Shalese added and was graced with a smile.*

"We should definitely get together for drinks soon," *Dr. Jessie said before moving on.*

She tried to keep the names, faces, and professions straight, but she was having trouble concentrating. There was no sign of Janelle Anderson, no irritating accents in the crowd. The wine was good, the food a little rich for her taste—Brie, a caramelized onion-and-fig spread, chunks of sourdough, some raw fish things Shalese didn't recognize, and a pate. Pate? Isn't that like goose liver? she smirked inwardly. Toward the end of the evening, she sat down next to Jenny at a mostly empty table.

"Listen, do you think we could talk about your recent experience sometime? I'd like to tell you about my project—it might be something that you'd be interested in," *Shalese said. And even if you're not, I'd sure like to see you again, Shalese thought.*

"How does next Saturday sound? Mid-morning? Ten-ish?" *Jenny offered.*

Shalese bit her lip to keep from saying, I've got a bad wrist, so I don't play ten-ish. She felt awkward—like a teenager—and stupid. She corralled her adult and said, "Ten is good. I really appreciate it." *They said their goodbyes and Shalese left, wondering if she could find her way back to the parking lot.*

Granny, she appealed to her dead grandmother with whom she had a special working relationship, what's wrong with me? I'm comin' undone, and over a white girl, no less.

Chapter 5

The day after her interview with Jenny Pond, Shalese climbed the stairs to her makeshift office—a walk-up room over a Mexican restaurant—to type up her interview. With her laptop on the fritz, she sat hunched over a Corona manual typewriter with a missing "q" key. The phone jangled on the desk and jarred her concentration. It was Sunday, for God's sake—who calls on a Sunday?

"The First Step—this is Shalese," she said, trying out the name she'd come up with for her project. She felt the impatience in her voice, and tried to convince herself that it was the interruption of thought, not the obsession with Jenny, that irritated her.

"This is Florence Wilson," the woman said, in a cultured yet reedy voice of the elderly. "I'm an acquaintance of Jenny Pond. She said you might be looking for staff for your halfway house." Florence was nothing if not adept at utilizing her resources. Now that she'd established a friendship with Jenny, what better way to manipulate the relationship between Shalese and Jenny than to be an integral part of Shalese's dream? With any luck, no one would get harmed. Well, no one she didn't wish to be, that is.

"Ah, yes, Mrs. Wilson. I just interviewed Jenny yesterday and she mentioned your name." Shalese circled the woman's name in her notes, drew an arrow to the margin, and wrote *possible staff.* "I'm afraid I'm not at the point of being able to afford a staff at this time. I'm still looking for funding, but—"

"I'd like to volunteer my time to help you, dear," Florence interrupted. "I know some influential people," she continued, "who helped me out when I most needed a hand. Perhaps we could meet for tea?"

Tea? Shalese was in no position to turn her back on free help. "I'm meeting Jenny this evening after work at the wine bar, K Syrah, on Third Street. Care to join us?" *Crap,* Shalese admonished herself silently. She was hoping to step out of her comfort zone a little—well, a lot, actually—and get to know Jenny better. Having Florence there would be a real buzz kill to the excitement of that possibility.

"Thank you, dear. I've been looking for a good cabernet. Sixish?"

Tenish? Sixish? *Must be a rich folk thing,* Shalese surmised. "Sixish is good. See you then." Shalese hung up the phone. "This should be interesting," she said to her reflection in the window. "So what do you wear to a wine bar?"

In the tiny parking lot of K Syrah, there was an open spot next to Jenny's silver Miata—a car that smacked of white privilege in Shalese's book. She eased her old Honda in, turned off the ignition, and sat listening to the chatter and laughter of the early crowd on the patio. She unbuttoned the top button of her shirt, took a deep breath, slung her dressy jacket over her shoulder, and gently opened the car door, hoping to avoid the usual skreek of the hinge. *Skreek.* "Damn," she muttered.

The old stone building looked like a place where you'd find big-bosomed wenches draped over fat squires drunk on ale. The cobblestone pathway led to an intricately engraved oak door that opened into a dimly lit bar. Small red shades dripping crystals hung over low watt bulbs giving the bar a womb-like feeling. Wine glasses glinted overhead, suspended upside down from a light oak rack. Soft music, something mid-eastern with zithers, gongs, and chimes, subdued the clink of glassware and china.

Shalese spotted Jenny and Florence at a corner table. Introductions were made and the usual small talk gotten out of the way while they squinted in the dimness at the oversized menus. A New Age Earth goddess named Brie guided them through the specials and returned shortly with the first round of wine and a variety of tapas to begin their evening. Shalese felt like she'd stepped into an ad in one of those pretentious California living magazines, but Jenny seemed quite at home, as did Florence in her matching sweater set and pearls.

Florence swirled her cabernet, checked the color and clarity, and took a sip. "Mmm," she moaned, "when you start with the best, where else is there to go? So tell me dear, how did this dream of a halfway house come about?" She leaned back in her chair, hands folded in her lap, and looked at Shalese the way people watch pigeons from a park bench.

Jenny was absorbed in spreading soft smelly cheese drizzled with truffle oil on a crisp of bread, her mouth puckered in concentration.

She wore a serpentine green sleeveless dress the color of her eyes, and her blonde hair was caught back in a casual bun with wisps curling along her cheekbone.

If I were in the desert, she'd be one long, cool sip of water, Shalese thought. She unglued her eyes from Jenny and with difficulty fixed them on Florence. "Long story short," she said, "a friend of mine was married to an abuser. When she recovered from the latest near-death beating, she bought a gun and shot him in the . . . well, crippled him for life. Went to prison, and a week after she got paroled, he hunted her down and killed her." Shalese sat back with a sigh, reached for her chardonnay, and then changed her mind, unsure that she could swallow right then. Memories of Vanessa's petite body lying in a pool of blood on the living room floor came rushing back. She shook her head slowly. "She never had a chance to start over."

"So, that's what you want to do—give women a chance to start over," Florence said, "create a different life for themselves." She forked a bacon-wrapped scallop into her mouth and chewed thoughtfully. Shalese nodded.

Jenny swallowed a bite of butternut squash orzo and smiled. She fingered a strand of small amber beads that hung around her neck and looked at Shalese from under long blonde lashes. "Where did she go when she got out—your friend? Where did he find her?" she said, joining the conversation.

"My house. I was at work. I couldn't protect her. Will you excuse me for a moment?" Shalese said, blotting at her eye with the corner of her cocktail napkin as she left the table.

"Oh dear, that poor girl," Florence said.

"Shalese or her friend?"

"Both," Florence said and took another sip of her cabernet.

Shalese stumbled into the ladies' room and splashed water on her face to wash away the memory—front door ajar, place tossed, a bare foot sticking out from the other side of the couch. She tasted bile in her throat, and grabbed the sink counter to steady herself until the feeling passed. Post-traumatic stress, the therapist had said, sometimes will sneak up on you and take you by surprise. *Damn straight,* she thought.

"Sorry," she said as she slipped back into her chair moments later. She looked away when she caught Jenny gazing at her.

"Understandable, dear," Florence said. She reached over and patted Shalese's hand.

"Thank you," Shalese said, and cleared her throat. It had been a very long time since anyone had patted her hand. "So, Florence, what is it about my project that catches your interest?" she asked, trying to regain her composure.

Florence took a moment before answering. Her jaw set, her eyes narrowed, and her shoulders seemed to square themselves. "The idea of justice, I believe. It comes in many forms," she said, her voice husky with emotion. "Women unfairly imprisoned, unable to start their lives over, victimized by the system, and cast out from society," she leaned forward, her eyes ablaze, "need a hand correcting the wrongs done to them." She pounded the table emphatically with her fist and made the silverware clink.

Shalese glanced around, hoping no one had noticed. "Do you believe Jenny was unfairly imprisoned? She did, after all, kill a man, and it wasn't self defense."

"He was a scourge on society." Florence's breathing became labored as she continued, "He thought he was invincible."

"The DA said he was schizophrenic," Shalese offered.

"He traumatized an upstanding citizen by killing a poor, defenseless animal right in front of her—with an illegal handgun in broad daylight, no less," she wheezed. "Unforgivable! Urban justice, that's what Jenny provided," she said, her earlier genteel demeanor replaced now by that of a crazed vigilante.

Shalese noted the transformation and struggled to stay focused. "Jenny told me your friend was killed by a man with a handgun. Did he go to prison?"

It was as if a dark shadow wrapped itself around Florence as she recalled the night she watched the life drain out of the congressman through the small caliber hole she had just put in his head.

Yes, they'd all been drinking—heavily, truth be told. But that was no excuse; it did not give him permission to put his filthy hands on her friend, make lewd suggestions about the three of them slipping off to his cabin. When her friend had screamed and slapped him, he'd twisted her arm behind her and forced her onto the floor. In the struggle, he ripped her skirt and called her a whore. She fought harder, and he'd pulled a gun from his pocket and shot her. Just shot her. It all happened so quickly. Florence snapped out of the fear-induced paralysis she'd been in and kicked the gun from his hand. It had been self-defense—well, friend-defense, more accurately, she supposed. She shot him just as Gloria ran into the room, screaming loud enough to wake the vineyard owners down the hill. Florence silenced her and swore her to secrecy.

They found an unbelievable sum of money stashed in his pockets and briefcase—who knew congressmen carried that much cash—probably from an off-shore account, possibly traceable. Money being the least of her worries and knowing she was going to have to make herself scarce for a while, she figured burying the money for later retrieval would be the safest move. As a last minute thought, she drew a cryptic map on a sheet of paper and hid it where only she or Gloria would remember.

Florence pursed her lips for a moment, stretched her neck like a bird about to preen its feathers, and then said to Shalese, "He met with an unfortunate accident before he could be apprehended." She patted her forehead with her napkin, shifted in her chair, and stared at her empty plate.

"Urban justice?" Shalese ventured, and noticed a twitch of a smile rearrange Florence's lips.

Chapter 6

The next morning, Shalese phoned Jenny. "I'm afraid she's a bit of a maverick, maybe even a loose cannon," she said of Florence. "I don't want to step on your toes, Jenny, but how well do you know this woman, really? Do you know her family or where she's from? Do you know how long she's lived here? Have you met her husband?"

"Well, no," Jenny said. "I guess maybe she knows me better than I know her—but she's been such a support to me. Really, Shalese, I think she's harmless. She's just passionate about righting what she believes are wrongs, like women not getting a fair shake after having served their time. She has some wealthy friends, influential people. I think she could be an asset, Shalese and you're going to need a board of directors."

"You don't suppose those 'influential people' were responsible for the 'unfortunate accident' that befell her friend's murderer, do you? Something about her really creeps me out." Shalese glanced down at the paper she was doodling on—a noose. She flipped the paper over. A shiver wiggled up her spine. *Granny, you trying to tell me something?* She sent the question up into the ethers.

"You're sounding a little paranoid," Jenny teased.

"I'm concerned that somewhere in her twisted mind, you're some kind of a hero to her for wiping out yet another bad guy. I don't want to be used to further someone else's warped agenda."

"How could she use you? Honestly, Shalese, you should hear yourself . . ."

"Yeah, you're probably right. It's just—oh, forget it. Are you free for lunch by any chance? I mean, I thought we could go over the proposal I've written up."

"Sure," Jenny said, sounding enthusiastic. "It's a beautiful summer day. Why don't we meet at the Square and grab some hot dogs from the vendor. We'll have a picnic. Noon?"

"Noon it is," she said. Shalese noticed that each time she spoke to Jenny, she felt like she was not the one in charge. Jenny was headstrong, direct—qualities Shalese usually liked in a woman, but she had to admit, Jenny scared her a little. Shalese chuckled. Her granny would laugh her ass off at the thought of Shalese scared of some little white girl.

As Shalese took the downtown exit, she recalled Granny also said if you call ahead for a parking space and tell God just where you want to pull in, there'll be a space for you right where you requested. She said a lot of other crazy things too, but it was close to noon, so she gave it a try. A BMW signaled to pull out right in front of her, leaving a meter with an hour of parking left. "This is my lucky day," Shalese said. *Thank you, Granny,* she added, as thanking God wasn't an option since she didn't know if she really believed in him, her, whatever. She knew she believed in her granny.

Jenny smiled and waved to Shalese from a picnic table in the middle of the Square. A woman in a wide-brimmed hat sat opposite Jenny. All the tables scattered about seemed full of yuppie business people on their lunch break eating yogurt or salads.

Jenny nodded and started walking toward Shalese who had pointed to the hot dog stand at the corner of the Square. *Uh oh, onions or no onions?* She'd have to see what Jenny did.

"Looks like we'll have to share a table," Shalese said, trying to keep the disappointment out of her voice.

"Oh, yeah, it's always like this at noon. I'm starving," she said. Jenny grabbed Shalese's hand and led her toward the hot dog stand. A shock wave went up Shalese's arm. Damn, she never knew what to expect from this woman. "Hey Arnie," Jenny addressed the vendor, "two with the works, a couple sodas, and some chips." She looked over her shoulder at Shalese and squinted against the sun, "That okay with you?"

Shalese nodded, struck mute by the light sprinkling of freckles on Jenny's nose and cheeks that made her look like some classy pixie. She reached for her wallet.

"Your money's no good here," Arnie said. Before Shalese could work up a proper amount of indignation, he explained, "You're a friend of Ms. Pond's, you're a friend of mine." He handed them their order with a wink.

"Thanks, Arnie," Jenny said with a wave. "He used to work for my grandpa," she explained as they headed for the table where the woman in the sun hat still sat.

The woman sipped lemonade from a paper cup and blotted her lips daintily with her napkin. "Hello, dear," she said, as Shalese pulled out the bench.

"Florence?" Sufficiently disguised behind the wide brim and the Ray Bans, only the pearls gave her away. *Scratch that lucky day thing,* Shalese thought.

"Jenny tells me you've finished your proposal. I can't wait to read it," she said, fingering her pearls. "I have a friend who might be interested in funding just this sort of thing. I could connect you," she said with a smile that prickled Shalese's skin like gooseflesh. Or maybe it was the soda she was holding. *I've never been one to trust easily,* Shalese chided herself silently.

"Oh my God, Shalese, private funding. Wouldn't that be great?" Jenny said as she unwrapped her hot dog. "You wouldn't be stuck in the non-profit world of the well-meaning poor." She took a big bite, chewed sensually, and looked at Shalese expectantly. Okay, maybe Shalese imagined the chewing sensually part.

Shalese studied her own hot dog. "Yup, it has everything," she muttered, stalling until she could think of a noncommittal response to Florence's offer.

How long, Shalese wondered, could she get away with staring stupidly at her hot dog? Another thing her granny had told her was to trust her gut. Granny would have given this old dame a run for her money; Shalese almost smiled at the thought. Then again, Granny didn't get very far in life.

"You must have some very wealthy friends, Florence," Shalese said. "Why would someone I don't know be interested in funding my project?" She took a bite of her hot dog and chewed thoughtfully. Florence's expression was hard to read—smug, conniving maybe. Shalese held up one finger to delay Florence's response until she could swallow, and then continued. "I'm thinking if I apply for government funding, rather than accept private funding, I'd be obligated on a professional level rather than a personal level. Does that make sense?"

"Obligated how, dear?" Florence said, her voice sounding genuinely curious. "People with the means to do so invest in causes they believe in all the time. That's one of the greatest things about our country, don't you think?" She folded her napkin neatly and placed it next to her lemonade cup. "Philanthropy is alive and well among my friends, and yours is such a worthy project. I do so wish you would let me help," she said.

Jenny stopped munching potato chips long enough to say, "Chance of a lifetime, Shalese. Don't let your pride get in your way. You deserve this." She reached a finger over and wiped a smear of mustard off Shalese's chin.

A shiver ran down Shalese's spine, and for a moment, she forgot what they were talking about.

"Why don't I borrow your proposal," Florence said. "I'm assuming this is a copy, right? I'll have my friend look it over, and if he's interested, he can call you. Better yet, he can let me know and we'll all do dinner and talk it over then." Florence reached for the neatly bound papers. Shalese put her hand on top of Florence's to stop her. Jenny placed her hand on top of Shalese's. They looked like they were about to shout, "Go team," and break.

"C'mon, Shalese. What would be the harm?" Jenny said, fixing those green eyes on Shalese.

Chapter 7

Snake-charmer eyes, that's what Shalese decided Jenny had. She felt like she could be twisted into a pretzel by those ocean-green eyes, talked into throwing herself off a high building, cajoled into crossing the freeway blindfolded. Or even more horrific, convinced to hand over financial control of her dream to total strangers. There was something she didn't trust about Florence. "One disc off the plow makes the whole row crooked," Granny used to say.

She supposed she couldn't continue to use her concern about Florence as an excuse to see Jenny. She was pretty sure Jenny was straight, even though Lawrence seemed to be the end of some sort of personal era in Jenny's life. Was she misreading the clues? The glances through those eyelashes? The unabashed honesty and no-nonsense way of expressing herself? The subtle touches in passing? Maybe Shalese's gaydar needed a tune-up, but she didn't sense Jenny pulling back when Shalese so obviously fell all over herself whenever they were together. "Let it go, let it go," she mumbled as she lost herself in her work.

A week later, Shalese sat at her desk watching the sun go down on the horizon in between apartment houses. She'd been rifling through her files on model recovery house programs and making notes for the last hour without a break. She rubbed her temples and contemplated wrapping up for the night when the phone rang. "The First Step," she answered.

"Isn't that a little premature," Jenny said, "considering you don't yet have funding?"

"Just practicing," Shalese said. "What's up?" Hearing Jenny's voice, she felt a smile spread across her face.

"Do you like jazz?" Jenny asked without formality.

Shalese chuckled. "Are you asking me out on a date?" she said, barely able to suppress the hopefulness in her voice. Immediately, she censored herself—too presumptuous. It was just a question. Now she'd really blown it.

"A date? No. I just wondered if you liked jazz." Jenny sounded slightly offended.

"Why would you want to know if I liked jazz?" Shalese felt confusion blow through her mind like a swirl of dust and leaves in autumn. *And why can't I just say yes,* she admonished herself.

"I have this great jazz collection and too much spaghetti. Do you like spaghetti?" Jenny countered.

Okay, now she was intrigued and a little amused. "I like jazz, and I like spaghetti. Is this leading somewhere, or do you just randomly call people and ask them odd questions?" Shalese said. She heard Jenny giggle.

"Would you like to have dinner with me and listen to some jazz?" Jenny asked.

"Ah hah," Shalese teased, "it is a date."

"Not a date. I find that I don't have as many friends as I used to— before I became a murderer, that is—and I'm lonely. You don't seem to mind my felon status, and you don't look like you're on a diet. So how about it?" Jenny said.

"Not on a diet? Is that a slam of some kind?" Shalese asked.

"No, I mean that in a good way. Like, you're healthy-looking . . ." her voice trailed off. "Listen, if you're busy or something—"

"When?" Shalese interrupted, fearful that Jenny would slip away if she pushed her too far. "Really, I'd love to come for spaghetti and listen to jazz. When?"

"Now?" Jenny suggested. "I mean, the spaghetti is done." She gave Shalese her address.

"On my way," Shalese said, grinning broader than she had in a very long time. She grabbed a bottle of Chianti, her jacket, and was out the door in a minute.

Jenny's one-bedroom apartment was in the Marina district, overlooking the ocean. It was a mild evening, and a crescent of moon could be seen high in the sky in place of the usual marine layer. Shalese pressed the doorbell and heard a faint chime.

Jenny opened the door. Dressed in cutoffs, a ragged sweatshirt, hair tucked behind her ears, and barefooted, she stood looking at Shalese.

"You did mean now, as in 'now,' right?" Shalese grinned.

"Oh, sorry," Jenny said, and stood aside so Shalese could enter. "It's just that you look really good. I mean, dressed up. This isn't a date, you know," she reiterated.

Shalese rolled her eyes. "I was working today; I didn't take time to change." She shook her head and followed Jenny up a flight of stairs and through a doorway on the left. The Modern Jazz Quartet was playing softly in the background. "Whoa, killer view," she said as she looked out the ceiling-to-floor window. Prior to this, she had only seen Jenny's kitchen, which looked out onto row upon row of apartments so crowded together even weeds couldn't grow. She walked over to the fireplace. "Soccer? Let me guess—championship?" Shalese asked, noting a framed picture on the mantle of a bunch of happy looking teenagers in team uniforms.

Jenny nodded. "Boarding school," she said. She pointed at two other pictures. "Trip to Italy," she said of one where she stood in front of a museum along side a tall brunette. "Habitat project in Guatemala," she said of the other where she stood surrounded by smiling, brown-skinned children.

"You've done a lot," Shalese said appreciatively.

"I don't just go around killing people," Jenny said. Shalese chuckled.

They exchanged minutiae about their days as Jenny dished up the spaghetti. Shalese tossed a salad together from ingredients Jenny had set on the granite kitchen counter. Jenny opened the Chianti and then pulled a loaf of sourdough from the oven. They moved the feast into the dining room, an extension of the living room and the great view.

"You're not from here, right?" Jenny said. "You've got a little bit of an accent thingy going on that I can't quite place."

"Detroit. Mama worked in the factories," Shalese said around a bite of warm bread. "Mmm," she said with a shiver of pleasure.

"What about your father?" Jenny asked.

"Never knew him. He bailed before I was born. Mama was a single parent with an eighth-grade education who worked herself right into the grave so I could have a better life than the one she had. My granny pretty much raised me. How about you," she asked, her eyes on Jenny who sat unblinking across the table.

"Ohio. Cleveland Heights. Dad's a retired CEO, Mom is a career socialite. Only child. Mary raised me, mostly," Jenny said. Her eyes misted over for a moment and she swiped at them with her knuckles.

31

"Who's Mary?" Shalese asked.

Jenny shifted in her seat, looked out the window, and mumbled, "Our housekeeper." She shot Shalese a look that had a dare in it.

"Great spaghetti," Shalese said. "So, after boarding school, did you go to a university?"

"Yup, communications major," Jenny said.

Shalese covered a bark of surprise by putting her hand over her mouth as if she'd coughed. She cleared her throat for good measure.

"Something funny about that?" Jenny asked with arched eyebrows.

"No. No, it's just that you have an . . . interesting communication style. I'm guessing you didn't learn that in school," Shalese said with a grin. To her surprise, Jenny snorted.

"I have an idea I'd like to run by you," Shalese said, then forked in a bite of salad and chewed thoughtfully.

Jenny squinted in mock impatience and drummed her fingers noisily on the table until Shalese swallowed.

"An educated and currently unemployed woman such as yourself," Shalese pointed to Jenny with her fork, "with a background in communications, could be a wonderful asset to a halfway house. Would you consider being on the staff—I mean, once I get funding and a location and all that?"

"Really? You'd want me? I could do bookkeeping and record keeping, like I did for the investment managers," Jenny offered. "Could I still take part in the program? I mean, I'm in need of whatever rehabilitative services you've got up your sleeve, as well as a job."

"I don't see why not," Shalese said. "I'd like to run the house more like a collective, you know, where everyone gets a say in what happens."

"Don't you think that might be a little naïve? I mean, some of these women are bound to be right off the street. The place could run amok with too much *choice*," Jenny said.

"There was a time when I was right off the street," Shalese said, her voice tinged with bitterness. "Anyway, we'd have the veto," she reassured Jenny. "Think about it, okay?"

"Does this mean you're considering Florence's offer to fund the place?"

Shalese was quiet for a moment. "Considering," she said.

"I wish you'd at least consider my financial offer as—"

"No," Shalese said, bringing an abrupt end to that conversation.

They finished the meal, the Chianti, and several more albums. When it was so dark that all they could see in the plate-glass windows were their own reflections, Shalese offered to help Jenny with the dishes before heading home.

"You want to load my dishwasher?" Jenny said with a smirk.

Maybe it was the wine, but the way Jenny said that, all sexy and taunting, made Shalese blush. "I'll save that for when we have a date," Shalese said.

Jenny's lack of smile was belied by the dimples on both cheeks. "Thanks for coming over—really," she added.

Back in her car, heading across the city on autopilot, Shalese's mind drifted back to their conversation. "Damn," she swore and banged her fist on the steering wheel. "I forgot to ask about Lawrence."

Chapter 8

"Florence, this is Shalese DuBois," Shalese said into the phone. She took a deep breath to steady herself. It had taken a week of mostly sleepless nights to reach her decision.

"Shalese, how wonderful to hear from you, dear. I hope you're calling to tell me you've considered my offer and will accept our funding for your halfway house."

"I don't know how I could refuse. This is such a generous offer," Shalese fought off the feeling that she was selling her soul to the devil. *She's just a rich old lady, with rich old friends,* she admonished herself. Jenny had reminded her that just because she didn't understand wealth, she didn't have to reject it.

"I'll have the papers drawn up and delivered by the end of the week. Will that do?" Florence asked.

"That would be great. I'd also like to take you up on your previous offer to join the staff. I have a part-time administrative position open. Would you be interested? I mean, I know you're retired, but—"

"Oh, thank you, Shalese. You can't imagine how much that means to me," Florence said, interrupting her. "Yes, I'd love to serve in whatever capacity you see fit. I'm awfully good at interviewing," she added, a frisson of excitement running up her spine.

"Wonderful. That's one of the first things that has to happen," Shalese said, feeling some relief at having delegated the task.

"When you've gotten the papers and are ready to sign them, perhaps we can meet?"

"Uh, yes—good idea. I'll call you. Thanks again, Florence," Shalese said and hung up. For a moment, she was left wondering who was in charge.

Feeling light-headed, she paced her office until she'd gotten back her bearings. This decision called for a celebration. Most of her friends and colleagues were in the East Bay, and she wasn't up for the drive. She dialed Jenny's number.

"What?" Jenny answered.

"What?" Shalese said. "You can't answer the phone by saying 'What'."

"Caller ID. Knew it was you. What's up?" Jenny asked.

Shalese toyed with the idea of taking the direct approach. "I'm picking you up to go out with me for a drink to celebrate. Florence is sending over the financial agreement. I'll be there in twenty minutes," she said, mustering all the bravado she could.

"Is this a date?" Jenny asked.

"We'll talk about it," Shalese said, and hung up the phone. It took a moment to realize her toes were curled tightly under, she was gritting her teeth, and her shoulders were up close to her earlobes. "Jeez," she said, and shook the tension out of her body.

When Shalese picked her up, Jenny was dressed in linen slacks, a beige silk blouse, strappy little sandals, and diamond stud earrings. Her hair hung loose and swung back jauntily when she tipped her chin up in greeting. Shalese, speechless, motioned towards her car.

They drove to a quiet, upscale neighborhood bar, ordered their drinks, and sat looking at each other over the glow of the candle on the table between them.

"Congratulations," Jenny broke the silence. "This is a really big step. Your mama and granny would have been proud of you."

"Thank you for saying that," Shalese said. She sat back and appreciated the vision of Jenny as their drinks were served. "You look beautiful, by the way," she said when they were alone again. "Okay, so I'm just going to come out and ask you. Do you date women? I mean, I don't know much about boarding school, but I've heard rumors . . ." her voice trailed off.

"I've only dated guys, but I suppose all girls go through that latency period of curiosity, you know. You're like, full-time gay though, right?" Jenny asked. "Did you ever date men?"

"Uh, well, no, but . . ." Shalese stammered her confusion at trying to answer both questions. "I mean, yes, I'm gay, and no, I've never dated men. I knew when I was eight years old that I wasn't like other girls in the neighborhood." She paused, cocked her head, and asked, "Weren't we talking about you?"

"I kissed a girl in boarding school once—"

"The one in Italy?" Shalese interrupted. "The one in the picture?"

Jenny pursed her lips a moment, then said, "Yes. Just wondered, you know, what it would be like."

"What was it like?" Shalese persisted.

"Different. Nice—really nice. But that option definitely did not fit in my program. Well," she amended, "my mother's program for me— you know, finish school, get married, have kids."

"How did Lawrence fit in to all this?" Shalese asked, leaning forward, elbows on the small table.

"Lawrence was from a good family, studying law, crazy about me—or at least crazy about marrying someone his parents would approve of. I guess I fit the bill." She took a sip of her Manhattan and studied Shalese over the rim of her glass. "Something just wasn't right. After a year of engagement, I broke up with him. My mother nearly disowned me," she chuckled. "Since prison I haven't dated. I suppose Mr. Right could be out there, but truthfully, I haven't been looking that hard."

Shalese took a big gulp of her drink to brace herself. "Would you consider dating me?" she asked.

"I thought this was a date," Jenny said. She smiled and batted her lashes playfully. "I mean, I'm all dressed up, we're out in public, you're buying me drinks . . ."

Shalese grinned. She felt a blush coming on. "So, can I take that as a yes?"

"Whoa, not so fast," Jenny said and swirled her drink. "What part of 'I've only dated guys' didn't you hear?"

"I heard the 'I haven't been looking that hard' part." Shalese leaned forward and fixed Jenny with a stare.

"Hmm," Jenny said, buying time. "I'm not sure that . . ." She stopped mid-sentence, glanced at Shalese, and then looked away. "I don't know—it could get complicated, us working together and all," Jenny said, a quizzical look on her face.

Is she considering this? Shalese wondered. She sat back in her chair to give Jenny some space. "Could. Doesn't have to," Shalese said. She wondered if Jenny could hear her heart pounding away in her chest. "Let's just take it slow."

"Okay. Maybe. I can do slow," Jenny said.

"Good. How about dinner tomorrow night?" Shalese asked.

"Tomorrow? That's slow?" Jenny said in mock surprise.

"Hey, by all accounts, we should be moving in together by then," Shalese chuckled, referring to the popular lesbian stereotype.

At the end of the evening, Shalese walked Jenny up to her doorstep. There was an awkward moment where both women shifted about on their feet.

"Do you want to try that girl-kissing thing again?" Shalese said, keeping her tone light while sweat broke out over her body.

"Not yet," Jenny said, putting her hand on Shalese's shoulder to keep some space between them, "but eventually. Maybe. Okay?" She ran her hand slowly down the length of Shalese's arm, gave a little squeeze at the wrist, and turned to go inside.

"Your call," Shalese said.

The financial papers arrived two days later in the form of a two-page, clearly written agreement with a minimum of legalese—no need for a lawyer. Shalese reviewed them with a mixture of elation and skepticism. Her dream could be funded by nothing more than a signature. A place, furnishing, all equipment needed, money for staff, all bills paid (Florence would open the account and monitor transactions), and cash available on request, indefinitely. Her life was about to be underwritten, with no obvious strings attached. Florence would be the liaison between the halfway house and the funding source, which was to remain anonymous, so Shalese could be free to direct the operation. If this was life in the wealthy lane, perhaps Shalese should just put on her turn signal and move on over.

Chapter 9

"I still feel like I'm dreaming," Shalese said, a week later, as Florence handed her the key to a two-story Victorian right in the middle of the city. Tears pooled in her eyes. *I will not cry, I will not cry,* she swore silently, and turned toward the street.

"The house is a tax write-off dear. It's been sitting uninhabited for months. You'll be doing my friend a favor by putting it to good use," Florence said, pretending not to notice the tear streak on Shalese's cheek.

Shalese tossed the key in the air and caught it, looked down the length of the porch, across the street, and checked out the neighborhood. She took an uneven breath and on the exhale ran her hand slowly across her chin and down her neck as if trying to swallow a lump.

Jenny shifted her weight from one foot to the other. "Will you open the door already? A girl could grow moss waiting to get inside."

Shalese's fingers felt numb as she fumbled the key into the lock and opened the beveled glass door. Excited and disoriented, like a contestant on one of those reality shows where they build a new house for a family, she stepped through the threshold to take her first look around. This was it, her dream come true—The First Step. *Granny,* Shalese sent a thought into the ethers, *I may have been wrong about the old broad.*

They *ooh*-ed and *ahh*-ed their way through the six bedrooms, four baths, formal parlor, dining room, industrial sized kitchen, and a small study, all with cathedral ceilings, and windows spilling in so much light that you just couldn't hold on to a bad thought.

"Look at these floors," Jenny gasped. The well-polished oak was covered with comfortably worn Oriental carpets thoughtfully left behind by the owner.

Lost in her fantasy of holding the first group in the parlor of this safe haven for women recreating their lives, Shalese didn't notice that

Jenny, standing close to her, had taken her hand until Jenny gave it a little squeeze.

"So, this is The First Step," Jenny said smiling hugely.

Confusion washed over Shalese, and she blushed in embarrassment for a moment at her misconstrued notion Jenny was referring to the handholding thing. "Looks like it," she said, and grinned sheepishly.

It all happened quickly: furniture arrived, utilities were connected, a computer was installed, a bank account was opened by Florence—into which Shalese transferred the bulk of her life savings to offset feeling like a complete charity case—and office supplies were put in place.

"I think you should be the one to hang this," Jenny said, and handed the business license framed in oak to Shalese. Shalese stared at the license that marked the beginning of her new career. "The study would be nice," Jenny suggested. She took Shalese by the hand and led her down the hall.

In the study, a stack of applications rested on the roll-top desk. Florence had volunteered to sort them by criteria set by Shalese so ten lucky women could be chosen to take their first step into a new beginning. She hung the license over the desk and stepped back to admire the effect. "This is all real, isn't it? It's really happening," Shalese said. Jenny, eyes moist, nodded, slipped her arm around Shalese's waist, and gave a hug that set Shalese's toes a-tingle.

Jenny was in charge of all things kitchen and set about creating a warm and inviting environment and a well-stocked pantry. A friend of Arnie's, a retired caterer, was hired to prepare the evening meals.

Later that afternoon, Shalese, Administrator and Program Director, curled into an overstuffed chair in the parlor and reviewed her program notes. Jenny wandered in from the kitchen.

"So, here's the program," Shalese said. "We'll have group therapy, individual therapy, 12-Step meetings, yoga, exercise, nutrition classes, living skills, and an arts and creative expression group. What do you think? Oh," she rushed on, "and I know this law student who will come in for free once a month and help the women with legal issues. And a woman who is a professional job coach has offered herself as a resource." A self-satisfied smile made her look like a happy—though exhausted—ten year old.

Jenny grinned. "What about a spa day?" she said, plunking herself into a comfy chair across from Shalese.

"A what?" Shalese wrinkled her brow.

"You know, once a month we'll get someone to come in, do haircuts, manicures, pedicures, massage—"

"Jenny, these are ex-felons, not socialites," Shalese interrupted. "You're coming from that white privilege place. I'm talking about skills they'll need to survive."

"May I remind you that I am an ex-felon. I happen to think self-care is important to building self-esteem, regardless of your skin color or economic status. It's every bit as important as learning how to balance your checkbook. Maybe it's your blue-collar mentality that needs some updating."

A sound of skepticism escaped Shalese before she could clamp down on it. Jenny shot her a fiery look. In the end, Jenny won.

Shalese decided there would be two women to a room, with one room saved for overnight staff. Shalese and Jenny would each take a night and hire someone to cover the other five nights. As staff, Jenny would be there days and take part in the program, but maintain her own apartment off site, as would Shalese. Or that was the plan. Somewhere in the back of her mind, Shalese hoped that plan might change.

Florence, who had been arranging flowers in the parlor, stuck her head into the study, her coat and bag slung over one arm. For an old woman, she sure held up well under the rigors of move-in day, Shalese thought.

"Well then, I'll see you two bright and early Monday morning," Florence said. Jenny and Shalese walked her to the door. "This is so exciting. Thank you, Shalese, for letting me be a part of it. What you're doing here is going to make a huge difference in the lives of some very deserving people," Florence said, her lips somewhere between a grimace and a smile.

Shalese paused a moment before responding. Her gut was sending up a red flag. She ignored it and said, "I certainly couldn't have done any of this without you, Florence. See you Monday."

Shalese closed the door and turned around. Jenny threw her arms around Shalese's neck and planted a big one right on her lips. "I'm so proud of who you are, of what you're doing," she said. Pulled into the tide of Jenny's sea green eyes, Shalese stammered, "So I guess this really is *the first step*," and kissed her back, this time with no misunderstanding.

Chapter 10

Later that evening, Jenny kicked off her Birks and sat yoga-style on her couch. "Well," she said aloud as she extracted the cork and poured herself a glass of the cabernet she'd picked up at K Syrah. "Well," she repeated. She swirled the wine, appreciated the deep garnet-plum color, the mushroomy oak bouquet, and then took a hardy gulp.

She unfolded her legs and padded across the floor to her favorite overstuffed chair, and sat staring out the window. The late August night sky reflected back her image in the glass which felt strangely reassuring as she didn't want to be alone with her thoughts, but who could you call to talk about something like this—her quasi-liberal parents back in Cleveland Heights who wouldn't mind that Shalese was black, but would definitely mind that she was a woman? She didn't think so. It was Friday night and she had no one to call. She leaned into the pathos of it all.

Her cell vibrated in her pocket and she jumped as if zapped by a cattle prod. "Damn," she swore as she fumbled the flap open.

"Did I catch you at a bad time?" Shalese's voice made her feel weak, like she was coming down with the flu or something. Truthfully, it was more the *or something*.

"I kissed you," Jenny blurted out.

"You certainly did."

Jenny could hear the grin plastered across Shalese's face. "But, I'm not—"

"Interested in anything more?" Shalese ventured.

"No. I mean, yes. I mean, no," Jenny said, stumbling over mental boulders. This was definitely not a trail she'd ever hiked before.

"So," Shalese said, dropping her voice to what she hoped would be a sexy register, thoroughly enjoying Jenny's discomfort, "you're still not sure if you're interested in a relationship? Or you're still not sure if you're a lesbian?"

"I guess if I were interested in a relationship with you, it would make me a lesbian," Jenny's voice cracked on the last word, making it sound like *a lezzie*. "Oh, God, I can't believe I said that. How completely politically incorrect and totally stupid. You must find me—"

"I find you irresistible," Shalese interrupted. "I can't stop thinking about you. You're gorgeous, smart, fun, and a damned good kisser," Shalese said, knowing that for the first time since they met, she had the upper hand. "We'll also be working together. Is that going to be a problem?"

"I don't want to screw this up," Jenny said, her voice softening, "I need this program. I need the job. I need—I need to figure some things out. Can we finish this tomorrow?"

"Sure. Jenny, regardless of what does or doesn't happen between us, your job is not in jeopardy, nor is your participation in the program. There are no strings attached, I swear. Okay?" Shalese waited for a response.

Jenny's breath was audible on the other end of the line. *In. Out. In. Out.* "Okay," she said quietly into the phone and hung up.

Saturday morning she drove to the Castro district—otherwise known as San Francisco's gay Mecca—and parked her Miata. The phrase, "That which you resist persists," ran a loop in her mind. *Immersion therapy*, she thought. Like some sort of baptismal sacrament she'd start at one end of the street and walk, one step at a time, through the most heavily populated gay, lesbian, bi, trans, queer, questioning, intersex street in the world.

By the time I reach the end, I'll know where I belong, she promised herself. She passed men leaning against storefronts, holding hands as they strolled in and out of shops, kissing over coffee in sidewalk cafes, cruising each other as they walked their too-cute dogs. *Where are the women*, she wondered.

She passed a number of transsexual men who'd been born on the wrong side of the fence, and a couple of trans women, one who could have used a personal shopper from Macy's. *Where are all the lesbians already*, she fumed silently.

There's one, she thought, spying a woman pulling alongside the curb on her Vespa. *Nope*, she sighed, *just another transvestite*.

"Hey, baby," a guy called to her as he gave her the eye. On closer look, it wasn't a guy after all but a very butch woman who was making kissy noises in her direction. Jenny hurried on down the street.

This was not turning out to be the soul-freeing, spirit-embracing, homecoming she'd hoped for and she was no closer to taking a definitive step in the lesbian direction than she had been last night. She stopped at a pretzel stand and was squirting mustard on her pretzel when she sensed a presence just behind her.

"Could you save a little for me?" The woman's voice was deep, suggestive, sensuous like velvet.

Jenny shivered as if someone had just blown on the back of her neck. She turned to face a stunning woman with short-cropped auburn hair that shimmered in the minimal sunlight available at that hour of morning. She was slightly taller than Jenny and wore a casual pantsuit. Her eyes were a deep brown and almond shaped. Her skin was creamy and smooth. Jenny gasped and squirted mustard all over her thumb.

The woman smiled. Her gaze never wavered from Jenny's as she took Jenny's hand in her own and slowly trailed her pretzel down the length of Jenny's thumb.

"I think that was the last of the mustard," she said. She took a bite of the dough and chewed slowly.

Oh, my god, I'm going to pee my pants, Jenny thought, her body vibrating like a plucked string.

"My name is Jane," the woman said.

"Jenny," was all Jenny could manage. Her heart was pounding.

"Coffee?" Jane said, nodding her head toward a place across the street.

"Uh, maybe another time. I'm meeting my girlfriend and I'm running late," she lied effortlessly. She backed away from Jane, turned and hurried back down the street.

"Wait . . . can I get your number?" Jane called. The question hung like mist in the morning air of the Castro.

Panting, Jenny reached her car. She had to steady her shaking hand to get the key in the lock. She rolled down the window and sat, breathing slowly until her heart stopped banging in her chest.

"Lesbian. I'm a lesbian," Jenny said aloud, trying on the words. She had never given serious thought to the idea and yet here she was, swooning over a perfect stranger—a woman, no less—who wanted her number. *Do I look like a lesbian*, she wondered. *Lesbians don't hit on straight women, do they?* The memory of Jane's eyes sucked Jenny in like a piece of litmus paper. With a tissue, she blotted at the moisture that had formed on her forehead and upper lip.

Latent. She'd heard the term related to women who hadn't a clue about their true gender preference. My god, she was a latent lesbian.

That afternoon Jenny puttered around her house. She sat at the kitchen table with a crossword puzzle from last week's Chronicle but couldn't focus. She'd promised Shalese she'd call this weekend, and she would—eventually. She needed to get over the prickle of guilt she felt, as if she'd cheated on Shalese by finding another woman attractive. *Oh no, is this what it was going to be like*, she wondered. Shalese. Just the thought of her warmed Jenny's heart and made her smile.

"This is big," she said aloud, "this is really big." This was the kind of big you didn't keep to yourself, but whom was she going to tell? Florence? That would shock the garter belt right off the old gal. There was one person in the world who she knew would love her unconditionally—well, okay, two.

Around seven o'clock Jenny called home. She pictured the phone ringing in the family room of the two-story, wood-framed Colonial with a wrap-around porch. "Pond residence," a familiar voice said, her words, shaped by Midwestern dialect, sounded like *Pound rezdents*. Jenny smiled.

"Mary, it's so good to hear your voice," Jenny said.

"Sweet Jesus, is this our Jenny all the way out in California?" the housekeeper asked. "Tell me all about your life, child. Oh, but wait," she caught herself, "you're probably calling to talk to your folks, aren't you?" she chuckled on the other end of the line.

"I am," Jenny agreed, "but you first. Mary, I'm a lesbian." There, she'd said it. Jenny waited, searched through the empty space as if she was looking for a document in a file cabinet. "Mary?"

"We don't have many of those back here, I don't think," Mary stated flatly. "Are you happy honey? Is there someone special?"

Jenny's eyes filled with tears, her bottom lip quivered, and she sniffed. More than anything, she wanted to crawl up into Mary's lap as she did as a child and have all her booboos soothed away. "She's pretty special all right. Her name is Shalese, and we work together at a halfway house for ex-felon women just like me."

"Well, that's just fine then. Oh, Jenny, I see your mamma coming down the hall. You want me to put her on?"

"No," Jenny grinned, "but put her on anyway. I love you, Mary," Jenny said around the knot of affection that threatened to close up her throat.

"I love you too, Little Bit," Mary said, using Jenny's childhood nickname. "Here's your mamma."

"Jennifer. Are you in trouble again?"

"No, Mother. I've never been happier in my life," Jenny said, knowing the truth of those words deep in her heart. "I've fallen in love," she said surprising herself with the admission.

"Well, nice of you to inform us before the wedding," Pauline Pond replied, her voice crisp and dismissive. "Is he employed? The one before Lawrence was an artist or something." Jenny sensed the wrinkled nose around the word artist. "I still don't know why you left Lawrence. I believe he's seeing that Totsie Baulderaux now," Pauline offered as an aside. Jenny heard Pauline's muffled words, "Mary, this is a private conversation. Please close the door behind you, and don't look at me like that."

"I'm in love with a lovely and powerful black woman who is the director of the agency where I'm employed," Jenny offered, redirecting the conversation.

"Oh, Jennifer," her mother heaved a weary sigh, "must you continue to individuate in such a blatant manner? Wouldn't it be easier just to reject your trust fund or something?"

"I just thought you should know," Jenny said, her voice sounding much younger. "Is Daddy there?"

"It's ten o'clock at night here. You know your father retires at nine."

"Will you tell him I'll call him tomorrow? Don't tell him why—I want to do that myself."

"I wouldn't dream of disclosing your news, Jennifer. Yes, I'll tell him you'll call. Please, dear, don't take this too seriously. It's probably just another phase. Regardless of what you believe, your father and I wouldn't want you to get hurt—again."

They said their goodnights and Jenny snapped her cell phone closed. She stared at her feet. "Well, that went rather well," she said. Her toes wiggled an affirmative.

Jenny poured herself a glass of Merlot, curled up on the sofa, and watched the sun set over the Pacific. As the last shard of color left the sky, she glanced over her shoulder toward the kitchen, hoping by some force of will she could conjure up dinner. A strange lethargy had settled into her body. She felt spent as though she'd run a long marathon only to collapse just over the finish line. She left the lights off and poured herself another glass of wine. The marine layer rolled in, swathing the stars in a swirl of white as Jenny poured herself yet another glass of Merlot.

Chapter 11

Sunday was overcast and an unseasonable wet chill seemed to seep into the flat through the plate-glass. Jenny lifted a heavy eyelid and slowly perused the damage: red film around her wine glass, bottle empty, a dim, ghostly outline of something not quite human reflecting in the window across from her. She wiped the crust from the other eye and lifted the eyelid with her finger. A car horn honked in the street, sending a shard of icy pain through her skull. Her mouth tasted like a cat box. Her feet were tingly cold and she retrieved the afghan from the floor and wrapped it about her.

Her cell phone, which was set on vibrate, sounded like an angry wasp buzzing on the wooden table next to her. She glanced at the schoolhouse clock on the wall—9 a.m. The nerve.

"This had better be good," she said by way of greeting. The deep-throated chuckle that answered caused the corners of her mouth to lift involuntarily.

"Well, aren't you just the sunshine we need today," Shalese teased. "Did I wake you?"

"No. I'm glad it's you," Jenny said. A wave of vulnerability set her at sea and she struggled to regain her emotional balance. "I came out to my mother last night," she said.

"Whoa, Jenny, I don't know what to say." The tease had gone right out of Shalese's voice. "Does that mean . . ."

"That I'm interested in a relationship with you? That I am a lesbian? Yes, and—I guess, yes." Jenny's heart was fluttering like a fledgling bird on the edge of the nest. "Will you come over? I feel kind of shaky," she said.

"On my way," Shalese said, her voice as soothing and vaporous as a cloud.

They talked all day, all night, until after midnight. Shalese fought to keep her eyes open, wanting nothing more than to attend to Jenny gently and lovingly as she grappled with this new emergence of her self.

"Will you stay?" Jenny asked, snuggling into the warmth of Shalese's arms as they curled up together on the sofa. "I don't want to be alone."

Shalese gently kissed Jenny's eyelids, took her by the hand, and led her to the bedroom. They held each other close under the down comforter, their breath matching in rhythm, until sleep overtook them. There would be plenty of time for more—a lifetime, Shalese hoped.

Chapter 12

The door swung open when Shalese tried the latch of The First Step early Monday morning. The aroma of French Roast greeted her like a long-lost friend. The door to the study was ajar, and a light shone at the end of the hall. *How did she get here before me?* Shalese wondered. *We left at the same time. Must have been the traffic on Valencia.*

"Hey honey, I'm home," she called down the hall, a grin sliding from ear to ear. She swallowed down the excitement she felt at the memory of last night's time together. *I just want you to be happy*, she heard Granny say in her mind. Shalese was very happy.

"Good morning, dear," Florence said, sticking her head into the hallway. Shalese stopped short as if she'd just hit a plate-glass wall. "Pink becomes you," Florence said, commenting on the blush washing over Shalese's face like the incoming tide. "Pour yourself a cup of coffee," she directed, "we have work to do."

Shalese headed toward the kitchen, wondering how to take charge of this situation. She stopped at the doorway. "No thanks, Florence, I'm a decaf kind of gal myself." There, that should do.

"Of course you are dear. I remembered that from the restaurant. It's French Roast decaf. Now hurry along."

Shalese let out a little huff of air. *What is it with these pushy women in my life,* she wondered. Yesterday Jenny had declared them a monogamous couple. Shalese didn't object, but she also hadn't had much say in the matter. She poured herself a cup of coffee and headed for the study.

Florence glanced at her watch. "Is Jenny coming in this morning?"

"She'll be here in a minute," Shalese answered, still feeling unguarded and vulnerable after a tender night with Jenny. Too late, she realized what she'd implied.

Florence's face screamed, "ah-HA!" but her voice merely said, "Here's the stack of applicants I've chosen. What do you think?" She shifted to the side chair so Shalese could slip into the chair behind the desk. "They're all available and could be moved in by the end of the week," she added.

"Let's schedule interviews for Wednesday," Shalese suggested, "and we'll go from there. Could you set that up for me?"

"Of course. I would very much like to sit in on those interviews," Florence said, her voice calm. "In addition to the questions you've outlined, I'd like to assess whether or not we need to get restraining orders. We'll need to know where the abusers reside, I think."

This made perfect sense to Shalese. "Good idea, I hadn't thought of that." Florence was turning out to be quite an asset after all. She glanced at Florence, whose mouth resembled that of a turtle—stretched wide, lips pressed together, not exactly smiling, but self-satisfied. A little shiver jiggled down Shalese's spine.

"Hi honey, I'm home," Jenny's voice rang down the hallway. Shalese pressed her fist to her mouth to hide a grin and shook her head.

"We're in here, dear," Florence called.

"Oh . . ." Jenny said, chagrined.

"There's decaf in the kitchen," Shalese called out.

"Decaf? Why bother?" Jenny said as she poked her head into the office. Florence acknowledged her with a raised eyebrow. "I'm putting on a pot of leaded. Back in a minute," Jenny announced.

The morning passed quickly with each woman carving out her part of the daily routine. Florence scheduled ten interviews: five on Tuesday and five on Wednesday. Jenny met with the cable guy and wrangled a few upgrades without increased cost. Shalese worked on the budget and made some phone calls. Jenny and Shalese moved awkwardly around one another, avoiding touch and prolonged eye contact in an attempt to keep their new relationship to themselves.

They broke for lunch at one o'clock. Over lox and bagels, Jenny said, "I'm so excited about next week when all the women will be here. It's sad though . . ." she paused, "that there are so many women waiting for what we have to offer."

"Yes, no end to the number it seems," Florence added, sounding oddly upbeat.

Later, Florence lifted the receiver quietly in an upstairs bedroom and listened to make sure the line was clear. She dialed, glanced at the door, hoping she'd remembered to close it, and waited for the answering machine to click on in Sidney's mansion across town. "Friday," she said quietly, "I'll know by Friday at the latest. I trust you'll make the appropriate calls." She hung up and sat for a moment feeling a surge of power light her from within. "Omniscience becomes you," she smiled at her reflection in the mirrored panel across the small room.

Chapter 13

"Jenny," her father's hearty voice tumbled through the phone lines from the Midwest and wrapped itself around her like a big hug. "I'm sorry I missed your call, sweetheart. Early tee time, you know," Victor Pond offered his excuse with a chuckle. "How are you, honey?"

Tears trickled down Jenny's cheeks and she swallowed, sniffed, and cleared her throat before she was able to speak. "Never been better, Daddy," she said.

"And that would make you cry because . . ." her father asked in confusion.

"The tears are just because I miss you so much. The good news is that I've fallen in love with the most amazing woman. Her name is Shalese, and she's the head of this halfway house where I'm working. You'll love her Daddy, I know you will." Jenny stopped to take a breath.

"I see. Hmm. Well, I see," her father said, fumbling with the complexity of such an announcement. "You know, honey, I haven't seen you since your trial. I think it's time your mother and I came for a visit and met this wonder woman. I'd love to see the halfway house too. What do you say?"

Jenny was silent for a moment. *Okay, just say it,* she told herself. "Daddy, do you think you could sort of leave Mother at home?"

Victor chuckled conspiratorially. "I suppose I could be called away to the West Coast to handle some business. Even though I'm retired, they call occasionally and ask me to help them out of some mess they've made of things. Perhaps they'll need me the very same week as that big charity event she has scheduled. God, I loathe those things," he said. "How does mid-September sound?"

"I can't wait," Jenny said, noting the happy feeling in her stomach. "Love you, Daddy. Bye."

"Love you back, Little Bit. Bye," he said.

Chapter 14

"Doris, you are just the sort of woman we're looking for," Shalese said to the first applicant Tuesday morning. "Would you be able to move in this Friday?"

"Oh, Shalese—may I call you Shalese?" she asked uncertainly. Her freckles rearranged themselves as she smiled shyly.

"Of course."

"You have no idea how this is going to throw me just the life line I've needed to get back on my feet. I have nowhere else to go, no means of support until I can get a job. I'll be here first thing Friday morning."

"If I may interrupt, dear," Florence glanced first at Shalese, then at Doris. "In order to secure your safety here, and that of all the women, we need to take certain precautions. In case a restraining order might become necessary, I'll need the physical address of your abuser—in this case, your former boyfriend."

"Oh, sure. 537 Maple Drive," Doris offered without hesitation. "I'm glad you've thought of that. I've heard horror stories. Sam's just the kind of person to try something stupid and vengeful," she added. "I've been told by others to live my life quietly, very low profile, when I got out of prison so he won't find me."

"Before your time with us is up, dear, you'll be able to live your life out loud," Florence reassured.

Jenny had slipped into the parlor toward the end of the interview. "This is Jenny Pond," Shalese nodded to Jenny. "She'll show you to the room that will be yours. We'll see you Friday, Doris." Shalese stood and shook Doris's hand.

"Welcome to The First Step," Jenny smiled warmly. "This way please."

Shalese rubbed her hands briskly. "This is it, Florence," she said as she straightened the pile of intakes on the desk before her. "This is exactly what I was meant to do and I owe it all to you," she said grinning broadly.

All five women were appropriate candidates and by the end of the day, Shalese was running on the adrenaline of a job well done. "How about if I take you two lovely ladies out for dinner? There's a sushi bar a few blocks from here I'd like to try," Shalese offered.

"I'm rather done in, dear," Florence said. "How about a rain check? I have some work yet to do at home."

"Rain check it is then. Jenny?"

"Let me close up the office and grab my coat," Jenny said. "Florence, I'll see you in the morning."

Over sake, calamari, and spring rolls, Jenny said, "You still haven't hired an overnight staff for next week. That's cutting it pretty close isn't it?"

"I've been thinking," Shalese paused to take a sip of sake and squinted. She gave a little shiver as the fumes found their way up her nostrils. "Just hear me out on this, okay?" Jenny nodded. "Consider how much money we could both save if we gave up our apartments and moved into The First Step as staff in residence."

"Both of us?" Jenny gasped. "At the same time? Isn't that sort of a cliché?" she asked.

"What do you mean?"

"What do lesbians do on their first date?" Jenny asked, and answered without pause, "Rent a U-Haul."

"Very funny. Anyway, we're past our first date. Think about it, it's a big room," Shalese said weakly. "I mean, you could have your own bed if that's the problem. I just think it would be practical is all. I mean, no obligation or anything," Shalese stammered. "I think I'd like to move in, make it my home. It's so much more than just a job for me, Jenny. It's a commitment, a way of life." A fine line of sweat had broken out on Shalese's top lip.

"You're serious," Jenny stated the obvious. She moved a piece of octopus around with her chopstick. "Let me sleep on it, okay?" Shalese nodded. "Alone," Jenny amended. "I'll let you know in the morning," she added.

Shalese tossed and turned all night, got up and drank straight from the milk carton in the refrigerator, peed, went back to bed. Half an hour later, she was up again, pacing her apartment. She turned on the public radio station and listened to a few minutes of Art Bell. Even at this hour of morning, he was too far out for her. Nothing but infomercials on TV. "Crap," she said, "it only makes sense." She climbed back into bed, threw the covers over her head, and eventually fell into a fitful sleep.

Across town, Jenny sat propped up in bed against a stash of pillows and swirled half a glass of Merlot. A paperback novel lay face-down on the bed beside her. Jo Khool played on the stereo—an irritating piece with rhythms too erratic for early morning listening. She kicked the covers back, got up, and turned off the stereo. She glanced at the digital clock on her desk: 2 a.m. She put on her robe, wandered out to the living room, and sat staring out into the night.

There were obviously some things she hadn't thought through, like giving up her apartment. Who in their right mind would give this up? She also knew Shalese would pull that 'white privilege thing' if she offered that as an excuse. It's true, she supposed, that if she didn't have a relationship with Shalese, hadn't been hired on as staff, she would be just another resident, giving up her apartment and sharing a small room with a total stranger for the next year. "Well, hell," she muttered. "Carpe diem and all that." She promised herself she'd call the landlord later this morning. She tossed the pillows on the floor, turned off the light, and fell into a heavy and dreamless sleep.

At 6 a.m., Shalese was woken by the ringtone on her cell. Bleary-eyed, she looked around the room trying to remember which pocket she left the damn thing. Stumbling out of bed, she shoved her hands into the pocket of the jacket hanging from the bedroom doorknob. Jackpot. "Yes?" she muttered into the phone. Her mouth felt like flannel.

"Okay," Jenny said on the other end of the line and hung up.

An hour later, Florence closed the door quietly to the office of The First Step. "No more than one every few months, Sidney," Florence spoke clearly but quietly into the phone, "we don't want to draw attention." She eyed the pile of papers on the desk in front of her. "Someone is bound to make the connection at some point," she fretted.

"Darling Florence," Sidney reassured, "stealth is our guiding principle. You do remember Marco Sanchez, right?"

"Oh, Sidney, that was masterful. Right over the rail in midday. How did you pull that one off?" Florence smiled at the memory. "The body was never recovered, if I remember correctly."

"So true, so true," Sidney said. "To our advantage, people die all the time in a city this large. It hardly ever makes the papers anymore. Accidents are just that—accidents."

"This first crop of women will move on in eight months to a year," Florence said. "There will be less connection as time passes," she added.

"And a never-ending renewal of resources," Sidney said sounding wistful. "Will Victor's visit be a problem?"

"Shouldn't be. He hasn't seen me since he was a child, and I was using the other name back then. Just as a precaution, I thought I'd take a few days off at the end of the month when he's here. Someone's coming. Stay in touch." Florence hung up quickly, slipped out of the chair, and opened a nearby file drawer.

"You're here bright and early," Shalese said as she entered the office. She slung her jacket over the back of her chair.

"There's just no end to paperwork," Florence said with a smile. She rifled through a file then closed the drawer. She hung Shalese's jacket on the coat rack in the corner.

"Jenny will be here in a moment. We thought the three of us should have a little talk, if that's okay," Shalese said her voice edgy with nervous energy.

"Is everything okay?" Florence asked, alarmed. The last thing she needed was to raise suspicion in this goldmine of opportunity. She made a quick mental check. No, there was no way in which she had slipped up.

"Oh, yes—better than okay. Well, um, Jenny should be here soon," Shalese mumbled. She sorted through the stack of papers on her desk, putting an end to the conversation until Jenny arrived.

The three sat for an uncomfortable moment around the dining table. Shalese cleared her throat, pushed her chair back, and stood, hands braced on the table. "You're probably wondering why I've called you here," she said, looking out across the room.

Jenny giggled. "There are only three of us here, and two of us already know."

Shalese shot her a look and sat back down. "I haven't done this for a long time. I'm a little rusty."

Florence spoke up and with a shake of her head said, "Oh for heaven's sake—if this is about your relationship, could we just cut to the chase?" Shalese and Jenny exchanged a caught-with-hand-in-cookie-jar look. "I may be old," Florence continued, "but I'm not blind and certainly not stupid. You two are such a natural match I was wondering why it took you this long to figure it out." She smiled, self-satisfied.

Shalese let out the breath she didn't realize she'd been holding. She hesitated before saying, "I hope it won't be a problem, then, if Jenny and I move into the staff bedroom and become on-site house parents."

"It certainly isn't a problem for me. We have work to do," Florence said with a nod. She excused herself and left the dining room.

Jenny glanced at Shalese who had that perplexed look on her face that often accompanied an exchange with Florence.

"Why do I always have the impulse to say 'yes, mother' to that woman?" Shalese asked.

By Wednesday afternoon, ten women were signed on as residents of The First Step. Maren, down to earth; Gabriella, a socialite; Doris, hypervigilant and fearful; Chandra, a brazen ex-prostitute; Paulina, a quiet potter; Margot, with a penchant for bee keeping; Beth, a practicing herbalist; Madigan, barely literate but street savvy; Analise, a former flight attendant; and Kendra, classy in a five-star restaurant hostess sort of way.

By the end of the day, Jenny had notified her landlord and arranged to pay for the extra month, scheduled movers to haul her furniture—or as much as would fit when blended with Shalese's—over to the resident staff room on Thursday, and had secured a storage unit for the remainder of her life possessions.

"A commitment, indeed," she said, as she clicked off the light in the office.

Chapter 15

Thursday was cacophonous as the last of the furniture was delivered and placed in the residents' rooms. Jenny and Shalese had culled the best choices from their respective apartments. Shalese's oak desk and a favorite lamp made the cut—the rest had been collected over the years from Goodwill and The Salvation Army and were returned to the source. Shalese grinned as Jenny's memory-foam mattress was set in place. *You're the one that wanted me to be happy, Granny*, she said, knowing that her granny would be rolling her eyes at such luxury.

Friday morning, ten women sat in a circle in the group room and shared their stories of abuse. The themes were the same: learned helplessness, low self esteem, no one to turn to, financial dependence, imposed isolation, and wanting so badly to believe that he could change—if only she could figure out how to make him happy.

The outcomes were the same: each woman had reached her breaking point and had struck back with a vengeance after one too many broken bones, facial lacerations, missing patches of hair from her head, pets abused, trips to the ER with 'the lie' well rehearsed.

The consequences were also the same: they'd all been thrown in prison for assault with a deadly weapon, battery, attempted murder. None of them believed in justice anymore; all of them had lost their ability to trust the system to keep them safe. Their lives were a shamble of fear and futility, and it was Shalese's mission to give them hope and tools to get them back on track.

When it was Analise's turn to share, she wrinkled her nose slightly at the memory of her life, as if sensing a bad smell, like a gas leak. She scanned the gathering of women. "I know Jordan didn't mean to push me over the edge; I don't know why I just snapped," she confided.

"That sucker stalked you, sabotaged your job with the airlines, wouldn't let you out of his sight. I'd have poisoned him too," Chandra piped up—she'd gotten the skinny on Analise's life earlier that day.

"It's important to be able to tell our stories and examine our own behaviors," Shalese interjected. "And we're here to learn new ways of handling bad situations."

"I guess that's a good thing," added Beth, their resident herbalist. "Otherwise, we just keep using what we know." She turned to Analise and said, "And I know a couple of good lethal potions I could have suggested . . ." her voice trailed off. Several of the women chuckled.

"I think we should just focus on our healing," Paulina added in a quiet voice, "and let karma deal with our abusers."

"Let's hope this Karma fella knows how to kick some serious butt," Madigan offered.

Weeks passed smoothly as the women developed a routine and got to know one another. They focused their energies on their classes: life skills, money management, self-esteem, boundary setting, and how to create a resume from almost nothing. Shalese was beginning to relax and consider that Jenny might have been right—if you expect trouble, you'll probably get it. She even found herself looking forward to the next spa day.

Across town, two men stood unseen in the shadows as the chilly drizzle made halos around the lampposts. A short and stocky man pulled his collar up against the unseasonable September rain.

"I had a mail-hold sent to the post office for five days," a tall man in a gray rain slicker said under his breath as they jiggled the lock loose on the gate at 537 Maple Drive. The gate sat back from the street and thick twists of Paper White vines that ran along the tall wooden fence obscured the view from the sidewalk. Somewhere in the neighborhood, a dog barked. The tall man paused, and then pushed open the gate.

"Trip-interruptus, heh, heh," Short and Stocky said, chuckling as he opened the gate. His partner admonished him with a noisy, "Shhhh!" They slipped through unnoticed in the silver gray dusk. "Poor dude didn't even know he was goin' anywhere."

"None of this poor dude stuff. You know what he did to that girl," Tall Man said.

"You're sure the plant said his luggage was on the top shelf in the bedroom closet, right?" Short and Stocky asked, lowering his voice.

"Hey, the plant's a pro," Tall Man whispered back. "If she said that's where it is, that's where it is. We just make it look like it fell on his head while he was pulling it down. Snap! There goes the neck."

"From one suitcase? What's he got in there, bricks?" Short and Stocky was a little skeptical about this one.

"It's a stack of suitcases, one inside the other. That would be enough if you weren't paying attention," Tall Man said. "Okay, so here's the plan: he answers the door, we grab and subdue him, snap his neck, drag him into the bedroom, and set the scene."

"Piece of cake," Short and Stocky said as Tall Man wrapped sharply on the door.

At 9 a.m. Saturday morning, the women gathered for a shorter version of group therapy with Shalese as facilitator. The air was subdued, the usual bantering suspended. Maren sat scrunched down on the couch nibbling her thumbnail. Chandra, with studied nonchalance, stared at the carpet. Doris tapped her foot to a beat no one else could hear.

"So, what's going on this morning?" Shalese asked.

"Did you hear about Doris's ex?" Paulina asked. "Someone whacked him last week."

"I saw the article in the paper," Shalese said. "I'm sorry, Doris, that must have been quite a shock for you."

"Shock?" Doris raised her chin to meet Shalese's eyes. "It was the best news I've ever had. I just don't know if I can really believe it." Tears glistened on her lashes.

Doris had served time for a hired hit gone bad on her abuser husband. She could have avoided a stint in the pen, as the guy wound up dead anyway in a freak accident—a suitcase fell on his head breaking his neck. Doris appreciated irony.

"If it's true, I'm free—actually free," she said, her voice quivering with emotion. "No more looking over my shoulder when I walk down the street; no more double checking the back seat every time I walk up to my car." She heaved a sigh. "I am in debt to whoever did this, and believe me, someone did."

A little chill ran through Shalese. Please let this be a coincidence, she sent a silent prayer into the universe. If any connection was found between this man's death and the residents, it could mean the end of The First Step.

"Wish someone would whack my old man," Chandra said. The rest of the hour was spent with each woman imagining how her life would be with her abuser no longer alive.

After group, Shalese and Jenny met in the office. Shalese closed the door. "I don't like it," she said to Jenny. "In a city this size, what are the chances that a guy gets killed in a fluke accident after surviving a hit gone wrong by one of our residents?"

"Yeah, weird," Jenny agreed, "and a little too close to home. What possible connection could anyone make though? Like you said, it was a fluke accident."

Shalese stood with her hands balled into fists in her pockets. She sighed. "I guess. It just makes me nervous. What time is your Dad due?" she asked, changing the subject.

"Soon. He said he'd be here after lunch. I can't wait to see him," Jenny said, her eyes sparkling.

Chapter 16

At the back of the house, Jenny was just crossing the hall from the kitchen to the office when she heard the front door open. She turned just in time to see a distinguished gentleman in his early fifties step inside and tentatively call out, "Anyone home?"

"Daddy!" Jenny squealed, ran down the hall, and threw herself into Victor's open arms. He spun her about as if she were the six year old who would attach herself to her father the minute he entered the room.

"Little Bit, how is it possible that you've grown even lovelier since my last visit?"

"I dumped the prison orange," Jenny said with a chuckle, "and added a few pounds."

Victor beamed at his daughter. A movement to his left caused him to glance at the woman standing awkwardly nearby. "And you must be Shalese," he said, and extended his hand. "You're every bit as stunning as Jenny described."

Shalese half-smiled, took his hand, and mumbled, "Good to meet you." She forced her eyes to stay focused on his and added, "Welcome to The First Step." Her throat was constricted in nervousness and she shot Jenny a get-me-out-of-here look. Jenny beamed at her.

"I'll let you two catch up and join you later," Shalese said and excused herself.

"Dinner is on me this evening," Victor called out as she walked down the hall. "Sort of shy for such a powerful looking woman," he commented as he sat next to Jenny on the sofa.

"I don't think she's used to the meet-the-parent thing, or the black-and-white thing, or the this-is-my-new-girlfriend thing," Jenny said. She reached out and took Victor's hand. "Are you really okay with this?"

"I have no reason not to be, sweetheart," he reassured her.

"Florence said she's sorry she wasn't able to be here to meet you; she was called out of town by a sick friend. You would have liked her," Jenny said to her father as she led him into the den, a small sitting room next to the office. "She's a real firecracker for an old gal."

"Florence. Now that's a name you don't hear much anymore. Your grandmother Gloria had a friend of sorts named Flo when I was young. Must be something about those Italian names; she was a firecracker as well," Victor said with a shake of his head.

"What's a friend of sorts?" Jenny asked. She kicked off her shoes and folded her legs underneath her.

Victor settled back on the sofa. "Well, the whole thing was a bit of a scandal as I recall. Your grandfather used to call them the Flo and Glo Show," Victor smiled at the memory. "That's before things got serious."

"Excuse me," Shalese poked her head into the den. "Could I offer you some coffee or something to drink, Mr. um, ah . . ."

"Please, call me Victor," he said warmly. "I'm fine for now, Shalese, but thank you for offering." Shalese nodded and walked back down the hallway.

"Before things got serious . . ." Jenny prompted.

"What? Oh, yes, the story. The word incorrigible would best describe Flo. Your grandmother started wearing pants, smoked her first cigarette, was even heard muttering a swear word under her breath on occasion after spending time with 'that woman,' as Father referred to her." Victor chuckled softly, then was quiet for a moment. "Oh, and the pearls—I remember Flo wore these ridiculous pearls even with her trousers. Considered herself a real trendsetter. Occasionally the two of them would slip off to a ranch in Santa Rosa. God knows what kind of trouble they got into over there," he finished with a shake of his head.

Jenny grinned appreciatively. "That doesn't sound so bad."

"No, some of it was playful. They used to make recipes with odd names, like Millionaire Mulligan Stew. I remember Mother laughing as she'd write them down. I imagine she thought I wasn't old enough to pay any attention. I watched everything she did. I was fascinated by her." He sat quietly for a moment with a wistful look on his face, lost in the childhood memory.

"That was just the beginning, though," Victor said, bringing himself back to the present. "Flo seemed to believe herself invincible. Harmless pranks at first, even a few light brushes with the law that her father smoothed over by calling in some favors with the good old boys who had positions of power in the city." Victor's tone had become glum. "Too big for the britches she insisted on wearing, it was said. Then there was a rumor that Flo had killed a man."

"No," Jenny gasped.

"Yes. It was labeled as an act of vengeance, some love triangle mess with another woman. Again, it was mostly kept out of the papers.

"Grandmother wasn't involved in *that,* was she?" Jenny asked, horrified.

"Oh, heaven's no," Victor replied. "Well, not to my knowledge," he amended. "Your grandfather forbade your grandmother to spend time with Flo—bad for the family name and all that," he said with a sardonic smile. "You know your grandfather."

"And I know Grandmother," Jenny added. "I can't imagine she took that gracefully."

"No, that she didn't. In fact, that's when she packed me up and moved the two of us back to Ohio to stay with her family, to give Father a little time to miss her and come to his senses, I suppose."

"And then what happened?" Jenny leaned in.

"Flo disappeared. Mother of course packed our bags and we came right home, but by the time we arrived, there was no trace of Flo. Some thought she was hiding out in Europe with friends."

Jenny looked stricken. "My gosh. Grandmother could have been mixed up in all that. Whatever happened to Flo?"

Victor shrugged. "She just sort of faded out of existence. She was never heard from again. After a few years, your grandmother stopped trying to find her. It just about broke her heart. For all I know, Flo died overseas."

"What an awful story," Jenny said, and slumped back against the sofa.

"Sweetheart, I didn't mean to upset you. I can be so insensitive sometimes. I'm sure your Florence is a delight." Victor stretched and looked around the comfortable room. "How about a tour of the house? Oops," he caught himself. "That is, if men are allowed beyond the den?"

"Yes, like repairmen or," Jenny grinned, "my Dad . . ." she reached over and squeezed his hand, ". . . if they're accompanied by staff. The women are all upstairs at the moment, so we can take a quick tour without bothering anyone." Jenny led her father down the hallway to the kitchen.

Chapter 17

"Sorry I didn't get to spend time with your Dad, Jenny. What sort of crisis was it? Someone sick or something?" Shalese curled up next to Jenny on the sofa in their bedroom and snuggled the bowl of popcorn between them. She reached for the remote control.

"No, nothing like that. Some work emergency. Story of my life," Jenny sighed. "That place almost fell apart when he retired. He still gets roped into troubleshooting." She reached for the salted, buttered, gooey popcorn. "Mmm, decadent," she mumbled around a mouthful. "I know you wanted to watch *Casablanca* tonight," she said when she'd swallowed, "but could we talk for a little while?"

"Sure babe. You sound upset. Is it about your Dad?" Shalese turned to face Jenny.

"No, not my Dad exactly, but a story he told me about my grandmother and a friend of hers—Flo." Jenny relayed the story, capturing all the details and nuances. "Grandmother has always been sort of a hero to me, the epitome of the strong woman. To think that she followed this Flo and could have gotten herself in a lot of trouble, well, I guess it really upset me." Shalese pulled her close and nuzzled her neck.

"Odd though, isn't it?" Shalese said over the top of Jenny's head, making little wisps of hair dance with her breath. "Both tough old birds, your grandmother's Flo and our Florence, with Italian names. And the pearls," she smiled. "What's with those pearls?" They both giggled. "What if they're the same person," Shalese joked, "and she's come back to corrupt you?" She hummed a bar from *The Twilight Zone* theme song.

"Okay, now we're into horror story material," Jenny chuckled. "Don't give up your day job," she chided.

"You've got to admit, it would make a great movie," Shalese said, wiping a drizzle of butter off Jenny's chin with a napkin.

"Thanks for listening," Jenny said. "I'm ready for *Casablanca* now."

Later, as Jenny snored softly beside her, Shalese slipped out from under the covers, slid her feet into her scuffs, grabbed her robe, and quietly closed the bedroom door behind her. She'd been joking about Florence being Flo, but the thought worked itself around in Shalese's mind like an embedded thorn keeping sleep at bay. She thought of all those times she had ignored her own intuition about questioning Florence's motives. Florence had craftily inserted herself into Shalese's plans, had taken control without seeming to, and had manipulated most decisions made at The First Step. What did they really know about Florence? And was there a connection between the suitcase death and Doris having been chosen by Florence as one of the residents? And what about those pearls—just a coincidence of old lady fashion? Her mind was going squirrelly on her.

She padded softly down the stairs and let herself into the den, closed the door, and turned on the lamp by the phone table. She stared at the phone. "Bad idea," she said aloud. Granny would have said, "Let sleeping dogs lie," or maybe, "Don't go pokin' at snakes." She walked to the window and looked out into the night. The fog had rolled in and made halos around the streetlamps and cast an eerie shimmer of light over the dark street. Shalese crossed the room, picked up the receiver, and dialed the phone.

"Mab?" she said when a woman answered.

"Shalese! Is that you, baby? What you doing calling me at this hour? Your girlfriend dump you or something?" Mab chuckled heartily.

"My girlfriend is just fine," Shalese said with exaggerated patience, suppressing a grin. "I need to talk to you, professionally." There was no response. "Mab, are you there?"

"I'm always here for you sugar-doll," she said, thick and sexy. Shalese rolled her eyes. There was a time when that sort of stuff made her knees weak.

The next morning, Shalese stuck her head in the office where Florence was just hanging her coat and said, "I'm going to run a few errands this morning. When Jenny comes down, would you let her know I'll be back in a while?" Florence nodded. "Thanks," Shalese said and hurried out the back door to avoid running into Jenny.

She knocked three times on the glass door of the Lavender Rose Café and allowed herself a smirk at the CLOSED sign that had never applied to her. Memories of the back room brought an uncomfortably warm and sticky feeling that clung to her like perspiration. She took a deep breath and squared her shoulders.

The hanging bells jingled as Mab turned the lock and opened the door. "Hey, sweet thing," Mab greeted her. "Déjà vu all over again, huh?" she chuckled, as all three hundred pounds of her jiggled like chocolate Jell-o.

Shalese stepped through the doorway and gave Mab a peck on the cheek.

"Hmfp," Mab snorted, the sound an old hound dog makes as she flops over and finds a new position for a snooze.

"Good to see you, Mab," Shalese said, her throat tightened with a moment of nostalgia.

Back in her twenties when Shalese had first moved to the city, she met Mab, who was tending bar at the Lavender Rose Café—the local lesbian watering hole and meet market—and selling a little real estate on the side. Mab had taken her under her ample wing, introduced her to a few hand-selected women, and had even seduced her for a few memorable one-night stands. Mab was not a relationship kind of gal, and she had the skills that come only with years of experience and diligent practice.

Now Mab owned the Lavender Rose. Her staff was loyal, and the place practically ran itself. By day, she sleuthed around as the local dyke PI. She'd gained her reputation staking out unfaithful partners, gathering evidence in petty crime cases, and investigating hate crimes.

Mab and Shalese sat knee to knee at the bar on tall stools padded in purple faux leather. A coffee pot and two mugs were the focus of the first uncomfortable moments of conversation. "Cup o' Joe?" Mab offered, lifting the pot.

"Sure," Shalese said and scooted her cup closer. "Your coffee was always the best."

"My coffee, huh?" Mab bounced her eyebrows suggestively. Shalese chuckled. "So what is it you want to talk to your old friend Mab about," she asked, filling Shalese's cup and then her own, "that was so urgent it couldn't wait until a decent hour of afternoon?"

Shalese recapped her story of meeting Jenny, and then Florence through Jenny. She told Mab about the halfway house and the sudden funding, all the times she ignored or overrode her own intuition that something wasn't right, seduced by the promise of being able to manifest her dream.

"So some rich, pushy old broad has decided to make your dream come true," Mab summarized. "Yup, sure sounds like trouble to me," she said with her elbow on the bar and chin in her hand.

"Florence sort of put herself in the position of interviewing which women we'd accept for rehab. I noticed when going through the files that they were all victims of domestic violence, women who'd stood up, fought back, and wound up incarcerated for their efforts, whose male partners were all living free lives here in the city," Shalese said.

"Well, shame on her, wanting to help all those battered women," Mab offered.

"That's not the point," Shalese banged her fist on the bar. "There were deserving women who weren't considered, women whose spouses were also in prison; women with children; women who were in prison for other reasons. It's like Florence had her own agenda and was using The First Step to fulfill it."

"Uh huh, go on," Mab said, the sarcasm having left her voice.

"Then she wanted to know the addresses of their partners—something about possible restraining orders."

"That makes sense, don't you think? You know about retaliation. God bless Vanessa's soul," Mab said quietly.

"One of those partners recently wound up dead under unusual circumstances." Shalese added the story about Flo and her suspicions that Flo and Florence might be one and the same, right down to the detail of their shared penchant for pearls.

"Oh, well, that's the cincher; they both wore beads," Mab chided. No response. "Something like that used to get a rise out of you. Either you're losing your edge or you're serious." She waited a beat. "You're serious, aren't you?"

Shalese watched the steam rise from her coffee for a moment. "Something just doesn't feel right, Mab. Could you look into this for me?" she reached out and took Mab's pudgy hand.

"Anything for you, baby girl," Mab said.

Chapter 18

Jenny and Shalese sat on the back stoop, carving pumpkins in the midday heat. The residents were having free time, and no one seemed to be in the holiday mood. Jenny swiped at the sweat that trickled down her temple and managed to trail pumpkin goo along her cheek. Shalese reached over to wipe it off.

"Don't touch me, I'm still mad at you," Jenny said with a pout. She waggled the dull carving knife menacingly. "You waited a whole month to tell me you've been seeing your old girlfriend?" Jenny said, all in a pique. She slammed the knife down and bumped the coffee mug that was sitting next to her on the stoop. French Roast splashed over the edge of the mug and ran in a little stream toward her leg. "Shit," Jenny exclaimed brushing it away with her hand.

"I said I called her—to ask for help. It was her idea that we meet." Shalese knew that sounded lame.

She reached over Jenny with a paper towel and mopped at the coffee. "I'm not seeing her, as in *seeing* her," Shalese explained patiently. Jenny expelled a little huff of breath and rolled her eyes. "I met with her professionally, to ask her to run a background check on Florence," Shalese continued, "and she's not my old girlfriend—exactly," she amended. This did not have the effect Shalese had hoped. Jenny's mouth squinched in an angry pucker and her eyes squinted accusation.

"You went behind my back to have Florence checked out by your *not-exactly* ex-girlfriend, and I'm supposed to be happy about that?"

"Look, I just couldn't shake the thought that Flo and Florence might be one in the same." Shalese's voice had a timber to it she knew she'd regret later. "I knew you wouldn't take me seriously."

Jenny stared at the floor. When she looked up, her eyes were rimmed with tears. "Are we having our first fight?" she asked in a shaky voice.

Shalese scooted next to Jenny and pulled her into a tight embrace. "Honey, Mab is the best PI around. I shouldn't have called her without talking to you first. I'm sorry," she apologized. "Will you go with me if she unearths anything?"

Placated, Jenny turned her chin up and received a kiss on her nose from Shalese and a smile that still made her heart race. "You don't think I'd let you go without me, do you?" Jenny said with a coy smile.

As if on cue, the phone rang. Shalese wiped her hands on the coffee-soaked paper towel and grabbed the kitchen extension. "The First Step," she said. Jenny studied Shalese's face as she spoke.

"Hi. Yes, okay. Really?" Shalese's voice registered alarm. "How about tomorrow? We'll be there." Shalese hung up the phone and looked at Jenny. "You've got your wish. That was Mab."

Saturday morning Jenny and Shalese sat sipping coffee across from Mab in the back room of the bar.

"This coffee is strong enough to curl my eyelashes," Jenny said goodheartedly.

Mab reached over, took the cup from Jenny's hand, and put it on the table out of her reach. Jenny looked baffled. "Wouldn't want anything to mess with those beautiful eyelashes, girl. Those lashes are lady killers," Mab smiled, showing several gold capped teeth.

Jenny blushed and glanced over at Shalese. "I told you to watch out for her," Shalese chided playfully.

Mab returned Jenny's coffee cup and scooted her chair a little closer. "So, here's the thing," she began, "there were several weeks of articles in the local paper from back when your Dad would have been a child," she said to Jenny. "There was suspicion that a Flo Lorenze may have been mixed up in a love triangle, but apparently money and connections spoke pretty loudly, and the whole thing was buried. Rumor had it that she went into hiding in Europe, but there's no trace of her once she left the states. It's like she vanished into thin air." Mab sighed and looked at each woman for a moment. "However, I did come across something last month in the local paper that I want to run by you."

Mab reached for an article she'd clipped and handed it to Shalese. "Tiny little article buried on page 17. It wouldn't have caught my eye if you hadn't given me the list of your women's partners. Maple Drive sound familiar? Wasn't that where Doris's boyfriend lived?"

Shalese studied the article about a man who was found in his home after dying of a snapped neck. "Yeah," she said skimming the article, "a suitcase fell on his head." She raised her eyebrow and said, "This is the one I told you about."

"I suppose it could happen," Mab said, "but why do you suppose it happened to *that* man?"

Shalese shot Jenny a glance. Jenny shrugged. "Why would we think Florence had anything to do with this?" she asked. "If we do the math, that would put the date of death on a Tuesday, and she is at The First Step on Tuesdays."

"Florence is no spring chick, right?" Mab ventured. "Let's say she has an accomplice, or maybe a bunch of them."

"Like a gang of old sociopaths who go around offing bad guys?" Jenny snorted her disbelief. "Have you ever thought of writing fiction?" she asked Mab.

"That does seem a little farfetched," Shalese said, "but I trust your instincts." Shalese looked from Mab to Jenny and noted that Jenny was working herself into a pout at that little infraction of loyalty.

Mab looked at Jenny and said, "I'm just sayin'," she held her palms up in mock surrender, "I have a few decades on the streets behind me that have taught me not to take anything at face value— even kindly old women."

Jenny sighed. Shalese reached over and tucked a runaway strand of hair behind Jenny's ear.

"Did she ever talk about relatives, or friends, or people she knew?" Mab asked.

"There's her husband, of course. And she has a sister-in-law," Jenny offered.

"She mentioned she had some influential friends who helped her out when she needed it. Remember, Jen? That's when she was trying to convince me to take the private funding," Shalese recalled, "but she never said who they were."

"And you never asked? You just took thousands of dollars from this woman's friends without knowing who they were?" Mab's voice was somewhere between incredulous and horrified. She shook her head.

Chastised, Shalese stared into her coffee. Jenny squirmed in her chair.

"Okay, who do you make the rent out to?" Mab tried another approach.

"There is no rent. Florence opened a bank account for The First Step, and money is deposited by our benefactor to cover all our needs," Shalese said, feeling more gullible by the moment.

"Mother of God," Mab said, rolling her eyes.

"I knew I shouldn't have trusted a rich, white woman," Shalese muttered. "Didn't I learn anything from my childhood?" She got up and paced the small room.

Jenny cleared her throat. "May I remind you that *I* am a rich, white woman? What you just said is highly offensive, even if it did come from childhood pain." The clench of Jenny's jaw told Shalese she'd just stepped in it, big time. "And I am not the bad, rich, white woman who did you and your mother wrong. You've got to get past this. You have no reason not to trust me—or most white women," Jenny said, "but you've lumped us all in the same category."

Shalese had stopped pacing and looked at Jenny. "You can't imagine I was talking about you," she began to defend herself. "I just meant—"

"I'm with Jenny on this one," Mab said, cutting her off. "It's like folks saying all us fat people are jolly. It's what they call a stereotype—and those hurt," she finished.

With her head hung, Shalese said barely audibly, "I'm really sorry. And really embarrassed," she added.

"Okay," Jenny said, and after a moment got up, went to her, and put her arms around Shalese. "Just think of it as an opportunity for awareness," she said and kissed Shalese on the cheek.

"How about a kiss for the grumpy, fat woman?" Mab joked. She was rewarded with a big smack on each cheek from Shalese and Jenny. With the mood lightened, Mab promised she'd do a little more digging around on the case. "I've got two staff people out next month at the Café, and I'll be picking up their hours," she said, "but I'll do what I can."

November passed without incident. Shalese figured the women of the house were still in the honeymoon phase. Thanksgiving was one big old love fest of appreciation and gratitude. Florence stopped by with a pecan pie, but was planning to spend the day with her husband and his sister's family.

It was an early Monday morning in December, and the sky was sheet-metal gray. It had been raining for a solid week, and Shalese's mood was as gloomy as the weather. The call from Mab the previous night—the Café staff was back from their travels, and she was ready to launch a full-on investigation—hadn't helped. This could be the beginning of the undoing of her dream.

"We'd better get breakfast started," she said leaning against the refrigerator. "What was I thinking giving our cook the morning off?" She grabbed the large frying pan from under the cupboard.

"You were thinking that it was more important for our cook to watch her daughter dance in the third grade's version of the Nutcracker, than to scramble up some eggs for a bunch of ex-felons," Jenny answered, "and I happen to agree," she said with an affirmative nod of her head. "I'll do the bacon," she offered reaching into the fridge. "Oh . . ." Jenny stopped short.

"What? Are we out of bacon?" Shalese asked.

"No. How weird will it be when Florence comes in this morning? I mean, we both know she's being investigated, but she doesn't have a clue. Is that fair?" Jenny pulled out a pound of bacon wrapped in cellophane and closed the refrigerator door.

"Hopefully, she'll never know—if she's innocent. Mab's pretty good at staying invisible. It's fair for us to protect ourselves, The First Step, and the women we serve," Shalese said opening the carton of eggs. "It won't be weird at all," she concluded.

"If she's innocent," Jenny added. "I hope we're not overreacting," Jenny said as she laid strips of bacon neatly next to each other in the frying pan. "Your old girlfriend does have a little of the cloak-and-dagger about her."

"She's not my old girl—" Shalese stopped mid-sentence when she heard the front door open and close, followed by the *click, click, click* of Florence's heels down the hallway.

On her way to the office, Florence stuck her head in the kitchen and called, "Good morning. Something smells good." Her smile froze on her lips and her eyes narrowed in suspicion. "What? Did I forget to comb my hair?" she asked.

Both Jenny and Shalese stared at Florence, frozen, like kids playing a game of Statue. The only thing that moved in the kitchen was the bacon grease that sizzled and popped in the frying pan. Suddenly, both women jerked into action and became preoccupied with their tasks at hand. Shalese cracked eggs into a bowl with studied concentration. Jenny flipped a strip of bacon with careful precision. "Good morning," they said in unison.

"Well, good heavens," Florence said in a huff of exasperation, "you two are acting stranger than usual this morning." She clicked on down the hall and into the office.

"You're looking a little green around the gills," Jenny said later in their bedroom. Shalese was sitting on the edge of the bed; Jenny knelt behind her and massaged the muscles in Shalese's shoulders and neck.

"Mmm," Shalese groaned appreciatively. "Have you thought about what would happen if we find out that Florence is connected in some way to that guy?"

"To her? Probably prison. Wouldn't that be ironic?" Jenny chortled. "I could go visit her this time. Bring her cookies. Maybe when she got out she could come here for rehab." She giggled at the thought.

"Except there wouldn't be any here *here*," Shalese said, her voice serious. "No Florence, no funding, no The First Step."

Jenny's arms fell to her side. "Shoot," Jenny said, "I hadn't thought of that."

Chapter 19

"Sidney," Florence's voice held that scolding tone that made Sidney want to reach through the phone line and smack her, "we really shouldn't talk business in public anymore. Now that we've begun taking action, we can't risk any leaks."

"You're letting paranoia rule you, my dear," Sidney chided. There was an edge to his voice. "Let's put this in perspective; we were in the Plaza with about a hundred other people; the din was terrible, and we were almost whispering. There wasn't a soul near our table." His foot hurt, and he was short on patience today—even for Florence.

"Still, I would feel much better if we firmed up arrangements by phone from here forward." Florence knew Sidney understood this was not merely a request.

"Very well, Florence," Sidney said in an even tone. He couldn't remember exactly when it was that she had gained the power in this organization—perhaps when she'd returned to the states last year. If he hadn't known she was coming, he may not have recognized her— amazing what a change of hair color can do, and time, of course. He ran his fingers through his own thinning hair. "I've confirmed that unfortunate mugging at the water's edge at Ocean Beach next week. With all the detective shows on TV, you'd think a person would know not to struggle," Sidney shook his head slowly. "That's how one gets one's throat cut. More's the pity," he *tsk*ed.

"It's good to be doing work we love, isn't it my friend?" Florence smiled, feeling particularly invincible in the moment.

Chapter 20

Tuesday afternoon a week later, Jenny grabbed the office phone. "Hello, The First Step," she said, bracing the phone between her ear and her shoulder as she set down the stack of files she'd pulled for review.

"Jenny, it's Mab. How you holding up, girl?" To Mab's relief, she had ceased being 'the enemy' in Jenny's mind. She could almost see what Shalese saw in Jenny—still too vanilla though, for Mab's particular taste.

"Mab, what's new? Shalese and I were just talking about you this morning," Jenny said as she switched the phone to her other ear, pulled out the desk chair, and collapsed into it. She kicked off her shoes and wiggled her toes.

"Uh oh," Mab joked. "Guess I should be flattered. Lot a people don't even notice a three-hundred-pound black woman; it's amazing how color and fat make you invisible," she chuckled.

"Oh, Mab, that's not—"

"Honey girl," Mab interrupted, "believe me, sometimes it works to our advantage. I heard something at the Plaza that I think you and Shalese might want to know. Can y'all come on over?" Mab ran a damp cloth over the bar with her free hand.

"Let me see if Shalese can get away. Give us an hour, okay? The Financial Freedom group is just finishing up," Jenny said as she checked her watch.

"Guess you got that one nailed," Mab said good-naturedly.

"Thin ice, my friend—thin ice," Jenny joked back. "Bye."

The Lavender Rose Café was virtually empty at four o'clock, which made Sanna chuckle when Mab called out, "Hey, Sanna, keep an eye on the place for me for a little while, okay?" Sanna stuck her turban-wrapped head out of the kitchen and gave a quick wave to Shalese and Jenny, then disappeared again.

Mab ushered them into a booth at the far end of the bar so she could watch the door, an old PI habit. A pot of coffee, three mugs, and three slices of pecan pie awaited them.

Mab filled the coffee cups and slid the plates of pie in front of each woman.

"I saw Florence sitting at one of those little round tables in the Plaza with an old dude, some upper-crust, money-lookin' kinda guy. They were having coffee. No one else nearby." Mab paused, took a gulp of her coffee. "So, I figure to aristocrat types, people like me are invisible; we mop floors, pick up garbage—you know, not like real people." She forked some pecan pie into her mouth and chewed slowly, savoring the flavors.

"Wait a minute, isn't that a stereotype?" Shalese raised her eyebrows and shot Jenny a look.

"Yeah, but it's an accurate one," Jenny grinned. Mab nodded and chewed her pie.

Jenny and Shalese leaned forward, elbows on table, neither had touched their coffee or pie. "Mab," Shalese said, her chin jutted with impatience, "you're killing us here. What happened?"

"They were deep in conversation," Mab said. She stopped to wipe the corners of her mouth. "Florence kept glancing toward the entrance, nervous-like. I swiped a cloth from a cart near the counter, sashayed right up to the table next to them, and started mopping it off like I worked there."

"You didn't," Jenny said, shaking her head. "Did they stop talking when they saw you?"

"Honey child, I'm telling you, we're invisible to the likes of them. I overheard something about an accident at Ocean Beach, scheduled for next week."

"You don't schedule an accident," Jenny said, then slapped her hand over her mouth. "Oh my God."

"I moved to another table nearby, but I couldn't hear anything more than that. They left soon after. I followed them to the parking garage, which wasn't hard—he had a limp that slowed him down. He doffed his fedora as Florence got in her car. Then he got in his Alpha and drove away—but not before I got his license plate. It's registered to a Sidney Harrington—lives here in the city."

"What do we do now?" Shalese asked, balancing a piece of pie on her fork.

"I suggest you eat that piece of pie before it falls in your lap," Mab said and poured herself more coffee. "I thought about a stake-out, but I don't think that will get us very far. The guy's too old to pull off something like an accident at the beach by himself; probably hire someone."

"What about a phone tap?" Jenny offered.

"Gets tricky. You have to get into his house to plant equipment. That's breaking and entering," Mab said.

"Only if you get caught," Jenny added. Shalese looked at her with a mixture of admiration and disbelief.

"Maybe it's time to turn this over to the police," Shalese suggested.

"We don't have enough information yet," Mab said, wiping pie crumbs from the table onto her plate with her thumb. "Let me do a little more sleuthing and see what I can come up with. Call me if Florence takes any time off from work, or hangs up the phone quickly when you come in, or does anything suspicious."

They finished their coffee and pie and promised to check in by phone in a few days.

Chapter 21

Shalese sat rigid in her chair as the women talked excitedly. She wiggled her jaw slightly to unclamp her teeth and forced herself to breathe rhythmically until group was over and she could talk with Jenny alone.

Jenny's eyes darted among the women speaking. She glanced at Shalese who was staring at a spot on the floor.

"Let's try to not read too much into this," Jenny suggested, her voice barely heard among the chatter.

"All's I can say, girls, is we're on a roll," Chandra said. "We've got some kinda guardian angel looking over us, is what I think." The women in the therapy group nodded, grinned, and high-fived their agreement.

"It's kind of creepy though," Maren said, her voice tentative. "I mean, his neck was sliced over a wallet?"

"Hey, you live like trash, you die like trash," Paulina offered.

"What he did to me, no death's bad enough for the bastard," Chandra said, years of impotent rage fueling her bravado. "Idiot probably thought he could bully his way out of being mugged. If I'd have been there, I'd have given that mugger a piece of ass as a reward." The set of her jaw and the glint in her eyes made Chandra look like someone you wouldn't want to mess with in a dark alley. Maren giggled nervously.

"For now, I think we'd best write this off as a coincidence," Shalese suggested. She stood, held out her hands, and the others joined hands around the circle. "God, grant me the serenity . . ." they began the prayer that ended each meeting.

Jenny excused herself right after lunch to return a call to the officer who had left a message earlier that morning. Shalese was dealing with a mini-crisis between two residents about acceptable levels of clutter in their shared room. Jenny closed the office door behind her and sat in the swivel chair next to the computer, spine rigid, eyes wide. She willed her teeth not to chatter.

"Yes, Officer O'Flaherty, it is strange that both victims have been ex-spouses of two of our residents. Very strange indeed. Quite a coincidence, actually, in a city this large," Jenny rambled, nodding her head vigorously. "Yes, of course I'll call you if we hear anything, anything at all, related to this case," Jenny promised.

She hung up the phone and collapsed in the swivel chair like a spent mop. Panting, she ran a shaky hand over her brow where a film of sweat had begun to chill. Issues of confidentiality, safety of the residents, scandal, and professional censure fought for space in her mind.

"Florence," she called out. There was no answer. After a moment, Jenny pulled herself together and checked the dining room, the study, and finally the kitchen. She stood for a moment, fuming. She opened the back door and scanned the outbuildings. No Florence. Jenny turned to go look for Shalese when she saw a yellow Post-It on the kitchen counter that read: *Slipped out for some errands. Back in an hour.* Florence had signed the note with a flourished *F*, which led Jenny to hurl an expletive without a flourished *F*. "Slipped out when you saw the message to call the police," Jenny said.

Shalese, having quelled the crisis between roommates, was in the office at her desk attacking an ever-growing mound of papers, months old by now, that she'd promised herself she'd file before one more day went by. She smiled at the efficiency of Jenny's filing system. Thank God for Virgos. When she unearthed a sheet of paper filled with real estate listings, she shrugged. Must be something Mab left behind, she reasoned, and set it aside with Mab's name on it.

"Damn it, damn it, damn it!" Shalese heard Jenny shout from across the hall. She bolted from the office into the kitchen in time to see Jenny kick the blue recycling bin across the floor.

"Jen, babe, what happened? You're all flushed—you're going to give yourself a heart attack," she said, approaching Jenny tentatively like you would a feral cat.

"Shalese, we've got to put an end to this. I can't take it anymore," Jenny sputtered, raking her hands through her hair.

Shalese shrugged her bewilderment like a bad-fitting coat. "Jenny, I don't know what you're talking about. What . . ."

"I'm talking about the police called. I'm talking about they're wondering if there's a connection between that guy with the slit throat and the guy with the broken neck and our residents. That's what I'm talking about. And Florence flew the coop," Jenny added.

"Flew the—" Shalese was interrupted by the ringing of the office phone. She crossed the hallway and caught it on the third ring. From the kitchen, Jenny heard her exclaim, "What? Oh my God, what do we do now?"

Jenny, braced against the office doorway, breathed shallowly, every muscle in her body on high alert. "Who is it?" she mouthed to Shalese. Shalese put her hand up and turned her body away from Jenny.

"Okay, yeah. Call us the minute you hear anything at all. Thanks," Shalese said, and hung up the phone. "That was Mab. She was sleuthing around and found out Florence is gone," she said to Jenny.

"That's what I was trying to tell you," Jenny began.

"No, I mean she's really gone," Shalese said. "Her house is empty. No sign of the Wilsons. The neighbors have no idea when they left or where they might be. It's like they vanished into thin air."

"Again," Jenny added. Her legs no longer able to hold her up, she slid down along the doorjamb and sat numbly on the floor. She looked up at Shalese who sat on the edge of the desk, a blank look on her face. There they sat like mannequins in a Macy's window. At some point, someone would have to move.

Chapter 22

After the women were settled in their rooms for the night, Shalese, Jenny, and Mab sat in the parlor across from Officer Shirk and Officer O'Flaherty. Jenny cried jerky little sobs and wiped at her tears with a soggy tissue. Mab's lips were clamped shut like a snapping turtle. She crossed and uncrossed her thick ankles and shifted her bulk uncomfortably in a wing-backed chair.

Officer Shirk looked over the two-page agreement, signed by Shalese. "This is it? This is your business contract?" A look of skepticism accompanied the repeated clicking of Officer Shirk's pen. "You're serious?"

"Look, I'm telling you," Shalese said, her voice quivered with frustration, "I don't know who owns the property. I don't know who pays the bills. I figured this is just the way rich people do business. Yes, it's stupid, and yes, I'm ridiculously gullible," she said as he took notes on a spiral bound pad. Shalese fought off tears that wanted to leak relief down her cheeks, months of dark little suspicions confirmed. She gritted her teeth and took in a hissy breath.

"When were you planning on sharing your concerns with the police about this woman who you believe might be connected to the recent murders?" Officer O'Flaherty asked. His voice sounded like a game show host. He could have just as easily been asking her if she knew the capital of Bolivia.

Mab leaned forward. "I've been doing some investigating on this case." She introduced herself and explained that she was looking into Florence's background, and that they believed Florence might indeed be Flo Lorenze who had been cold filed decades earlier.

O'Flaherty merely blinked. He opened his mouth as if to speak, then closed it again. He crooked his head at Officer Shirk, and said, "Why does that name sound familiar?" Shirk shrugged.

Unable to hold it together any longer, shoulder-shaking sobs overtook Shalese. "What's going to become of The First Step?" She turned to Jenny. "I don't know what to do," she cried. Jenny wrapped her in a wet hug. Mab sat on her hands and stared at the floor.

"Have you checked your bank balance?" Officer Shirk asked. "Did Mrs. Wilson have access to your account as well as your files?" His forehead wrinkled in anticipation.

"Oh my God," Shalese groaned. Jenny gave Shalese's hand a quick squeeze and said, "I'll check that right now." She excused herself and went down the hall to the office.

Shalese shook her head slowly in disbelief. Her life savings, her retirement were in that account. "I feel like such a fool for trusting someone this much."

Mab reached over and patted Shalese's hand. "We're gonna get through this, baby," she murmured. The officers glanced at each other, then at the door where Jenny would reappear with the answer as to whether larceny would be added to the list of charges.

Jenny returned looking like the ghost of all holidays past. Her lip trembled as she said, "The account has been closed." She stood rigid in the doorway. Shalese gasped. Her hands flew to her face as if to make sure she was still there. Mab muttered, "Jesus, Mary, and Joseph."

"That's not even possible is it, to close an account that quickly? Aren't there rules or something?" Shalese asked of no one in particular.

"Depends on who you're connected to," Officer O'Flaherty said. He looked at his partner. "I just remembered why the name Lorenze sounded familiar." He shook his head as if he couldn't quite believe it himself. "I'm thinking we're going to be re-opening that file on the AA."

"Alcoholics Anonymous?" Jenny said. "I knew Florence drank, but . . ."

"The Angels," Officer O'Flaherty corrected.

"You think they're resurfacing after all these years?" Shirk asked. "Thought they were all dead."

"The Hell's Angels?" Mab asked, and tried to block from her mind an image of Florence on a Harley.

"No, ma'am. The Avenging Angels. Group of corrupt elite from back in the 1940s. Got away with murder—literally," Shirk said. "They became sort of famous. The Academy uses them as an example of how to avoid stereotyping criminals."

"Seems they thought themselves to be above the law," O'Flaherty added. "Turns out they *were* the law. Their members included judges, police officers, lawyers, doctors, educators—people with money and influence."

"That dame, Lorenze," Officer Shirk added, "was suspected of murder. Vanished."

Mab looked at Jenny. "And you laughed at me," she reminded her. "Fiction, you said." Jenny's mouth hung agape.

"Why did they call themselves The Avenging Angels?" Shalese sensed the answer before she even finished asking the question.

"Back then, seems they'd take up a cause. Sort of a vigilante group bent on righting wrongs done to the 'little folks,' the poor folks who couldn't defend themselves. A type of Robin Hood complex or something," O'Flaherty explained. "There must be a new generation of them crawling out from under the rocks."

"Righting wrongs," Shalese echoed. "She chose which women we'd admit," she said aloud to herself.

Jenny sat down next to her. "They all had male partners who battered them and who were still alive and in the area, right?" Jenny added. "I remember you saying something about how that seemed unfair to others who were also qualified."

"Do you think that's the connection? That The First Step was just being used as a front for them to do their getting even?" Mab asked.

Shalese leaned back against the sofa hard. She looked at Jenny. "You and I didn't know each other until we were introduced by a friend of Florence's who works at the junior college in Women's Studies."

"Women's Studies?" Jenny sounded crushed. "The bastion of feminist philosophy? Women supporting women?"

"Ain't nothing sacred, that's what I say," added Mab.

"I'll need the name of that contact," Officer Shirk said, flipping to a fresh page in his notebook.

The whole interview had taken two hours. Shalese closed the door behind the officers and walked heavily back into the parlor where Jenny paced and Mab sat with her bare feet propped on the coffee table.

"What are we going to tell the residents?" Shalese said, collapsing into a rocking chair by the window. "They have nowhere to go. We have no money. We can't pay the cook, or the utilities, or . . ." her voice trailed off like vapor.

"We'll call a meeting right after breakfast and just tell them the truth. Maybe among all of us we'll come up with an idea," Jenny said. She came and sat next to Mab on the sofa. "Will you stay over tonight? There's a pull out bed," she said and patted the sofa cushion.

Mab took a moment before answering. "You don't think I'd just abandon you here, do you?" she said gruffly to cover up her tender heart that needed to be needed. "There's some emergency money in an account a defunct lesbian political action group kept open. Left me in charge of it. Shoulda known better," Mab chuckled. "I think they'd be okay with helping us out."

"Us?" Jenny squealed and threw her arms around Mab.

"I've been thinking it's about time I invest in a good cause—that is, if you'll have me as a partner," Mab said, suddenly looking as vulnerable as a kid on the edge of the playground.

"Welcome aboard," Shalese threw a mock salute from across the room. "Let's talk about that account tomorrow. My brain's too tired to hold one more thought tonight," Shalese said. "We'll bring some blankets and a pillow down. G'night."

"Thanks, Mab," Jenny said and planted a big smack on her cheek. "I'm so glad you're here," she added.

"Yeah, yeah," Mab made a shooing motion with her hand.

Before Jenny and Shalese turned in for the night, Jenny placed a call to her father. "I need to update him," she said to Shalese who sat on the edge of the bed next to her.

"Babe, they're all going to be asleep back there. Maybe you should wait until morning," Shalese suggested.

Jenny shook her head. "I won't be able to sleep," she said with a doleful look. "Damn, you're right," she sighed, "it's the message machine. Daddy, it's me. Everything's coming undone. I think Flo may still be alive. In fact, she may be Florence. Call me when you get this. I love you," she said and hung up the phone.

"Feel better?" Shalese asked. Jenny nodded. "How's your dad's heart? That was quite a message to start his day," she said.

Chapter 23

Shalese had slept fitfully. Her waking moments were cluttered with thoughts, words, phrases that would help her explain to the residents this new turn of events. At 3 a.m., Jenny had woken and said, "I know you'll find just the right words. Try to get some sleep." She turned over and almost immediately lapsed into a gentle snore. Rather than feeling reassured, Shalese just felt pissed off. She turned on her side with a little extra bounce on the mattress, which was pretty ineffective given the memory foam.

Early the next morning, before Shalese, Jenny, Mab, and the ten residents of The First Step gathered in the parlor, Jenny placed a call to her father. "Please, please let him be home," she pleaded into the phone.

"Pound rezdence," Mary answered, her voice like liquid amber. Jenny was so wrapped up in the comforting sound, she forgot to answer. "Hello?" Mary said.

"Mary, it's me, Jenny," she said grinning, and waiting for the effusive greeting she knew would follow.

"Oh, my lord, child, I can't believe it's your sweet self. How ya doin', baby?"

"Hearing your voice, Mary, I couldn't be better," Jenny said, and meant every word. Mary had always had that effect on her.

"How're things with that halfway house you're runnin' out there?"

"Well, that's sort of why I'm calling," Jenny said. "Is my Dad around this morning?"

"Standin' right here," Mary said. "The man doesn't have enough to do, 'cept listen to my calls," she joked. "Here's your Daddy. Love you, baby girl."

"You too, Mary," Jenny said.

"Jenny? I was just about to return your call," Victor said, his voice full of concern. "Honey, what on earth is going on out there? Florence might be Flo?"

"Daddy," she said, and felt the tears pool in her eyes. She told Victor the story of Florence's disappearance, their lack of funding, the need to move—everything.

"Sweetheart, you know you can count on me for assistance," Victor said.

"I was thinking about borrowing against my trust fund, actually."

"You could, sweetheart, but that's really for your future," he said. "You know I will gladly front you funding. I just don't want to step on any toes. If you, Shalese, and Mab can see a way I can lend a hand, please just ask. Anything I can do for you, I will," Victor reassured. "I can hardly believe that Flo has reappeared as Florence—if that turns out to be true—and has found her way back into our family by nothing other than sheer happenstance. She did enough damage the first time around, and now to put the recovery house at risk—truly, it makes me shudder. Let me know how I can help sweetheart. I love you."

"You're the best," Jenny said. "Love you. Bye."

Just as Jenny hung up the phone, it rang again. It was Officer Shirk reporting back that Janelle Anderson had never been employed by the junior college. *What? Surely there must be a mistake*, Jenny thought. She meant to share this with Shalese just before the meeting began, but was interrupted by a question from Chandra. The phone call drifted from her mind.

The mood in the room was somber. The women looked at Shalese with expectancy.

"Somebody say something," Chandra piped up, "y'all are creeping me out."

"Yeah, this feels familiar—like when my dad was about to go off on us out of nowhere," Paulina added. Others murmured and nodded their heads. They looked from Shalese to Jenny to the new big woman, trying to get a read on the situation.

Shalese sat for a moment, working her lips, although no words were forming. "There's no easy way to put this," she began. "You all know Florence. She sat in on your initial interviews, and you've seen her around here." The women nodded. Shalese looked at Jenny and then Mab for support. Jenny smiled weakly. Mab opened her mouth as if she were going to speak, and then closed it again.

"What you may not know is that Florence was the benefactor of The First Step. Without her considerable financial backing, we could not have opened this recovery house. We would not have been here for the, what—almost half a year, that we've spent together so far. Without her continued backing, we cannot continue to exist," Shalese stopped for a breath.

"She dead or something?" Chandra asked. Gasps were heard throughout the room. "Oh no," Maren cried. "What happened to her? Did one of our exes kill her for helping us?" Things were getting out of hand quickly.

"It has come to our attention," Shalese said, hating that she lapsed back into formal speech when nervous, "that Florence may be involved with a group of wealthy, influential people who were using The First Step to further their own agenda. It seems she may have been responsible, in some way, for the recent deaths of two of your exes—"

"Then she deserves a medal," one of the women spoke over her.

"—in addition to several felonies from some years ago," Shalese finished. "The police are looking for her now. In the meantime, she's gone, and so is all the funding for the house. Now, until we receive an official eviction notice, we can stay put, but . . ."

Shouts of outrage, cries of betrayal, and sighs of resignation seemed to fill the space and suck the air right out of the room. Shalese closed her eyes for a moment and focused on breathing.

Jenny stood up, stepped behind Shalese, and placed her hands firmly on Shalese's shoulders. "The bank account has been closed and there are several bills outstanding," Jenny added. "Our friend Mab," she nodded at Mab, who blinked acknowledgement to the women as she sat with her beefy hands folded tightly in her lap, "has a possible, but temporary, source of funding that will carry us through the next few months."

Mab sat up in the recliner and looked around the room. "Back in the early '70s there was a non-profit group that funded a bunch of different lesbian activities. Not much money involved, but a little seed money here and there, most of it donated by women who'd made it financially. Some of it came from fundraisers."

"We're not exactly a lesbian population," Gabriella said, crossing her legs primly. Analise nodded vigorously.

"No, no—that we're not," Mab agreed, "not most of us. The point is, for whatever reason back then, the group decided I would be the treasurer. When the group disbanded in the '80s, there was about eight hundred dollars left, which we put in a savings account. We voted, and

I wound up as the overseer of the money to be used at my discretion, as long as it went to helping women," she said.

"Savings account?" Maren piped up. "That means a couple decades or so of interest, right?"

"I 'spose it does," Mab said. "I can't think of a better use for that money than to cover our utilities here at the house until we get resettled."

"Mab, that's very generous of you," Shalese said, "but are you sure you're okay using it to support a non-lesbian group?"

"Hey, women are women, right?" Mab said. There were high-fives and shouts of appreciation all around. Shalese's shoulders dropped an inch in relief, and Jenny grinned hugely.

"I have every hope of finding new funding sources so we can continue. This month, however, we're cutting back to basic services—no yoga classes, no haircuts, no outside helpers," Shalese said, ready to continue the list of things they would have to do without.

"I can cut hair as well as that young thing that comes in here every month," one of the women said. "I've been paying attention in yoga; I can lead the class," another offered. "I used to be a short order cook," Maren offered, "I mean if there are any groceries left."

"We probably qualify for free food since there's no income, right?" yet another woman chimed in, and several others agreed.

Shalese, Jenny, and Mab exchanged smiles as the residents took on the task of making a list of all the ways they could keep The First Step alive.

Shalese stood, cleared her throat, and raised her hands to signal quiet and the din dropped immediately. Tears of gratitude choked her words. "You all are amazing," she said, and wiped at her eyes with the back of her hand.

"Hey, this is our house," Chandra called out. "We take care of what's ours. That's what you've been teaching us, isn't it?"

Shalese nodded, and then said, "The problem is, the house isn't ours. I don't know who owns it or how long we'll be able to stay. There are just some things I can't—"

A woman in the back of the room interrupted. "Well, we better be looking for a new place then, right?" The women shouted out their agreement. "So, how do we do that?" she asked. "What's the next step?"

"That's it," Mab blurted out. "That's the new name for our new place, The Next Step." Cacophony reigned as the women hollered out names of people they knew that might be able to help them find a new house. Mab slipped her arm through Shalese's. "It's just trusting the right people," she said with a grin. What had begun on a funereal tone had turned into a celebration of life.

Later, upstairs in their bathroom, Jenny said, "Promise you won't get mad if I tell you something?"

Shalese looked up from brushing her teeth and said, "I don't have a whole lot of tolerance left for bad news," Shalese said. She rinsed and spit. She caught Jenny's pout in the mirror as Jenny turned to leave. "Jen, I'm sorry. Of course I want to hear anything you have to say," Shalese said, catching Jenny by the hand.

Jenny reversed her pout and held her bottom lip between her teeth for a moment and then said, "Janelle Anderson was never employed by the junior college." Shalese's jaw dropped. Jenny stared at the floor.

"Don't tell me—this happened in close proximity to the time Florence disappeared?" Shalese said with a grimace.

Jenny nodded. "Officer Shirk told me over the phone. I'm sorry— I got distracted and it just completely slipped my mind."

"Better tell Mab," Shalese said.

"Already did," Jenny answered. "This just keeps getting creepier and creepier. I wonder who else is involved."

Shalese pulled back the covers, sat on the edge of the bed, and shook off her slippers. "I'm tired to the bone," she said with a yawn as she snuggled under the down comforter.

Jenny had slipped into her nightie and was sitting cross-legged on the bed, brushing her hair. Shalese turned on her side to watch Jenny, mesmerized. Shalese's hair didn't lend itself to being brushed. Stroke. Stroke. Stroke. She felt herself drift towards sleep.

"Just one more thing?" Jenny noted Shalese's heavy eyelids, but plunged ahead anyway. "I talked to my Dad this morning."

"What?" Shalese sat up and looked at Jenny. "Tell me you didn't . . ."

"He offered to help," Jenny interrupted. "I didn't ask, and he knew receiving money from him might be a problem for you," Jenny pleaded her case, "but there is money to invest if we want to borrow from it. I mean, what's the difference between that and a small business loan?" She reached over and set her brush on the nightstand.

"After our experience with Florence, I should think the answer would be clear," Shalese fumed. "We can't afford anymore handouts. Jenny, look what just happened." Shalese grabbed her pillow, gave it a good punch, and slammed it up against the headboard with more force than was necessary. Jenny winced.

"Are you comparing my father to Florence?" Jenny said, her lip trembling in frustration.

"I just think business should be done with businesses, not with individuals. Less messy that way," Shalese responded. She took a deep breath, released a heavy sigh. "I'm sorry," she said, taking both of Jenny's hands in hers. "I haven't been this scared for a long time. When I was thirteen, we got an eviction notice. It was about the scariest thing that ever happened to me," she said, looking deeply into Jenny's eyes.

"What happened?" Jenny asked, her own eyes beginning to brim with tears. At times like this, the disparity of their upbringings felt like a wedge between them.

"My momma's supervisor at the factory said we could come stay with her a while. Turned out to be a real nightmare. She never let Momma forget that we owed her for helping us out when we were needy."

"White woman, right?" Jenny guessed.

"Yup . . ." Shalese said, and sighed heavily again. "Damn," she muttered, "I hate that this is still a problem for me."

"Remember when Mab said you've just got to know *who* to trust?" Jenny leaned into Shalese.

Shalese nodded. "Okay, we'll consider the Pond money as a possible back-up. How's that?" she said, and kissed Jenny on the nose.

As they snuggled under the covers, before turning off the light, Jenny turned to face Shalese and said, "What a long strange trip this has been, huh?"

"You know it, babe. No one could make up stuff like this," Shalese said. She turned off the light and pulled Jenny close.

Chapter 24

It was late morning, the last week of June, and the marine layer was beginning to thin enough to promise sunshine for their trip an hour north of the city.

Six months had passed since the morning Shalese had gathered the women in the group room and told them that Florence had flown the coop and taken all the money with her. The women had banded together in an impressive brainstorming effort to keep their recovery house afloat.

Along with the funds Mab secured from the now defunct lesbian political action group, Margot had been reading up on bee keeping. Chandra was studying to renew her cosmetology license—she'd given up prostitution along with alcohol and meth while in prison, although the quick, tax-free income still held some allure. Beth was trying her hand at candle making, and Paulina had pulled her potter's wheel out of storage.

More substantially, Victor Pond had offered to underwrite the halfway house for six months. Issues of white privilege aside, Shalese gratefully accepted the gift.

Although they still hadn't received an eviction notice, at the top of Shalese's list was finding a place to relocate since they were currently stranded, rent-free but with no visible proof of tenancy, in the San Francisco Victorian. Mab had located two potential sites, a two-story open floor plan warehouse south of Market Street right there in San Francisco, and, through a multiple listing flier that had been sitting in the office at The First Step, a foreclosed guest ranch in Sonoma County.

Chandra's cousin Harold had a small fleet of limos, one of which he willingly lent to the soon-to-be-homeless women for a jaunt to scope out their options. He owed Chandra. Ten years her senior, he'd molested her behind the garage at a family barbeque when she was fourteen. No charges were filed, but he had been paying guilt dues ever since.

"I ain't never been in no limo," Madigan, who'd done time for serving her husband a not-quite fatal dose of rat poison, gasped as she hoisted her considerable bulk into the We Go Limo. "Where we headed again?"

"Downtown first since we're already here, then Santa Rosa," Jenny said as she took a quick head count of the ten women and extended her hand to help Shalese into the limo.

There was an air of excitement similar to a school trip as they pulled away from the curb and blended into mid-day traffic.

"Where's Mab?" Madigan asked. "She gotta be there."

"She had some business to take care of this morning. She'll meet us in Santa Rosa," Jenny assured. She took Shalese's hand and squeezed it. "I've got butterflies in my stomach from either excitement or terror, I can't decide which," she whispered in Shalese's ear as Harold weaved his way across the city.

Shalese, lost in thought, smiled and gave her a distracted kiss on the cheek. She hoped the abandoned ranch in Santa Rosa would be the answer to their dream; it would get them away from the noise, filth, and chaos of urban life, not to mention the danger. How they would afford this dream had not yet come to her.

Bypassing as much of the Civic Center traffic as possible, Harold headed toward the general vicinity of 11th and Market, an interesting mishmash of swanky restaurants, some spill-over S&M bars, abandoned warehouses, and desolate undeveloped lots of urban blight.

"What on earth are they doing?" Maren gaped at the sight of a man wearing a dog collar being led by his partner dressed in leather spats, a vest, and not a whole lot more.

"You don't want to know," Chandra said.

"That's it on your right," Shalese said to Harold. "Pull over there."

Jenny bobbed hear head to catch a view of the lumbering two-story abandoned warehouse missing several windows. "Oh, look—air conditioning," she said playfully. Shalese scowled.

The sidewalk in front was littered with debris, and a tattered blanket wadded up in the doorway marked someone's turf.

"This is going to take more than vision," Shalese mumbled as they exited the van. "Why are we even looking at this place?"

"Because Mab set up an appointment to see it. We wouldn't have to leave the city," she said as she looked up and down the block.

"There must be something redeeming about it," Jenny said, sounding less sure by the minute. A woman wearing a business suit and sensible shoes stepped out of the building and stood in the doorway. With one foot, she kicked aside the moldy blanket and turned a bright smile on the women emerging from the limo. Tentatively, she worked her way to the sidewalk.

"Cheryl Jasper," she said, extending her hand to Chandra who was the first to reach her.

"How ya doing, Cheryl," Chandra said, and pumped her hand. Cheryl blinked and scanned the group looking for someone in charge.

Jenny stepped forward, introduced herself and Shalese. "I'm not sure this is exactly what we're looking for, but Mab—who you spoke with earlier this week—said we should take a look," Jenny said, doubt coating her words.

Once inside, Cheryl said, "Follow me to the second floor. I think you'll see the infinite possibilities available." Chandra snorted in response. "The owner is willing to build out the space any way you want it," Cheryl said as they crossed the great empty span of concrete flooring. Her voice echoed as she spoke.

"Ahh!" shouted Madigan.

Startled, Shalese turned to her. "What's wrong?"

"Nothin'. Always wanted to shout in a tunnel and hear my own voice. Never got to. This works," Madigan said with a grin. Jenny cast a look her way and then followed Cheryl up the industrial stairway.

"I do like all the light," Gabriella said of the floor-to-ceiling windows on both floors.

"The space really is like a blank canvas," Paulina added, trying to be helpful. "And it is still in the city, close to all the action," she added.

"Depending on what kind of action you're looking for," Chandra said with a chuckle.

The women wandered about on the second floor trying to envision walls where there were none. Margot peered out a window along the back wall into a tiny cement courtyard.

"There's really no outdoor space," she said. "Certainly won't be doing bee hives here."

"No place for a pottery shed either," commented Paulina.

As they descended the stairs, Jenny took Shalese's arm and whispered, "I just can't do this. I feel like I'm back in prison here. Too much concrete. I'm sorry, I tried to keep an open mind."

"Thank God," mumbled Kendra who had overheard.

Shalese sighed in relief. "Cheryl, thank you for your time. I don't think this is quite what we're looking for," she said as she ushered the women out the door and back into the limo.

"Okay, *now* we gonna go 'cross the Golden Gate Bridge?" Madigan said, giddy at the thought.

"It would make more sense to go across the Bay Bridge and up 80 instead of crossing the city again," Harold offered, looking to Shalese for guidance.

"We can come home down 101 and across the Golden Gate Bridge," Shalese said to Madigan.

"What? No!" Madigan was adamant. "I gotta see it from both directions." Her eyes filled with tears of desperation.

Harold shrugged. "Hey, I'm just the driver," he said.

"And don't you forget that," Chandra shot back.

Harold started the engine and headed the limo west through morning traffic to catch 19th Avenue, which would take them straight through Golden Gate Park to the bridge. The women talked quietly among themselves and were in mutual agreement that the funky warehouse would not be home to The Next Step.

Madigan pressed her nose against the window and watched the park go by as they glided along 19th Avenue. She waved at an old man sitting at a bus stop. As the limo rolled over the Golden Gate Bridge, Madigan watched the city skyline recede. "Whooee," she said, "that sure is a lot of concrete. How come it don't just fall right in the water?"

"Are you saying you've never seen the city from this angle before?" Doris asked.

"I never been outta the Tenderloin, 'cept to the park once when I was a kid," Madigan confessed. "Ever-thing I needed was there in the 'hood."

Gabriella, world traveler and former wife of Dr. Parducci—ophthalmologist to San Francisco's elite—paled at the thought. The Tenderloin was the sewer of the city. The First Step was certainly an equalizer of social strata, she quietly mused—or maybe it was the time they'd all served in prison for fighting back against their abusers. "Really?" was all she could manage to say in response.

By the time the limo reached Petaluma, it had taken on the feel of a bus bound for summer camp, as another round of "Make New Friends" harmoniously wove its way from one side of the limo to the other.

Analise, sitting next to Gabriella, moaned softly and held her head. "Migraine?" Gabriella asked.

"Car sick," Analise mumbled.

Overhearing this, Beth, the resident herbalist, slipped her a bottle of Rescue Remedy. "Just a couple of drops under your tongue—fix you right up," she said.

"I don't think I should open my mouth," Analise squeezed the words out through clenched teeth.

"Sick? Somebody bein' sick?" Madigan said. "Stop the bus!" she shouted to the driver.

Jenny and Shalese exchanged a look. "Car sick or pregnant," Shalese said quietly with a shake of her head. "I'm not buying the 'I got tied up shopping' story for why she missed group a few weeks ago."

Jenny groaned. "Just what we need. That could start an epidemic of women returning to their abusers." She looked out of the window and watched the traffic flow by as Harold pulled the limo to the side of the highway and Analise threw up in the grass.

Back on the road, they reached Santa Rosa in twenty minutes and worked their way across the city to the frontage road that would take them to the ranch.

Chapter 25

Harold drove leisurely up the old frontage road through the vineyard, his elbow hung out the window; the fresh warm air lifted the strands of hair he'd combed across his bald spot that morning. As he passed through a gate, the road turned to hard-packed dirt and he slowed his speed. A few yards up the road and around the bend, the road became even more hazardous, forcing Harold to hunch forward in concentration and grip the wheel with both hands.

The limo spewed dust and rocks, clunking and pinging against the frame, as it lumbered slowly up the country lane, slipping in and out of tire ruts. Harold pulled onto a gravel turnaround in front of the abandoned ranch, turned off the engine, and ran his fist across his forehead. "Shit," he muttered.

"Hey, babies," Mab called out, waving wildly as the women spilled out of the limo. They clambered across the parking area and swarmed about the structures like an army of ants at a picnic.

"What the . . ." Madigan hollered. She covered her head with both hands and ducked.

"Just a hummingbird," Mab said, pulling Madigan into a big hug. "We city girls have to get used to all this wildlife. Hey girlfriend . . ." she called to Jenny who was picking her way across the dried grasses and knee-high weeds.

Jenny coughed and flapped her hand in front of her face at the dust as Harold pulled the limo around to the side of the ranch in search of shade.

"Oh my God," she said, slowly turning her head from one side to the other, taking in the semi-circle of six small cottages, three on either side of a main house. "Really, Mab, you said minor disrepair, not major disaster zone."

"Well, ya got to have some vision, is what I think," Mab said. "Like that pillar that fell in front of the door over there? We can put that back up—no problem. Not sure about the corner of that wall," she mused, hands on hips. "Looks like a truck backed into it or something." Jenny, head cocked to one side, pursed her lips and squinted at Mab as Shalese walked up to join them.

"You've got to admit," Shalese said, "it has more potential than the warehouse."

"About that warehouse . . ." Jenny said, raising her eyebrows at Mab, "what *were* you thinking?"

Maren wandered over and stood next to Jenny. "Mab, this is a-*maz*-ing," she said, scanning the property. "A diamond in the rough," she continued, a smile spread across her face.

"Always could spot one," Mab winked at Shalese. Jenny rolled her eyes.

"I doubt we'll be competing with any other bidders," Jenny murmured. She tagged along behind Shalese and Mab as they joined the other women waiting at the door of the main house. They navigated around the pillar as Mab unlocked the door, and moved like a wave into the reception hall.

"Eeee!" Madigan shrieked. Several other women, startled by her scream, shrieked as well.

"Well, that's gotta go," Mab said, pointing at the stuffed moose head above the fireplace mantle. "Can't hurt you, baby," she said to Madigan. "Been dead a long time, by the looks of the cobwebs on the antlers." Jenny groaned and Shalese shot her a look.

The reception area was wide and open, with a sunken conversation pit in front of the large flagstone fireplace. To the right was a dining area with an eight-foot wood plank picnic table and benches. Behind the dining area and through a doorway was a huge industrial kitchen. To the left of the conversation pit was a hallway that led to two bathrooms, a sizeable office, and a spare room with an attached bath. French doors on either side of the conversation pit led outside to a wooden wrap-around porch—complete with swing—and steps down to a lawn that sprawled to the right and left, connecting all the cottages. Several smaller buildings and sheds edged the wooded area along the perimeter of the property.

"My pottery shed," Paulina squealed and headed toward a small wooden structure, her copper-red ponytail bouncing along behind her.

"Right over there," Margot pointed to the right, "bee hives—can't you just see them?" She extracted a small spiral bound book from her bag, made a sketch, and jotted down some notes.

Maren appeared on the porch, breathless, flushed. "There's a double refrigerator in there, and an industrial stove!" she said, pointing back towards the kitchen. "Just *think* of what we can do for the holidays."

Shalese sat down on the porch swing next to Jenny and draped an arm around her shoulders.

"They do know we're just looking, right?" Jenny said with an edge to her voice.

"Honey, what's the matter? You've been a little snarky since we left this morning," Shalese observed.

A tear trickled down Jenny's cheek and she wiped it away with her finger. "I love that Victorian. I don't want to leave."

"That's not up to us, Jen. I love it too, but we've got to move on. Anything else on your mind?"

With downcast eyes, Jenny said in a little voice infused with embarrassment, "I think I'm jealous—of Mab. She's being so . . ." she twirled her hand in a circle searching for the right words, "so Mab, flirting with you, all energized and excited about this move. Ever since we made her a partner, I feel like there's not as much space for me. Does that sound petty?" she said, looking up at Shalese through long blonde eyelashes.

Shalese gave her a squeeze, smiled, and said, "Babe, Mab does take up a lot of space, literally and figuratively, but you have nothing to worry about. She's sort of like a best friend or older cousin to me. And if she pushes too hard, just push back—she can take it," Shalese chuckled. "Or talk to her—she can take that too."

As if on cue, Mab walked up the path towards the porch, rubbing her hands together briskly. "Boy, oh boy, this is somethin', ain't it?" Mab hauled herself onto the edge of the porch. "S'matter, baby-ette? You look like somebody punched a hole in your balloon," she said, looking at Jenny.

Jenny looked at Shalese, then at Mab. She put her head down, her hands over her eyes and sobbed.

"What the . . .?" Mab mouthed over Jenny's head to Shalese who shrugged. "Come on over here and sit by me," Mab said to Jenny, patting the porch. Jenny complied, her face splotched with emotion. She swiped at her tears with the back of her hand.

"I'm such an idiot," Jenny blubbered and sniffed.

Mab scooted her bulk next to Jenny and wrapped a meaty arm around her, holding her tight. "What is it, baby? You can tell Mab," she said, smoothing Jenny's hair back from her face. "This move got you all tied up in knots?"

Jenny nodded, shook her head, and then shrugged. "I've been jealous of you and Shalese, your history together, your presence in our lives now. I'm so embarrassed," she said through her tears.

"Green-eyed monster done bit you in the butt, did it?" Mab chuckled. "I wondered what those little puckered-mouth faces you been makin' at me meant." She handed Jenny a tissue from her back pocket and waited while Jenny blew her nose.

"Me and Shalese, we go back to the bad ole days, when neither of us had a nickel's worth of sense. Shalese was just comin' out, and I was in a goodly deal of denial around my alcoholism," Mab went on to explain. "Had us some times, didn't we?" she said and grinned mischievously at Shalese. "That's all past history now, baby girl. I'm so proud of the woman Shalese has become, and that she had sense enough to hook up with a smart, gorgeous, kick-butt gal like you. I'm truly grateful that you have allowed me to be part of this wonderful thing you two have created. Look at those women out there on the lawn—their lives have been changed because of The First Step," she said. "And now The Next Step," she added, to include the transformation they were all undergoing. "If I get too carried away," she said, tapping her finger on Jenny's chin, "you just tell me, 'Mab, shuck it a while now,' okay?"

Jenny nodded, grinned through her tears, blew her nose, and leaned into Mab's embrace. The other women, who had noted the tension and had stayed a respectful distance away, began to filter back up toward the porch.

"Can we get a look at those cottages?" Chandra asked. "I'm thinking I want one on the end so I can sneak out for a smoke at night."

"You don't gotta be sneakin' out for nothin'," Madigan said. "Ain't that right? We're all grown ups here and supposed to be learnin' good self-esteem and all that. You wanta smoke, you smoke— just stay way back from me while you're doin' it." She lowered her voice and said, "That's the way I see it, anyway." She glanced sideways at Shalese, hoping she hadn't misspoken.

"You got that right," Shalese said. Jenny added an affirmative nod.

"Leaps and bounds, baby, you growin' by leaps and bounds," Mab added.

As a group, the women went cottage by cottage, checking the structural versus cosmetic needs of each building and fantasizing how they would decorate their space. They turned on water faucets, flushed toilets, opened and closed windows, checked closets, and peeked under worn carpets.

An hour later, they reconvened in front of the empty fireplace in the conversation pit of the reception hall. Six of the women vied for the few pieces of abandoned furniture—an overstuffed leatherette couch with a rip down the front cushion, a rocker with a broken arm, and two matching recliners from which smatterings of mouse droppings needed to be swept away. The others arranged themselves along the stone shelf of the sunken room.

"We know it's up to Jenny, Mab, and me to make a decision about this place," Shalese said, looking around at each woman's face radiating anticipation and excitement, "but we want your input about—"

Before she could finish her sentence, the women broke into an enthusiastic debate, talking over one another, about the pros and cons of purchasing the property. The location was perfect versus the location was too isolated and too far from town; the whole thing should be razed and rebuilt versus some carpentry and paint would go a long way; there must be a reason it's been empty so long versus it's just been sitting here waiting for the right people, and we're the right people.

"It needs a whole lot of work, but mostly it needs some love," Margot offered. "We could do a lot of the work ourselves," she added.

"And for the rest, I know people who know people who could help," Chandra said. This was met with murmurs of skepticism—they all knew what kind of people Chandra knew.

"It hasn't been on the market very long, but it's pretty rundown," Mab said casting a glance around the room, "so I think we can negotiate a price below what they're asking."

"Which is?" Chandra asked.

"Which is $980,000," Mab said. What followed were gasps, sighs, forehead-slappings, women falling out of their chairs and onto the floor in exaggerated shock. "Hey, this is what they call prime real estate," Mab defended.

Shalese stood, wandered to the window, and looked out over the acreage. She turned and addressed the women. "So, are we willing to rule out the warehouse in the city?"

"Yes!" was the unanimous cry.

"There are other places we could check out," Mab said. "Maybe we should see some more properties and compare. Jenny, you're being mighty quiet. What are your thoughts?"

All eyes were on Jenny. She twisted a strand of hair around her finger and bit her bottom lip. "I think we've found our new home," she said simply. A cheer went up followed by clapping, stomping, and high-fives all around. "Let's see if we can make it work."

"That's my girl," Mab said with a satisfied and slightly smug smile. "Let's go get us some lunch and celebrate," she suggested.

"I'd like to take one more look around the kitchen," Maren said as the others readied themselves to leave. Shalese nodded as she corralled the women out the door. A few minutes later, Maren appeared at the limo carrying an old, hand-written, battered recipe book that diffused a scent of mildew. The faded covers and worn pages within were bound together with raffia. "Look at this!" she cried excitedly. "I found it in the back of a cupboard. Do you think anyone would mind if I took this with us?"

"Pe-e-uw," Madigan said, fanning her hand in front of her face. "I'm pretty sure that was left here on purpose."

To dampen the smell, Maren wrapped the treasure in her sweater she'd left in the limo, and held the book close as if it were a swaddled infant. The women climbed aboard the We Go and waved goodbye to the ranch.

From behind a stand of trees, a man with a silver moustache and a cowboy hat watched as the women departed. He stepped deeper into the shadows as they drove by.

Mab led the way in her green Pathfinder, navigating potholes like a pro. Harold carefully inched his way back down the rugged pathway, through the vineyard, and back onto the frontage road. Moments later, he signaled a right turn and followed Mab into the dirt-packed lot of an open-air fruit market where box lunches could be purchased and eaten at the picnic tables that bordered yet another vineyard. The vines dripped with clusters of large, deep purple, succulent looking grapes.

"Vintage grape," said Paulina to no one in particular. Beth cocked her head at the view Paulina was framing with her hands like a movie director. "That's what I'll call the new purple glaze for my pottery line."

"I read that grape seed oil has curative properties," Beth said, fingering the leathery texture of a large green leaf. The two women stood silently at the edge of the vineyard for a moment, each pondering the gifts of their soon-to-be new home that would eventually translate into money-making ventures to help support The Next Step.

From a bunkhouse surrounded by the vineyard just down the road from the ranch, the man with the silver moustache and cowboy hat lifted the handset from the faux antique black phone that clung to the wall like a spider and dialed. "They're interested," he reported, "but we need to move quickly. 'Bank-of-the-earth' may no longer be secure. Call me as soon as you get this message," he said and hung up the phone.

Chapter 26

Taking a little sunshine and a breath of fresh country air with them, the women headed back to the city. The marine layer that had lifted for their trip north had filtered back in on their way home and dropped the temperature fifteen degrees. Harold turned the air conditioning off and opened the front windows. Shalese and Jenny both noted that Analise was not bothered by "car sickness" on the return trip. Of course, it was mid-afternoon by then.

Harold pulled up in front of the Victorian on Steiner Street, turned his wheels to the curb, and ushered his cargo out of the limo. Chandra gave him a punch on the arm and said, "Thanks, cuz. See ya 'round," to which Harold grimaced, straightened his cap, got in the limo, and pulled away without looking back.

Shalese was the first to climb the steps and reach the front door. "What's this?" she said, removing a folded piece of paper tacked to the doorframe. Jenny looked over her shoulder.

"A three day notice . . ." Jenny read aloud. "Our utilities are going to be shut off? How can . . . Who do . . ." she sputtered.

"No lights?" "No heat?" "No gas?" "Do we still have water?" the women asked among themselves.

"I'll take care of it in the morning," Shalese assured them. "It's been a long day. Let's meet in the group room for a wrap up," she said as she unlocked the door.

As the women settled into the parlor, the festive mood from earlier became somber. Shalese rubbed her temples and stared at the floor, gathering her thoughts. Jenny sat with her fingers splayed across her lips as if to hold in her words, and Mab sprawled in a recliner with her face turned to the ceiling and her eyes closed.

"How much longer do you suppose we have?" Chandra asked.

"Well, we haven't received an eviction notice—yet," Shalese answered. She felt her chest tighten, and she tried to take a couple of slow breaths. "We just have to figure out how to keep the utilities on, at least until we figure out how to move," she said after a moment.

"That's a whole lot a figurin'," Madigan said, casting a worried look toward Mab, who finally opened her eyes and sat up.

Shalese stood up and addressed the women. "Before I met Florence, I was doing research for funding. There is some grant money available through the Department of Justice for programs like ours. I'll get right on that tomorrow."

"I'm pretty good with computers," Analise offered. "I can do some research for other money."

"I know a group of women entrepreneurs who make regular charitable donations," Gabriella offered. "That may be the best thing that came from marrying that lout," she said of her wealthy ex-husband, who she permanently blinded by a strike to the head with a poker iron after one too many beatings.

"I'll have a budget drawn up by noon," Jenny said. Others chimed in with suggestions and offers of help.

"This feels like some kinda family alright," Madigan said, wiping a tear from her eye. "We all pullin' together like this an' all."

Usually the quietest of the group, Paulina jumped up, fist raised, and declared, "That which does not kill us, strengthens us." Realizing what she had just done, she paled and cradled her fist to her chest. "Or that's what I read somewhere, anyway," she said in a small voice. Jenny reached over and gave her a hug. Paulina smiled shyly.

Before they adjourned, Maren, Doris, and Margot offered to make dinner, as the cook had been let go the previous evening.

Chapter 27

"Hey, sunshine," Shalese greeted Jenny in the kitchen the next morning. "You're up early."

"I wanted to get an early start on the budget," Jenny said, pulling Shalese into a hug, one that might have sent them back to the bedroom had it been the weekend.

There was a tap on the wooden doorjamb and Jenny jumped back as Maren peeked her head into the kitchen. "Sorry," she apologized. "Mind if I get a cup of coffee before I start breakfast? I don't want to interrupt anything . . ." her voice trailed off.

"No, sure, come on in," Jenny said, welcoming her into the room with a nod at the coffee pot. "What do you have there?" she asked of the book Maren had stuffed under one arm.

"It's that cookbook I found over at the ranch in Santa Rosa, in the kitchen. I've aired it out," she said defensively. A musty scent wafted up as she flipped to the back cover. "And look what I found stuck in the back." She extracted a thin piece of mildewed paper that she smoothed out carefully.

Wrinkling her nose, Jenny took the paper by one corner and cocked her head at it. The drawing was faded, but discernable. "Looks like a treasure map or something," she said.

"Yeah, that's what I thought," Maren said as Jenny handed the paper to Shalese.

"Or a love note," Shalese said, pointing to the inscription at the bottom. "F&G4ever," she read aloud. "And look at these squares at the back of the map. See how they're placed? Hmm. Interesting. That's sort of the way those sheds were lined up out in back of the ranch, remember?" Shalese said.

The three huddled closer around the paper. "I say we take a shovel on our next visit," Maren suggested. "There will be a next visit, won't there?"

"It's looking like it," Shalese said, her smile broadening. She winked at Jenny.

Chapter 28

Two days later, while Shalese was pitching a capital campaign and operational funding speech to two different groups of businessmen and women, Jenny caught a call in the office.

"Baby girl, you sittin' down?" Mab asked. Her voice was strained, and the tone made Jenny's skin prickle.

"What's up, Mab?"

"I'm over at that ranch in Santa Rosa. Ever since our visit, something just hasn't felt right. You know I always try and follow my intuition . . ."

"Mab . . ." Jenny interrupted, "focus."

Mab shot Jenny a *don't get sassy with me* look through the phone. "It's been vandalized. Well, sort of, anyway," she said.

"Either it has or it hasn't," Jenny said, wishing she could see Mab's face to see what she was holding back. Was it bad or *really* bad? Mab had an obtuse way of getting to the point.

"The kitchen's been torn apart. Gonna need a total remodel, I'm guessin'."

"Why on earth would someone tear up the kitchen?" Jenny spoke the confusion that was scrunching up her face.

"Oh, and there's holes all over out back," Mab finished.

"Holes? Where out back?" Jenny grabbed a pen and piece of paper and started jotting down notes. She'd call Shalese as soon as she got off the phone.

"Yeah, holes—you know, like big potholes, only dug where there aren't any roads, out there by those free-standing sheds. Dirt's dry in them, so they're not fresh holes, but they weren't there when we were checking out the property. It's the craziest thing."

"Shit . . ." Jenny slapped her forehead with her hand. All the pieces started quilting themselves together.

"No, I don't think anyone was planning any outhouses. They're too close together and not nearly deep enough . . ." Mab trailed off in thought.

"Mab," Jenny interrupted again, "how fast can you get here?"

"By two o'clock, if traffic is in my favor," she said. "What's up?"

"I think I might know what happened," Jenny said. "I'll call Shalese and have her meet us here. Do you think we should notify Officer O'Flaherty?"

"Probably. But let's hold off on that for now," Mab suggested.

When they hung up, Jenny went in search of Maren and found her creating mouth-watering smells in the kitchen.

"Oh my God, cinnamon rolls . . ." Jenny inhaled deeply. "I've gained five pounds since you took over cooking duty," she giggled. Maren blushed. "Can you be free at two o'clock for a meeting in the office?" she said more seriously.

Maren looked startled. She closed the oven door carefully, and stood up with her hands flat against her thighs. "Did I do something wrong?" she said in a small voice. Her eyes darted about the kitchen.

"No, of course not, Maren," Jenny said gently. She forgot sometimes how traumatized these women were. They were used to getting assaulted by people with erratic behavior. Even a change in tone, or a sudden movement, could trigger a fear response. "In fact, you may have done something very, very right," Jenny said. "And could you bring that cookbook and map you found along with you please?"

Maren's face that had blanched with fear was now pinking up with pleasure and the excitement of inclusion. When it looked as though Maren was going to be all right, Jenny excused herself and headed back to the office to call Shalese.

Chapter 29

At two o'clock, Shalese turned the group over to Chandra and excused herself. She joined Jenny, Mab, and Maren, already gathered in the office. Shalese took the remaining chair at the table and wrinkled her nose at the odd scent in the air. Jenny pointed to the cookbook, lying next to a musty, faded piece of paper that loosely resembled a map.

Mab retold her story of following a hunch and driving over to Santa Rosa earlier that day to have a second look around the ranch. The main door was ajar when she arrived. "Gave me willie-bumps, know what I mean?" she said. "I puffed myself up and used my big, mean voice sayin', 'y'all in big trouble now' as I stomped into the main room. No one there. So I eye the door to the kitchen and slam it open real loud, yellin' 'freeze' like they do on *L.A. Law*. I'm real glad no one was there, 'cause all I had with me was a pad of paper, a pen, and my cell phone," she chuckled at her dilemma.

Jenny sighed loudly and made a get-on-with-it gesture with her hand, Maren sat spellbound, and Shalese fought to keep from smiling at what she remembered of Mab's story-telling days.

Mab arched an eyebrow at Jenny and continued. "Hoo-ee, that kitchen was d-e-s-t-r-o-y-e-d," she drew out the last word dramatically. "Drawers yanked out, cabinet doors torn off, table and chairs upside down; even the refrigerator had been gutted of shelving, and the door was torn off its hinges. Somebody was looking for something, that's for sure."

Maren paled at the thought of her gourmet kitchen torn asunder. She made a little whimpering sound.

"And tell them about the holes out back," Jenny urged.

Mab told about the holes that had been dug at the back of the property. "They weren't random holes," she said, "they were all in a line, just a few feet apart."

"I don't get the connection," Shalese said, leaning her elbows on the table.

Maren was the first to put the pieces together. "Oh!" she shouted, stood up from her chair, and bent over the map on the table. She pointed at it excitedly and looked to Jenny for confirmation.

Jenny nodded her head and said, "You got it." Maren clapped her hand over her heart and sat back down heavily.

Jenny placed her hand on the paper. "This, my friends, is a treasure map. And these," she pointed to the squares at the back of the map, "are the out buildings behind the cottages." The three women leaned in for a closer look. "And the X's are where something important was buried."

"But the holes weren't where the X's are on this map," Mab said.

"Without the map, it would have been pretty much guesswork," Jenny said. "Either whoever was digging out back got frustrated and left, or is planning to come back and try again."

"Someone was looking for the cookbook in the kitchen," Maren surmised, "knowing that the map was hidden there."

"Someone perhaps with the initial of F," Jenny pointed to the F&G4ever.

"Oh, no," Shalese and Mab gasped, sounding like a Greek chorus. "Flo?" they said in unison.

"Who is Flo?" Maren asked.

"Well, Gloria is dead, so it only leaves Flo—back to dig up something that could incriminate her before blowing out of the country—again," Jenny said, looking from Mab to Shalese. "What are the chances of this being the same ranch?" Jenny leaned back in her chair.

"I'm guessing they're pretty high, about now," Mab said.

"We may be getting ahead of ourselves here," Shalese said. "We don't know that—"

"Who is Flo?" Maren interrupted.

"Florence," Jenny said. "She disappeared back in the '40s when she was suspected of killing a man over in Santa Rosa. My Dad told me his mother took him to Ohio around that time. Oh my God," she said leaning back suddenly. "This might implicate my grandmother—the G in F&G4ever."

Jenny stood up, lunged for the cookbook lying on the table, and frantically flipped through the recipes. "Here," she gasped, jabbing a finger on the page that listed the ingredients for Millionaire Mulligan

Stew. Her knees buckled and she collapsed back into her chair. "My Dad told me about this recipe," she said with a whimper.

Shalese grabbed her hand and gave it a reassuring squeeze.

"We need to get our butts over there and dig where those X's are," Mab said.

"Shouldn't we call the sheriff or something?" Maren asked.

"Not just yet," Shalese answered, "and I think maybe we should keep this to ourselves for a while longer. No need to upset the other women until we get more information." The other two nodded their agreement.

"I'll tell Chandra she's in charge while we're out. That ought to make her day." Jenny grinned and headed for the group room.

"We'll take my Pathfinder, it's already covered with dust. Maren, you got the map?" Mab had to turn her head to see Maren nodding vigorously; information overload had muted her. Moments later, Mab ushered the three women, each bearing a garden shovel unearthed from an abandoned tool shed out back, into her car.

It was late afternoon when they arrived at the ranch. "You're navigating these potholes and ruts like a real pro," Shalese commented from the passenger's seat.

"Getting plenty of practice," Mab cracked. She slowed to a stop just before they reached the gravel turn-around and cut the engine. All four silently scanned the scene. No cars. There didn't appear to be any action.

"Let's walk from here," Shalese suggested, "just in case . . ."

"Are we going to get in trouble?" Maren asked in a small voice. The three women shot her looks that could be interpreted as 'it's entirely possible.' She sighed.

As quietly as four women carrying shovels could crunch across gravel, they crept to the verandah. Mab turned the knob, and the door—with the lock still broken—swung inward on a creaky hinge. The women looked at one another. Not a sound could be heard. On tiptoe and in a tight cluster, they entered the main room and veered toward the kitchen. It was still in shambles just as Mab had described. They headed for the door that led from the back porch onto the stretch of ground behind the cabins flanking the main lodge; the door hung on one hinge. Maren pulled the folded map from her back pocket and studied the terrain.

"Looks like they were off by yards on each hole," she said, consulting the map. They walked to the out buildings, and by approximation, paced the distance back toward the lodge according to the drawing. Each woman stood at where she imagined an X fell.

"Okay, let's get at it," Mab said. "By the look of the other holes, we shouldn't have to dig too deep."

"That's a relief," Maren said. "Probably means there aren't body parts." Three heads snapped in her direction.

"Ugh," Jenny mumbled. "That hadn't occurred to me."

"Thanks for puttin' that image in my head," Mab snorted. "Wait!" she said, holding up her hand and cocking her ear like a spaniel. The women froze like statues. The rumbling of an engine could be heard coming up the path. "Best defense is a good offense," she said. "Stay put," she ordered. Mab laid her shovel to the side and charged back over the lawn, up the steps, and through the lodge. She took a slow, deep breath before she opened the front door, and then descended the steps.

"Ma'am," the older gentleman addressed her as he stepped out of his truck and walked toward her. He looked robust for his age, despite an obvious limp. With his fingers, he smoothed his silver moustache and doffed the weathered cowboy hat perched on his head.

Mab walked down the steps to greet him. "Hello there," she said, reaching her right hand out in greeting. "Mabel Montana, Montana Realty. Are you Mr. Greenwood?"

"Uh, no . . ." the man stammered. "I'm Lefty, one of the grounds men at the vineyard down the road." The man shuffled his foot in the gravel. "Heard your car drive up the path a while ago. Just keepin' an eye out on the property. It's been vacant a while. Sometimes kids come up here and get in all kinds of trouble, don't you know."

"Why, that's mighty neighborly of you, Mr. Lefty," Mab said. "Next car you hear should be a prospective buyer, unless I've been stood up," she chuckled good-naturedly. "We won't be much longer. Thanks for keeping an eye on the place."

"Well, good luck with your sale," Lefty said with a nod toward the resort. "Rumor has it the place is haunted. Not that I believe in such nonsense, but it's been sittin' here quite a spell." With a wave, Lefty backed his truck up and headed back down the lane. Haunted? Mab rolled the word around in her head.

When she returned to the back yard, the three women were standing frozen in the same positions as when she'd left. "At ease," she called out, and they all relaxed. "Good news, bad news," she said. "We can probably get this place at a steal . . ." The women grinned. "It's haunted," she said, and watched the smiles melt like candle wax. Mab told them about Lefty—their watchdog—and her cover story. "I'm thinking on the way back down the hill, y'all should maybe scrunch down in your seats, just in case," she finished.

Focused now on the task at hand, the women started shoveling dirt. Little mounds of earth grew next to each hole. Anticipation was thick, and didn't leave any room for conversation.

"Oh my gosh," Maren said after ten minutes of digging. The others turned to see her stoop down and scoop loose dirt out with her hands like a dog going after a buried bone. "It's a package," she shrieked, exhuming a foil wrapped bundle. Jenny, Mab, and Shalese dropped their shovels and rushed to her side.

"I didn't know they had aluminum foil in the old days," Mab said, bending down for a closer look.

"It was invented in 1910," Jenny said.

"Why would you know something like that?" Mab asked, astonished. Jenny shrugged.

Maren carefully peeled back the foil to find a stack of $1,000 bills. "Holy shit!" she exclaimed, then quickly covered her mouth with the back of her hand.

"How many?" Shalese said, leaning so close that her breath tickled the back of Maren's neck.

Maren flipped through the bills, brittle with age. "Twenty-five," she whispered, breathlessly.

The others bolted back to their holes in progress, digging with renewed vigor. One by one, they uncovered three more foil wrapped packages, each containing twenty-five $1,000 dollar bills. They sat on the ground, stunned.

"That's $100,000," Mab stated the obvious. "I guess that's worth tearing up a kitchen."

"Do you think it was stolen?" Maren asked innocently. Three pairs of eyebrows raised in her direction.

"Why do you suppose Florence would come back for the money now, after all these years?" Jenny asked.

"My guess is she got wind that someone was lookin' to buy the ranch and wanted to take what she figured was hers before the place changed hands," Mab reasoned. "Either that or she's the one who planted the notice that the land was for sale—keep one step ahead of us, if you know what I mean."

"Ugh," Jenny made a punched-in-gut sound. "What if she comes back, sees the other holes, and comes after us?" A shiver of fear passed through her.

"We don't know for sure it was Florence, right?" Maren ventured. "I mean, that was just a hypothesis, wasn't it?" The eyebrows all rose again, this time with heads tilted in disbelief.

"I'd swear on a moldy cookbook," Mab said. "I say we do like the movie title, and take the money and run." She restacked her pile of bills and carefully folded the foil around it. The others followed suit.

"Maybe we should fill the holes back up," Maren suggested.

Jenny shook her head. "Come on," she said. She threw an arm around Maren's shoulder and hurried her, shovel and all, back up to the lodge.

It was a quiet ride home with each woman lost in her thoughts about what to do with their fortune. Good fortune or bad fortune was yet to be determined.

Chapter 30

It was late by the time Mab pulled her Pathfinder into the driveway alongside her bungalow in the Oakland flatlands. She'd let Jenny, Shalese, and Maren off at the curb in front of the Victorian, turned down an invitation to dinner, and battled traffic on the Bay Bridge with the driving thought of getting home and putting this day behind her.

"I'm just pure done-in," she muttered as she unlocked the front door, kicked off her shoes, and padded her way down the hall to the kitchen. As unwelcome as a burglar, the red button on the second line of her phone flashed spasmodically, signaling a back up of missed calls. "Noooo," she groaned, throwing her backpack on one of the two kitchen chairs. "You're just gonna have to wait," she said toward the phone as she swung open the freezer door and extracted a frozen dinner.

Sitting in front of the television, with her feet propped on the ottoman, Mab watched a *Law & Order* marathon as she made her way through a two-person serving of lasagna, washed down with a mug of iced coffee. During a commercial break, she checked in at the Lavender Rose Café to make sure they were covered for the night.

She glared at the line-two button, still blinking away. The second phone line was a front for her PI business, so she could have a legitimate number to receive calls that was different from her home phone. It was listed in the Yellow Pages as Mabel Montana Realty. She'd had a realtor's license for years but unofficially retired it when the Café started taking up all her extra hours; she still got the occasional call from someone looking for property.

"You're working my last nerve," she said, as she poked the message-retrieval button. There were six calls, made within fifteen minutes of one another, all from Lefty, the ranch hand she'd met in Santa Rosa that afternoon. All had the same message to call as soon as she got in and his phone number. "What the . . ." she mumbled as she dialed the number. "Probably wondering if I sold the place," she said.

The phone rang several times before the message machine clicked on. After the beep, Mab said, "Lefty, this is Mabel Montana returning your calls. Sounds urgent. Call me back up until 11 p.m. Otherwise, I'll talk with you tomorrow." She hung up the phone and went back in to the living room to catch the rest of her program.

At 10:56 p.m., just as they were wrapping up the case, the phone rang. "Damn," Mab muttered. When she got to the phone, she noted it was line two, hit the speakerphone button, and answered, "Mabel Montana Realty."

"Mabel? This is Lefty. We met at the ranch this afternoon . . ."

"Yes, Lefty. What can I do for you?" She wanted to add, *at this hour*, but didn't. She drummed her fingers quietly on the file cabinet next to the phone.

"Thought you should know, your place burned down not long after you left." Lefty waited a moment for a response. "You there?" he asked.

Mab shook her head to clear the fog. "It what?" she gasped.

"Burned to the ground. Couldn't get the trucks up there quick enough with those roads. You know all that old wood, brush, and such—went up like a tinderbox."

"How long after I left?" Mab tried to patch the information together to make sense.

"Oh, about an hour or so," Lefty guessed. "Thought you'd like to know, since you were tryin' to sell the place and all. The sheriff will probably be calling you too, since you were the last one on the property—at least that I saw. They're thinkin' arson."

"Damn that old crazy woman," Mab muttered. Fury bit like bile in her throat.

"Beg pardon?" Lefty said.

"Oh, sorry—nevermind. Listen, Lefty, I have to make some calls. Thanks so much for calling me."

Knowing everyone at the house was probably in bed for the night, Mab made a futile call to The Next Step. The phone rang six times before the message machine picked up. She hung up, promising herself she'd call early the next morning. "Gonna give me a sour stomach, that's for sure," she mumbled as she headed to bed.

Chapter 31

"I was on the computer all afternoon yesterday," Analise reported over breakfast the next morning, "and you'd be amazed how much grant money there is out there for real estate." She went on to explain a buy-back program from the government, first-time buyer new building options, and a host of other programs.

"We just need someone to give us a truck load of money so we can buy that ranch," Madigan said. There was general agreement around the table.

Maren squirmed in her chair and cast surreptitious glances at Jenny and Shalese. Analise opened her mouth to say something more, then covered it with her hand, pushed her chair back abruptly, and rushed out of the room. Shalese and Jenny exchanged a look of dismay.

"What's wrong with her?" Madigan asked.

"Preggers," Beth offered. "I'll mix up an herb tea for her," she said, excusing herself from the table.

"How'd that happen?" Madigan asked, looking around the table. "Ain't nobody here got the right equipment."

"Day shopping trip," Paulina said, making quote signs with her fingers. A couple of the women snickered.

As they were finishing breakfast, the phone rang down the hall and Shalese excused herself.

Beth was in the kitchen across from the office, cooking up a potion for Analise. Shalese closed the door behind her as she slipped into the office. "The Next Step, this is Sha—"

"It's Mab," Mab cut her off. "Is anyone there with you?" Her voice held an urgency that made the hair on Shalese's arms raise like porcupine quills.

"No. What's—"

"It's burned down, babe. The ranch, it's gone," Mab said. She listened to the shocked silence on the other end of the line. "I'm thinking Florence knew we were there."

"What . . ." Thoughts flew through Shalese's mind so fast she couldn't hold on to them long enough to put a sentence together. "How . . ." she tried again.

"Lefty called late last night," Mab answered her unasked question, "you know, that ranch hand? I'll tell you about it later. I'm on my way. Better gather Jenny and Maren. This could be big trouble," she said. "I was the last one he saw leave the ranch."

Within the hour, Mab's heavy footsteps pounded down the hallway of the Victorian, causing the overhead chandelier to tinkle like wind chimes.

"In here," Shalese leaned her head out of the office door. Mab swung in, nodded to the three women, and poured herself a mug of coffee from the pot sitting on the hotplate. "Fire hazard," she pointed to the electric burner as she squeezed her chair in around the tiny desk. They sat knee to knee for a moment, no one quite knowing how to begin.

"Okay, I've got a question," Shalese broke the silence. "From whom were we going to buy the ranch? How did you know it was available?"

"I was wondering that," Jenny added. "We should at least be able to trace the owner to see if Florence was involved."

"I've known about that property for years, but only recently saw that multiple listing sheet you pulled out of the file in the office—that wasn't mine, by the way," Mab said. "That place has been empty as long as I can remember. A very legitimate property management company has been caretaking the property for over twenty years," Mab said. "The property is owned by a trust. People do that to keep ownership anonymous and untraceable," she explained. She slapped both palms down on her ample thighs and bubbled her lips, expelling so much air it ruffled a little stack of paper on the desk.

"The property management company . . ." Maren piped up, then shrunk back in silence. Shalese nodded to her to speak. "Surely they know who has been paying their bill all those years, right?" Jenny nodded her head in agreement.

"You'd think so," Mab said with a shake of her head. "Apparently, it was done by money order. Untraceable. Came every month like clockwork until a month ago, so they never questioned it."

"Until a month ago?" Shalese asked. "What happened then?"

"Money order didn't arrive, phone number was disconnected, address—which they never used—turned out to be bogus. Seems Florence thought of everything. Very tidy, that rabid old bat," Mab said.

"Insurance? That would be public record, wouldn't it?" Maren asked. "She must have had insurance that she'll try to collect if the place burned down, right? Maybe we could find a source in the claims department who could let us know if there's a claim filed—then we'll nail her," she said.

"You ever thought of a career in the PI field?" Mab asked. Maren blushed and looked down at her lap. "My guess is, we'll find the premiums—that were probably paid by money order—stopped being paid about a month ago. But I'll follow up on that," she assured Maren who sat slumped in her chair with a pained expression on her face.

"We could do a skip trace if she ever sets up business again," Jenny suggested.

"She's probably already cut her losses and fled the country," Shalese said.

"Yeah, on the lam," Maren agreed. Shalese, Jenny, and Mab all cocked their heads at her.

"You've been reading too many cop novels," Shalese said. "Damn, it's just so unfair," she vented her frustration.

"Her losses, our gain," Jenny said, bouncing her eyebrows mischievously, pointing at the safe in the corner of the room holding $100,000 more than it did the previous week. A smile spread across all four of their faces. It was cold comfort, but comfort nonetheless.

Just then, Mab jumped in her chair, slapped her hand on her butt, and shouted "Jesus, Mary, and Joseph!" The other three turned and gaped at her. "Sorry. I forgot I turned my cell phone on vibrate before the meeting," she said, smiling sheepishly as she extracted the phone from her back pocket. "I don't usually carry this phone."

"Guess we're all a little jumpy," Jenny said as Mab pushed her chair back from the desk and flipped open the phone on her way into the hallway.

"Montana Realty . . ." they heard her say. She came back into the office a moment later. "Sheriff's Department. I have to go over to Santa Rosa. We've got to get our story straight," she said, and gave them all a meaningful look. "They'll want to know who this Mr. Greenwood was that I was going to show the property."

"He didn't show up, right?" Maren said.

"You do know there was no Mr. Greenwood, don't you?" Jenny asked *sotto voce*, just to make sure. Maren rolled her eyes. "I just meant that the *story* is that he didn't show up."

"What about the holes out back?" Shalese asked.

"What holes?" Mab said, her expression blank. "I was just inside the front door waiting for my client—I hadn't looked over the whole property yet."

"But we . . ." Maren began. "Oh, I get it. We have to actually lie to the police. Oh, my," her voice warbled with worry.

"Do you want us to come with you for moral support?" Jenny offered.

"Oh, Lord no. No offense, but the fewer faces in this story, the better." She left with a promise to check in that evening.

The women dispersed. Maren, sworn to secrecy, rejoined her financial management group; Shalese booted up the computer ready to do some focused real estate research; Jenny headed downtown to straighten out their Pacific Bell account.

Over in Santa Rosa, the clanging of a triangle called the workers from the vineyard into dinner. The man with the moustache and cowboy hat stayed a moment longer in the bunkhouse washing up. When the room was empty, he dialed the phone and left a message: "Plan B has been implemented." He ran a comb through his hair and moustache then joined the others up at the main house.

After dinner, the office phone rang. Shalese was again sitting at the computer. She reached over distractedly, picked up the receiver, and heard "Hello? Hello?" on the other end of the line.

"Oh! I'm sorry. The First, I mean, The Next Step," she said, her confusion apparent.

"Girlfriend, you're not sniffin' that funny glue, are you?" Mab teased.

"I'm glad it's you," Shalese said, pushing her chair back from the computer and refocusing on the phone conversation. "I've been at this computer for hours. My eyes are crossing."

"It's your *T*s you're supposed to cross. You dot your *I*s," Mab said. "You're not gonna believe what happened over there," she said, waiting for a prompt.

"You going to make me beg?" Shalese countered. Their easy banter was a welcome break and reminded her of the old days when life seemed simpler, but was probably just as complex in a different way. "I'm guessing you're not calling from jail."

"Yeah, that part went okay. They believed I'd never met Mr. Greenwood in person and hadn't had reason to call him back on the phone number that was unfortunately out of service. I'm a plausible liar, it seems."

Shalese could sense the self-satisfied grin that was surely spreading across her friend's face. "So, our mysterious Mr. Greenwood is now a possible suspect, but you're in the clear?"

"We're in the clear," Mab said, emphasizing the collective *we*. "Here's the crazy thing, the owner of the Angelico Vineyard just below the ranch property left word with the sheriff to have me call him while I was in town. I'm not used to this small town everybody-knows-everybody stuff—kinda creeps me out," she said. "I mean, I've been in my condo in Oakland for years and don't even know the folks across the street."

"Mab, focus," Shalese said.

"You been hanging out with Jenny too much," Mab muttered. "So I called him back, and he said he felt real bad about the fire, but that they've cleared some land that hasn't been good for crops—two acres, I think he said—and he wondered if I'd be interested in trying to sell a subdivided plot right up there at the back of the vineyard."

Shalese's jaw dropped. "What's he asking for it?"

"Negotiable," Mab said. "He's looking at $350,000 for the land, and then we'd have to build on it. Probably nothing so grand as the ranch, but we could maybe pull this off. What do you think?"

Shalese shook off a brief daydream of green pastoral hills, rolling vineyards, the call of red-tailed hawks, the sensuous seasons of wine country. "I think I'm really glad you pulled your realtor's license back out of the drawer. Let's talk this weekend."

"Okay, baby. I'll see you Saturday. Turn off that computer and get some sleep."

Chapter 32

"What was all that ruckus I heard last night?" Madigan asked over breakfast the next morning. "Sounded like rats runnin' up and down the hall."

Beth glanced at Analise who was working her way through a stack of pancakes, scrambled eggs, and bacon. Analise looked at Beth, then at Madigan. "Just a little trouble with my, uh, stomach," she said. "All better now."

"Uh huh," Madigan said. "Looks like you won't be missin' anymore breakfasts. Am I right?"

Analise's lips twitched slightly as she stabbed another bite of pancake. Shalese sent a silent prayer of thanks into the ethers. Beth released a long, slow breath and relaxed into her chair. Beth's grandmother had said the recipe was tried and true, but Beth had never tried it before last night.

When she'd finished her coffee, Shalese stood, weak-kneed and wobbly, and tapped her spoon against her juice glass to get the women's attention. She cleared her throat and glanced at Jenny who nodded her head in support.

"I've been searching for the right words to say this," she began.

"Oh, no. Not more bad news," Chandra said. "I'm just plain full-up, no more room—sorry," she said, gesturing with her hands that there was no more room in her brain.

"Whatever it is," Beth said, "just say it and get it over with."

"Yeah," Madigan added, "don't keep us dangling while you go searching all 'round for the right words."

Shalese looked around the gathering of women at the table. They'd been through so much in their lives, so many losses and disappointments. They'd been so excited about this ranch. How could she tell them? She stood with her lips pressed tightly together. Tears brimmed in her eyes.

Jenny eased herself out of her seat and braced her hands on the table. All eyes turned to her. She took a deep breath and said quietly,

"The ranch has burned down. It's no longer an option. We're looking for another place. We have a lead . . ." her voice trailed off. As she sat back down, she was aware of the stunned silence. No more bravado, no can-do optimism—just a bunch of deflated, unhappy women with yet another shattered dream.

No one spoke. The women stared at their feet, or out the window, or at the remnants of breakfast congealing on their plates. Maren fidgeted in her chair and risked a glance at Shalese.

Eventually, Margot said, "I knew it was too good to last," which was met with murmurs of agreement around the room. "This always happens," she said.

Shalese, who had sat back down, leaned forward and banged her fist on the table, making the silverware—as well as the women—jump. "No!" she said adamantly. "This doesn't always happen. I don't accept that. If we lost the ranch, it wasn't that it was too good to last, it was that it wasn't good enough. We'll do better—we just need to think outside the box."

Unable to suppress herself any longer, Maren added, "And we can afford to do that now." All eyes turned on her as she slapped her hand over her mouth and tried to lean back in her chair and become invisible.

Shalese spoke up quickly to divert the attention. "We've found a source of money we hadn't anticipated. It will help," she said.

Jenny jumped in to back her up by saying, "Mab has talked with the owner of the Angelico Vineyard, and he made an interesting offer that we need to hear more about. For now, let's just see this as a rerouting, not a set back."

Skepticism played on the faces of the women, but no one challenged the suggestion aloud. Throughout the morning, Shalese answered the women's questions and reassured them as best she could. By lunch, there was an implicit agreement to table any more talk of the fire or the fate of The Next Step until Mab had met with Jenny and Shalese.

In group that afternoon, it was Analise's turn to share. Her eyeliner smudged as she wiped at a tear that threatened to break loose and run down her cheek. "I'm so thankful for all you women," she said, looking around the circle. "When I was growing up, no one ever thought about making informed choices, or the consequences of our behavior. Life was lived in the moment, impulsively. 'You made your bed, you lie in it' was the motto. Hence, the husband."

"I know that one," Madigan said, and others nodded.

"Like, if I'd have thought things through, I would have learned to use that gun before taking a shot at him," she chuckled and winked at Shalese to reassure her she was just joking. "No, really though, this is not the time, and he is not the person I want to be bringing a child into the world with." She glanced at Beth, gave her a quick smile, and mouthed the words 'thank you.' "And with Marissa's help," she referred to the law student who donated an hour a week of legal consultation for the women, "I'm starting divorce proceedings." A cheer went up with high-fives all around. "I'm choosing a different life," she said with a nod of her head as she finished her share.

The women adjusted in their seats, or stood and stretched, as they prepared to shift into the business portion of their meeting.

"Since Marissa was mentioned, let's start there," Shalese said. "According to her, we could probably just sit tight until we figure out our next move," she reported. "Nothing is official until we're served a legal notice of eviction." Shalese reassured. "I'm not convinced Florence is going to want to get involved with the law anytime soon."

The crease between her brow that had become part of Shalese's facial features seemed to have relaxed, Jenny noticed. She weighed that against her need for a reality check. "Unless the law and Florence aren't as far apart as we're assuming," she ventured. Damn, there was that crease again.

"Whoa, and I thought I was paranoid," Paulina joked.

"You aren't paranoid," Beth quipped. "Your husband really *was* trying to drive you crazy and get you locked up in the nut house." The women laughed good-naturedly. She pushed her chair back from the table. "Tea anyone?"

"Not if you're makin' it," Madigan said. Laughter trailed behind Beth as she walked to the kitchen to put the teakettle on the stove.

"Let's talk about what we want in our next home," Jenny suggested. "Not having the ranch gives us some room to dream." Paulina found a large pad of paper and some colored pens for their brainstorming session.

"Swimmin' pool," Madigan said emphatically.

"A kitchen that's right off the dining room," Beth said, returning from her trip down the hall.

"A fireplace," Margot added. "I really love this fireplace." Her voice broke as she stroked the cool green marble. "It makes me feel safe," she said and dabbed at a tear sliding down her cheek.

"We've all been pretty caught up in the concern about what's next," Shalese commented. "Maybe we need to spend a little time on the loss of a home as we've known it for the last almost year." She checked with Jenny to see if she'd be okay with changing the focus. Jenny gave an affirmative nod.

"This is the first home I've lived in where I didn't get hit if there was dust on the bookcase," Gabriella shared.

"This is the only place I've ever lived where I only had to share a room with one other person," Madigan said, "and she don't even snore." Doris reached over and patted her roommate on the knee.

"I've never lived in such a beautiful house before," Margot said. "At first I didn't think I deserved it; but through being with you all, I now know I deserve all the good I can handle—and I can handle a whole lot more now than I once could," she added, beaming at the circle of women.

"Respect for others, and respect for myself," Chandra piped up, "that's what I've learned here. People aren't just objects to be used to survive. Neither am I. We have worth and value. Growing up on the streets, and then doing time in prison, you forget that real fast."

"I've learned that who I really am is okay," Jenny added quietly. "I just didn't know who that was until I came here." There was a moment of reflective silence that felt soft and gentle as it expressed itself on the faces of the women gathered.

"I'm so proud of all of you, of all the work you've done, the growth . . ." Shalese swallowed hard and took a slow, ragged breath. "Anything left unsaid before we move on?"

"I'm serious about that swimmin' pool," Madigan said.

Chapter 33

Saturday morning broke with the promise of a beautiful day. It was as if the marine layer that usually obscures the transition from night to day had slept in, missed its call, and left in its stead a full-on sunrise of red, pink, fuchsia, and gold—colors godly enough to make a believer out of an atheist. Mab wouldn't call herself an atheist, more of a healthy skeptic who had her own version of a creative force that oversaw the running of the universe. The sunrise, and the news she carried across the bay, made her feel more at one with that creative force than she'd felt since she'd sobered up for the last time eight years ago.

She pulled up in front of the Victorian, jogged her bulky self right up the steps, down the hall, and into the kitchen where she was sure to be met by a fresh pot of coffee and a few smiling faces.

"You're here mighty early," Chandra noted. "The milkman drop you off on his rounds?" she joked. Chandra tugged at her wig in an attempt to make the sides lay even. Her hair had never grown back after her boyfriend-pimp yanked it out by dragging her down the fire escape and into the alley by a handful of it.

Jenny stifled a yawn as she wandered into the kitchen in her pink robe and matching fuzzy scuffs. She wiped sleep from her eye with the knuckle of one hand, while she held her mug out with the other, like a beggar, for Chandra to fill. "Morning," she mumbled. "You're here early," she nodded at Mab.

"Y'all really know how to make a girl feel welcome," Mab said, lining up behind Jenny for a cup of coffee. Chandra obliged.

"I'm on breakfast duty," Chandra announced. "French toast, sausage, and scrambled eggs coming up in about twenty minutes," she said.

Jenny and Mab nodded and carried their coffee across the hall to the office. Shalese was already behind the computer, a half-empty glass of orange juice balanced precariously on a pile of papers. "I can't find anything that even comes close to the ranch," she said. "That was just so perfect . . ." her voice trailed off in frustration.

"Yeah, except that we would have had to re-wire, re-plumb, and rebuild a good part of it anyway," Jenny said. "I don't know how we could have afforded all that." She sipped at her coffee and then set her cup down with a sigh.

"You ready for some good news for a change?" Mab said, looking like a cat left to guard the goldfish bowl. Jenny and Shalese gave listless nods.

"Last Thursday, I had another talk with the owner of the vineyard. I told him about the recovery house and the run of bad luck we've had. He was sympathetic. Said he thought we could probably work something out regarding the sale of those two acres. Then, yesterday he called me back after a little sit-down with his tax accountant. Seems it would be more profitable for him to write it off than sell it," she said, letting her words hang in the air.

"I'm not following you," Shalese said. "You mean like when the government pays farmers to not grow—what's that called, subsidized farming? That doesn't sound like good news."

Mab shook her head no.

"The only other kind of write-off I know about is as a gift or something," Jenny offered.

As Mab's smile broadened, her dimples dented her cheeks making her look more like a pixie than the super-sized woman she was. "A gift to *us*—if we're interested," she added. "The owner is willing to deed us those acres and write it off as a tax deduction."

Shalese's jaw dropped.

"Free land?" Jenny gasped. "Shalese, with the resources you've found, we can get blue prints drawn up for free, and most of the labor donated. That just leaves us with the cost of materials."

"We should be able to furnish the place with grant money and donations," Shalese said.

"Girl, you've got a Victorian full of furniture, kitchen stuff, and office equipment. What's Florence gonna do, sic the sheriff on you?" Mab said.

The walls of the office pulsed with the excitement of new possibilities as the women spent the next half hour brainstorming.

Only Chandra's knock on the office door—and announcement that breakfast was ready—cut into their reverie.

"You're sure this is legal?" Shalese asked as they walked down the hall to the dining room.

"I'll double check the legality, but I'm thinking we're in the clear here," Mab said. "All this happy has left me famished," she added as she took her seat at the big mahogany table along with the other women.

."I heard the word *legal*," Maren whispered to Jenny as she scooted her chair up to the table. "Is there a problem?"

"No problem," Jenny whispered back. "We'll tell you after group." Jenny turned to greet the other women as they trickled into the dining room.

At three o'clock, the women sat in rapt attention as Shalese called for a shift of focus from their process group to the business meeting. It was customary to take a ten-minute break. No one moved.

"Don't nobody have to pee," Madigan said, "just start talkin'." Mumbled consent filled the room.

"Okay," Shalese began, "here's as much as I know at this moment. We've been offered two acres of land, free of charge, up behind the vineyard—that property just before the ranch we visited—on which we can build The Next Step Recovery House." Whoops, clapping, stomping of feet drowned out any attempt to continue for a moment.

"We're going over tomorrow to check out the land," Jenny added when the women had spent themselves, "and we'll let you know tomorrow night if it looks do-able."

"If so," Shalese continued, "we'll be meeting with an attorney next week to check on the legality, and an accountant to see how this works with our non-profit status, but . . ." she paused for dramatic effect, "it's looking like we could build ourselves a new home real soon." Shalese's grin was mirrored around the room. Conversation spilled out excitedly as if a stopper had been pulled from a bottle.

"And," Jenny stood and raised her hand to interrupt the chatter, "between Mab, Shalese, and myself, we've found a firm who will draw up the building plans pro bono . . ."

"That means ain't gonna cost us a penny, right?" Madigan spoke up, pleased to be involved in such an important conversation.

Jenny nodded. "A-n-d," she said again, drawing the word out three beats, "a large part of the building materials will be donated," she said, ticking points off on her fingers. "We'll move what we have here over there; Shalese is researching a renewable grant from the Department of Justice; and she's following up on a commitment from the Rotary Club and the Soroptimists who are interested in operational funding as well as helping us build our new board of directors." She checked her fingers to see if she'd forgotten anything, and satisfied, sat back down.

Willing to leave old habits behind, the women allowed themselves to be infused with new hope. "Holy shit," Chandra sputtered, "it's like Christmas came twice this year."

Chapter 34

By the end of the following month, the plans had been drawn up, submitted, and approved, the transfer of land documents completed, funding secured, and a project manager—a fiery redhead named Kelly—was hired. The women had made a trip over to the site and liberally gave their input down to the most minute details. Madigan requested a lavender room with antique white trim. Kelly tilted the brim of her baseball cap back on her head, squinted at Madigan, and said, "You're kidding, right?" Madigan's argument in support of her request was merely, "I never had me one of them." With a shake of her head, Kelly added it to the many pages of notes in her lined notebook.

The two-story, Midwestern-farmhouse style home with a sprawling front porch, would sit toward the front of the two-acre lot, with outbuildings for a workshop, pottery shed, laundry, and a greenhouse in the back—and a lap pool on the south-east side. Like the Victorian, the large, high-ceilinged group room would sport a marble fireplace and floor-to-ceiling windows. An office, kitchen, dining room, a master bedroom with an en-suite bath, a guest room, and a partial bath would occupy the remainder of the ground floor. Upstairs would house five double-occupancy bedrooms, and three full baths, plus an open-balcony sitting area/library. The acreage was surrounded by rolling hills lush with grapevines, and a winery just down the road, out of sight.

Over the months of construction, Saturdays became field-trip days. Harold would park the We Go in front of the Victorian at 10 a.m. and help load picnic baskets, blankets, and the women into the limo for a trip up to Santa Rosa.

"I brought my plans for where the hives could go," Margot shared as she climbed into the We Go. "I think just behind and beyond the potter's shed would be the choice location." She handed Jenny the paper on which she'd sketched three hives and their proximity on the property. Jenny nodded.

"Bees?" Madigan bristled. "I heard bees give you that elephantitis shock."

"Anaphylactic," Beth corrected, "and only if you're allergic to them. The herbs we'll grow will counteract any problems along that line," she reassured Madigan. "And wait until you taste the honey," she rolled her eyes in mock ecstasy. "The pollination from the vineyards should make it just exquisite," she beamed. "I've already talked with the winery owner, and he's willing to carry the honey in their gift shop under The Next Step label."

"Along with my pottery," Paulina added. The women chatted excitedly about their planned contributions to the recovery house as they crossed into Sonoma County. Kendra's people skills that she picked up as a hostess in a four-star restaurant had already landed her the promise of a job in the tasting room attached to the winery. The fact that she was 5'8" and modelesque didn't hurt either. Analise had claimed a corner of the library where the residents' computer would be hooked up to do independent contract work in computer consultation. "Who knew being a geek would ever come in handy," she chuckled. Chandra found a salon in town where she could rent a station and resume her career as a stylist. All the women were committed to paying what they could in money or services to ensure the house stayed afloat.

Shalese reached over and squeezed Jenny's hand. Jenny turned to her expecting to see the excitement in the limo mirrored in Shalese's eyes. Instead, she found the dark, clouded look and wrinkled brow that spelled worry. "What's wrong?" she whispered, not wanting to alarm the others.

"Jen," Shalese answered quietly, "all these women will be graduating in a few months. They'll be gone. I don't think that's occurred to them. There will be new women who won't have the same level of commitment to the house. I don't want to rain on their parade, but . . ." her voice trailed off and she looked out the window for a moment.

"Let's talk about it at the house meeting tonight," Jenny suggested. "For now, let's just enjoy the day and what we've all created together that will hopefully outlast even you and me." Shalese nodded and smiled, but the smile didn't reach her eyes.

Chapter 35

That evening, back at the house, the women settled into the group room as Maren passed around bowls of popcorn. "A special treat to end a special day," she said amidst the appreciative mumbles.

All eyes turned to Shalese when she stood and cleared her throat. She looked around the room at the bright eyed, smiling faces, filled with hope, and then she slowly sat back down, emotion deepening the crease across her forehead. The room fell into the kind of quiet you might find at the bottom of a well as the women waited. Shalese buried her face in her hands and wept, loudly. Stunned by this unusual behavior, no one moved, except Jenny who slipped behind Shalese, wrapped her arms around her, and held her tight until her sobs subsided.

Across the room, Gabriella shot Jenny a derisive look that said, *you'd never catch me blubbering in front of this group*. With an exasperated little sigh, she reached for a box of Kleenex and passed it around the circle.

When the box reached Shalese, she took several tissues, wiped her eyes, and blew her nose. "I'm so thankful for all of you," she began. She took a ragged breath and continued. "I haven't prepared you well for what we need to talk about. With everything going on lately, I hadn't even given it a thought myself until just this morning."

"You're not sick or something, are you?" Madigan asked, panic straining her voice.

"No, no—nothing like that." Tears began to run down her cheeks again and she blotted them with another handful of tissue. She turned to Jenny and sent her a pleading look.

"Oh, no. You two are getting a divorce," Doris said. "This is just how it was when my Dad sat me down to say he was leaving my Mom. Aw, geez, what's going to become of us?"

Gabriella, fully engaged now, leaned forward, eyebrows raised in anticipation.

"Nothing like that," Jenny said, coming to the rescue. "So, here's the thing—good news, bad news. The good news is that we're about to face our first graduation. Many of you have almost completed the program, more successfully than any of us might have imagined." The women chuckled and nodded in agreement.

"The bad news is," she continued, "that many of you will be graduating—and leaving." Jenny's eyes misted and her lip trembled.

"All them tears is 'cause you're gonna miss us?" Madigan asked, astonished at the possibility.

"Yeah," Shalese said, with a feeble smile. "You've all contributed so much to the success of this place. You've left your individual mark on my dream, and it will be so hard to move forward without you. But the time will come, and sooner than later for some of you, when you'll be stepping aside for the next woman who needs what we have to offer here."

"I guess I knew that was coming," Chandra said, "but I figured I'd be staying in the area anyway, and maybe I could stay connected somehow. Help out, you know?"

"When women graduate from this program, they may still need some safe contacts on the outside as they move back into their lives, right?" Analise said. "Maybe we could be like a sorority or something, stay in touch, help each other out," she suggested. "And, you're going to need a webmaster once I get us up and running."

"What about joining the board of directors? Then we could really help sustain this place," Kendra added.

"I don't want to be a full-time bee keeper, but I'd love to set up a training program for women who want to learn that trade and market the end product," Margot said.

Shalese placed her hand over her heart. Her smile was so bright, her gold tooth glinted. "You all are just too much," she said. "And I mean that in the best possible way."

"Just so's you know, I'm not going anywhere until I've slept in that lavender bedroom and done a few laps in the pool," Madigan said. Once again, the mood shifted from anxiety-laden heaviness to optimism and excitement.

Chapter 36

In the midst of an autumn heat wave, the last of the moving vans pulled away from the circular drive in front of The Next Step—snuggled among the vineyards in the hills of Santa Rosa—and left Shalese, Jenny, Mab, and the ten residents to arrange furniture, stock shelves, hang curtains, and bring some form of order to their brand new digs. Madigan was overseeing the filling of the lap pool.

"Déjà vu all over again, huh?" Jenny commented as she handed the city business license to Shalese, who hung it on the wall over the desk in the new office.

"Well, with one huge exception," Shalese grinned.

"No Florence," they both said at once and giggled in relief.

Down the road and out of sight, the sound of a triangle being struck with a wooden spoon beckoned the vineyard workers in for lunch.

"I'll catch up with you in a minute," Lefty called to the others who were headed to the main house. He removed his cowboy hat and swiped at the sweat that glistened on his forehead. "Gotta change boots—my bunions are killing me." He limped down the path in the opposite direction.

Once in the bunkhouse, he looked behind the partition that divided the bunks from the sitting area to make sure he was alone. He lifted the receiver on the phone and dialed a series of numbers.

Book Two
The Next Step

Chapter 1

Madigan, all two-hundred-and-eighty pounds of her, was stuffed into a red and white polka-dot swimsuit. It was mid-afternoon, three days after the women of The Next Step recovery house had moved into their newly built digs.

"Hey there, old woman," Madigan turned her pudgy brown face downward, in the general direction of hell, to address her thoughts to Florence, who had just about ruined them. "Turns out your crazy old self is responsible for me havin' a new swimmin' pool. Hah!" She slapped her thigh for good measure. She stood at the edge of the lap pool and dipped her toes in. The California summer had warmed the water to a pleasant enough temperature, if you didn't lollygag. Temperatures could reach the high nineties mid-day, and then drop to forty-six overnight.

Madigan tossed her beach towel onto a nearby lounge chair and lowered herself step by step into the water. Squinting against the sun, she noticed a mass on the bottom, at the far end of the pool. She back-stepped herself quickly out of the water and glanced around frantically. "Hey! Help! Somebody . . ." she shouted back toward the main house.

Alarmed by the pitch of her voice, Shalese and Chandra, who'd been raking up construction debris, came charging around the corner of the house. "Effin'-A, girl, you better be drowning or something, yelling like that," Chandra admonished.

Shalese, seeing that Madigan was safe, cut her pace back to a walk and stopped where the two women stood, poolside. She followed Madigan's finger, which jabbed frantically toward the other end of the pool. "Come on, let's go take a look," Shalese said.

137

"Right behind ya—w-a-y behind ya," Madigan muttered. Chandra jogged to the end of the pool, knelt down, and peered into the water. "Looks like rats, three of them," she said.

"Rats? I almost went swimmin' with rats?" Madigan crossed her hands over her ample breast, holding her heart. Madigan grew up in the Tenderloin area of San Francisco—she knew rats. It didn't mean she wanted to swim with them.

"No problem," Chandra commented, "they're dead."

"That's strange," Shalese said, squatting next to Chandra. "If they just fell in, you'd think they'd be farther apart. They seem almost tied together."

"Jesus, Mary, and Joseph," Madigan called out plaintively as she crossed herself.

"You're not Catholic," Chandra said over her shoulder.

"Can't hurt," Madigan said.

"I'll go get the net and scoop them out, unless either of you has a better idea," Shalese said to the women.

"I ain't jumpin' in to haul their sorry asses out of the pool," Madigan said. "You could get the plague or something. We gonna have to drain the water out . . ." She rocked herself from foot to foot.

That evening, even though it was a weekend, and their regular house schedule was suspended, the ten residents and three staff met in the group room to process the afternoon's events. Jenny spoke quietly with Mab.

"We've been here a grand total of three days and already something creepy happens. I thought we left all that behind us in San Francisco," Jenny said.

Gabriella, who had overheard, turned to Jenny and said, "Along with our hearts." She smiled at her own cleverness.

Gabriella spoke for all of them—no one had wanted to leave the city. The suspicious deaths of several men—who were coincidentally the ex-husbands of women in the recovery house—was one reason The Next Step had relocated. It seemed likely, but still not proven, that Florence, with the help of the Avenging Angels, may have been responsible for those deaths. Florence's vanishing act had brought the unwanted attention of law enforcement to the recovery house. The residents, as a group of formerly battered women, did not believe that *the policeman is your friend.*

"Baby girl, let's not jump the gun," Mab turned back to Jenny, addressing her concerns. "We don't really know what happened yet."

"There were three rats, tied together by their tail, tossed into our swimming pool!" Jenny's voice raised a notch on the panic register. "This was no accident."

"No, not an accident," Mab agreed. "Could be a nasty prank though. All the vineyard workers are guys. Maybe they just wanted to see if they could get a rise out of a houseful of women. You know, sort of like a hazing or something."

"If this is their welcoming ritual, I'd hate to see what they'd do if they wanted to get rid of us," Jenny said.

Shalese stood and cleared her throat. Slowly, the conversations around the room fell silent and the women looked at her expectantly. Maren, who had assumed the responsibility as chief cook for the house, opened the small journal she kept with her, and poised her pen, ready to record her version of the minutes of their meeting. Jenny had seen a page of Maren's notes when the journal was left lying open on the kitchen counter. They were mystifying—mostly a list of words without benefit of context or sentence structure, occasionally an emotional term such as *heartbreaking* or *grievous*. Jenny supposed Maren knew what they meant, and after all, wasn't that the therapeutic value of journaling?

"Welcome home," Shalese began. The women smiled weakly.

"Be more of a celebration if this were the Year of the Rat," Chandra commented *sotto voce*. Those around her snickered.

"Regardless of the unexpected guests in our lap pool . . ." Shalese bounced her eyebrows to lighten the mood. Several women chuckled; Gabriella scowled. "We are not women who let that sort of thing stand in our way," Shalese continued. "I want you all to recall the journey you've been on from the day you fought back against violence." There were murmurs around the room.

"No one is ever going to tell me I can't be all that I know I can be," Beth, their resident herbalist, said. Grinning broadly, she stood and waved a white envelope she'd received just that morning. "This is my acceptance letter to that alternative medicine program." The women cheered. After ten years of marriage, being beaten, and belittled for her "hippie woo-woo" interest in herbs and potions, she was due to start the new program following graduation from The Next Step.

Beth had been sent to prison on attempted murder charges when her husband fell deathly ill from food poisoning. She couldn't prove that she didn't do it, and with her knowledge of herbs, she was the fall guy. Guilty or not, once a felon, always a felon.

"Beth, we're all so proud of you," Shalese beamed. "That's what I'm talking about. We're not going to let a few rodents get in the way of our success, right?" The women clamored their agreement. "Let's put all this behind us and get on with business as usual."

"That would be dinner," Maren said. She jotted down the word *rat* in her journal, closed it, and headed for the kitchen.

Moments later, a shriek from the kitchen brought the women on the run. Maren stood frozen like a mannequin, staring at the shattered bowl on the tiled floor. Around and through the shards of pottery, slithered four slippery eels. Their dorsal fins, like miniature mountain ridges along their backs, twisted and turned spasmodically.

"Them's snakes!" Madigan shouted. "What's snakes doin' in our 'fridge?"

As each woman tumbled through the kitchen door and noted the mess on the floor, they gasped, shrieked, or as in Chandra's case, let fly a host of expletives.

"First rats, now snakes," Madigan shook her head. "What's this world comin' to?"

"Those aren't snakes," Jenny said, "they're eels—*Unagi*, actually. Think of them as menu items at a sushi restaurant, and they'll be easier to pick up off the floor."

As if on cue, all the women took a hefty step backwards. "I'm not picking those things up," Maren said, wiping her hands on her apron. "They're disgusting." She grabbed her journal from the kitchen counter and left the room.

"Eel wasn't on the shopping list, was it?" Jenny asked Paulina and Doris, who were in charge of stocking food for the first week in the new house. Paulina shook her head so hard her copper-red ponytail slapped against her cheeks. Doris, who had her hand over her mouth, mumbled "definitely not," through slightly parted fingers.

Paulina, artist and potter responsible for having created the beautiful bowl that lay smashed on the floor said, "Well, for heaven's sake, if we're not going to eat them, we should probably take them down to the creek and hope they survive. They are kind of pretty, in a slimy-green-fish sort of way," she added.

Shalese handed her a big cast-iron pot with a lid, and a large spatula, and watched with gratitude as Paulina maneuvered the eels into the pot. Chandra swept up the shards of pottery, and Maren, who had gotten her second wind, ran a damp mop smelling of bleach over that section of the kitchen floor. Her journal lay open on the counter, and next to the word *rats*, was *eels*.

The last two events had left the women on edge. They checked in their slippers before stepping into them at night, left nightlights on in their rooms, peeked in the toilet bowl before sitting down. Madigan mumbled, "Can't let it get to me, can't let it get to me," as she climbed the stairs on her way to bed.

Chapter 2

Monday morning after breakfast, Jenny was in the group room, writing the day's schedule on a big dry-erase board. Life management group taught the women how to budget their money, open checking and savings accounts, write checks, pay bills. Even though she came from a privileged background, Jenny's father insisted she learn these skills at an early age. She was amazed at the number of women who were so disempowered they believed they couldn't handle their own money.

What Chandra knew about money when she first arrived a year ago, was if you didn't make enough of it to hand over to your pimp at the end of the night, you got the shit beat out of you. Budget was a business that rented cars.

In Gabriella's case, her wealthy husband made and controlled all the money, paid all the bills, and doled out a pittance of cash at the beginning of each month that was gone by the end of the first week. She got smacked regularly for not managing her money well enough.

"You spelled that wrong," Gabriella said, coming up close behind Jenny. She put one hand on Jenny's shoulder, reached around with the other and erased *n-u-t-r-t-i-o-n* with her index finger, took the erasable pen from Jenny's hand, and rewrote it with an *i* after the *r*. Jenny hunched her shoulder unconsciously and took a step sideways, out of Gabriella's close proximity.

"Thanks, I didn't catch that," she said, crossing the room to turn on the overhead light against the morning fog. "Spelling was never my forte," she said lightheartedly.

"Mmm. What is?" Gabriella asked. Her voice dripped seduction and challenge.

"Listen, Gabriella . . ." Jenny was interrupted by Beth, bumping the door open with her butt and backing into the room, arms full of books and pamphlets.

"I've never done a presentation on nutrition—or anything else actually—in my whole life," Beth babbled. "I found these handouts at the Health Department. Do you think anyone will read them?"

"Perhaps those who can read, will," Gabriella glanced at Jenny. Jenny shot her a look. Something was definitely up with this girl.

"That was thoughtful of you, Beth. Anything you want to share will be helpful. You'll do fine," Jenny offered with a smile and a light squeeze of Beth's arm. "We're all friends here." Across the room, Gabriella snorted and took a seat next to the chair Jenny usually inhabited.

Jenny finished the schedule as the women filtered into the room. Shalese entered in animated conversation with Doris. Jenny caught her eye and signaled with a nod of her head asking Shalese to meet her in the hall.

"What's with Gabriella?" Jenny asked when they were alone outside the group room. "She's acting downright peculiar and snotty today."

"She's been trying to get your attention for a week. Guess it finally worked," Shalese said with a grin. "I think she has a crush on you."

"Crush?" Jenny said, aghast. "She's the most homophobic woman here. Do you remember back at the house in San Francisco when Mab volunteered to use the money from that lesbian political group to help keep us afloat after Florence left?"

"Oh yeah," Shalese smiled at the memory. "Gabriella said, 'we're not exactly a lesbian population,' all huffy, right? What's that Shakespeare quote about methinks she protests too much?"

"Oh my God, what should I do?" Jenny said, casting a furtive glance at the door to the room.

"Nothing, for now. I guess you'll have to talk to her later," Shalese said. She took Jenny's arm and ushered her toward the door. "Don't look so uptight. I've got your back." Shalese ran her finger in a zigzag down Jenny's back and gave her a playful pat on the fanny before guiding her into the room.

At the end of Beth's presentation, the women gave her a standing ovation. She blushed with pride when Madigan said, "You so smart, you ought be teachin' that medicine class, not takin' it."

Following the nutrition class, they had a half-hour 12-step meeting, after which Shalese called for a ten-minute break before they shifted to their business meeting.

Under the business heading, Jenny had written, *Lions, tigers, and graduation—oh my!* on the dry-erase board. Gabriella leaned forward in her chair, blocking Jenny's attempt to get up and said, "That's very clever. Do you think anyone else will get it?"

Jenny looked her directly in the eyes and said, "We need to talk. Meet me in the office after group this afternoon, okay?"

Jenny inferred from Gabriella's huge smile that she'd misconstrued Jenny's meaning. With an internal groan and an invisible head-slap, she excused herself and headed to the kitchen for a cup of tea.

When she walked into the kitchen, Shalese lifted the teapot and pointed to a mug. Jenny nodded and slumped into a chair by the breakfast table. "This just has to stop," she said, referring to Gabriella's behavior. "She's acting like it's us against the world or something."

"Truth be told," Shalese said, glancing at the door to make sure they were still speaking in private, "you two have more in common, at least in background, than any other two women in the house. You're both well-educated, well-traveled only children from wealthy families." Shalese pulled the teabag out of her mug, squeezed it, set it aside, and took a sip. "She's probably just trying to connect," she assured Jenny. "She's never had friends, you know."

"Geez," Jenny sighed, "now I feel like a jerk." They drank their tea in silence.

Shalese smiled, took their mugs to the sink, rinsed them, and nodded toward the door. "Mab should be here for the business meeting. Let's go check."

As they walked back down the hall toward the group room, they heard the sound of musical instruments being—if not played, at least—handled. Guitar strings plucked tunelessly, a-rhythmic sounds from a bongo, something pingy that sounded vaguely like a ukulele. The women were gathered around Mab, talking excitedly. Mab looked like a delighted child who'd just gotten the last cookie. Her eyes twinkled mischievously.

"What the . . ." Shalese was at a loss for words as Doris gave a big squeeze on the accordion she was holding. A sound that defied description filled the room.

"Toys," Mab said simply. "Music store down in the city was going out of business. Made me a deal I couldn't refuse," she grinned. "Free."

The women whooped, shouted, and clapped until Shalese raised both hands—like the Pope blessing the masses—to call some order to the meeting. Maren played a few more notes on the keyboard she'd balanced on her lap before turning off the instrument.

"Thank you," Shalese said, smiling at Mab. "After all these years, I still never know what to expect from you. Okay," she cleared her throat and looked around the room until she had everyone's attention. "Jenny," she motioned for Jenny to take the floor.

Jenny pointed to the dry-erase board. "Lions, tigers, and graduation—oh my! Anyone know what that means?" She looked away from Gabriella.

Paulina spoke up. "It's from *The Wizard of Oz*—lions and tigers and bears were all things you might be afraid of—"

"Kinda like we might be 'fraid of graduation," Madigan finished for her.

Jenny beamed and resisted temptation to shoot Gabriella a look. "That's right. It's true there's been a lot going on this last month, moving in, getting settled, but it's time to start thinking about the fact that our year together will be up at the end of September." A pall settled over the room, as if someone had siphoned out all the air and removed any trace of vibrant color.

"That means we have this month and most of next to start planning two celebrations," Shalese took over. "One for all of us, and all we've been through together, the growth, the changes—"

"And another to welcome in the next crop of residents," Jenny finished.

"Kinda like flying up from Brownies to Girl Scouts?" Margot asked. "I always wanted to do that, but we could never afford the uniforms."

"Or like sorority pledge night, where the older girls welcome the new pledges," Gabriella offered. If Chandra hadn't been occupied picking gum from the bottom of her leather boot, she might have said, "What planet are *you* from?"

"Yes, all of those are good ways of thinking about graduating. You have all helped create something that works, something that will continue to help women get their lives back on track, find their direction, and feel good about themselves," Shalese said as her eyes moistened with affection.

"Now that's somethin' to celebrate, all right," Madigan said, puffed up with pride.

"We need committees," Analise, the most computer-savvy of them, said. "I'll make a chart. What do we need?" As the women shouted out suggestions—food, music, a ceremony, diplomas, speakers—Shalese, Jenny, and Mab exchanged a look that spoke volumes about the success of their first year, against great odds.

During the lunch break, Mab's phone rang. She excused herself and answered it in the hall. The residents snickered when her one-sided conversation clamored its way into the dining room.

"Say what? The stove caught on fire? You put that little pothead on the phone right now, you hear? I'm gonna be carvin' him a new one, all right," Mab hollered. Shalese excused herself from the table and stepped into the hall to check on Mab. "You see that he is," she continued her rant. "I'm headed back right now. Be there in an hour." She slapped the cell phone shut and muttered to herself.

"Trouble at the Lavender Rose?" Shalese asked, leaning against the wall.

"Little pothead almost burned the place down, caught the stove on fire," Mab fumed.

"You used to be that little pothead, don't forget," Shalese reminded her, referring to what they now called *the bad old days*, before Mab found sobriety and a Higher Power to yell at.

"I used to be a lot of things," Mab said, "but I never burned down my job. I gotta get back to the city. Sorry to miss the afternoon group." She reached in her back pocket and pulled out the keys to her forest-green Pathfinder. "Tell the women I'll see them tomorrow," she called over her shoulder.

Before Shalese could return to the dining room, Mab burst back through the door. "Son of a dirty double dog!" she yelled. Several women stuck their heads out of the dining room. A few stepped cautiously into the hallway. "Someone took one of the damned tires off my car. Who'd do a crazy-ass thing like that?" she stood, hands on hips, exasperation leaking out of every pore.

"This is getting mighty old," Shalese agreed.

"Do you think we should call the sheriff?" Beth asked.

Shalese, Jenny, and Mab glanced at one another. Maren stared at the floor. There were reasons they wanted as little to do with the local authorities as possible—reasons that amounted to $100,000.

"Let's just get Mab's tire back on for now," Shalese suggested.

Mab and two of the residents got the tools out of the Pathfinder and set to work. Maren returned to the dining room, took out her notebook, and next to the word *eels,* wrote *tire.* Jenny and Shalese herded the rest of the women back in to finish their meal.

"Who do you think is harassing us, and why?" Gabriella asked as she sat across the table from Kendra who moved the food around on her plate so it would look as if she'd been eating.

"I'm inclined to think it's the vineyard workers. Maybe they're homophobic," Kendra, model-thin, said with an air of chilled indifference, as she shifted her rice to where the salad had been moments earlier.

Gabriella flinched. "Homophobic? You mean because of the staff here? Do you really think someone would harm us because of that?"

"Happens all the time. You wouldn't know about that, of course," Kendra answered. While Gabriella pondered the possible message embedded in that answer, the gong sounded signaling an end to lunch and a shift to the afternoon agenda. The women cleared their plates and reassembled in the group room.

"Okay," Shalese began when the women had settled in, "lots of strange stuff has happened in a short amount of time," she conceded. There were murmurs of consent throughout the room. "But none of it has been actually dangerous."

"You don't think a three-wheeled car is dangerous?" Analise asked.

"I think if the tire had been loosened and left on the car, it would have been dangerous, yes. But the tire was laying in plain sight. It's harassment, and maybe some sort of message—"

"'Git the hell outta here' is my guess," Madigan offered.

"I think it might be wise to keep an eye out. These things are happening right under our noses, and in broad daylight," Shalese said. "Someone actually came into our kitchen while we were all in the group room to deliver our . . ." Shalese paused to clear her throat, "*Unagi.*"

"Maybe we could take shifts doing lookout," Maren suggested.

"Or hire someone, so we wouldn't have to miss group," Analise countered.

"I'm thinking Mab might know of a good alarm and surveillance camera system. That's sort of her expertise," Shalese said. Jenny offered to place the call to Mab while the women settled into their afternoon job skills group.

Chapter 3

After the last meeting of the day, the women had an hour of free time before dinner. Jenny caught Gabriella's eye in the hallway and motioned her to the office.

Gabriella settled into a chair across from Jenny. "You wanted to see me?" She smiled seductively and twirled a curl of hair around her finger. She crossed her legs and leaned forward, spilling cleavage from her low-cut blouse.

Jenny pressed herself farther back in her chair and forced herself to make eye contact. She could feel moisture on her upper lip. She'd always hated conflict. "I've been really uncomfortable with your behavior lately," she said, trying to keep her voice calm and non-threatening. "I have to admit, I don't understand what it is you're trying to do. I'd like to understand—I really would."

"I don't know what you mean," Gabriella said innocently.

For a moment, self-doubt clouded Jenny's thoughts. Perhaps she'd misinterpreted Gabriella's attention. Shalese's words ran through her mind, 'just trying to connect' and 'never had friends.'

Jenny flailed around for words that would make sense. "I feel like you want it to be us against the world or something—like an alliance that excludes the others. I know we have similar backgrounds, and it can be hard being thrown in with women whose lives you don't understand. I can imagine what prison was like for you—it was a real eye-opener for me, too—but, here at the house, we're all on equal ground." Jenny felt herself relax in her chair. The hardest part was over.

Gabriella's lip quivered and her eyes brimmed with tears. "I think I'm in love with you," she blurted.

Jenny blanched. Nothing could have prepared her for this, and she was clueless as to how to proceed. The memory of her own coming out, just over a year ago, flashed in her mind—the fear, the vulnerability, the confusion, the exhilaration. This called for the grace and delicacy of a tightrope walker, and at the moment, she felt more like a lumbering elephant.

"I've never been attracted to a woman before in my life," Gabriella said, as tears now ran freely down her cheeks. "I'm so jealous every time I see you and Shalese together, I feel sick to my stomach. I want you to like me, not her," she whined, sounding like seven year old. She buried her face in her hands.

Shit, Jenny said silently, and swallowed hard. She didn't want to encourage Gabriella, but she didn't want to throw her into shame, which was waiting just around the corner at a moment like this.

"Gabriella," Jenny said gently, "I do like you. You're a lovely, intelligent woman, and you've lived through years of abuse that no one should have to endure. But you're strong, and you made it through." She looked at Gabriella who was still sobbing quietly into her hands.

"You have your whole life ahead of you. And now you have this wonderful new part of yourself that you're just discovering. This is a good thing, and I'm glad you told me about it."

Gabriella wiped her tears with the back of her hand and sniffed. Jenny handed her a box of tissues. "You are?" she said, her voice catching between words. She blew her nose loudly.

"Yes," Jenny said, surprised at the truth of her words. "I'm honored that you find me attractive. I may be the first, but I surely won't be the last," she said. "And that green-eyed monster is no stranger to me," she added with a smile. "Between us," she leaned forward conspiratorially, "Shalese and Mab were girlfriends years ago. When I first met Mab, I wanted to scratch her eyes out."

Gabriella giggled through her tears. "But you're friends now? You seem to really like each other," she said.

"We do. Gabriella, there are some wonderful women out there, but the first step is to make friends with the new you, and this is a safe place to begin that process."

"I guess you're not going to be leaving Shalese any time soon?" Gabriella said with a shy smile.

"Nope, no time soon," Jenny said. She took a tissue out of the box and gently wiped a tear that lingered on Gabriella's chin. "Let's go have dinner."

Mab had returned, having dealt with the kitchen fire at the Lavender Rose Café. The insurance would cover the minor damages, the "little pothead" had been fired, and a new dishwasher was hired immediately. The café was fully staffed for the night, and Mab looked forward to sharing her ideas about surveillance equipment for The Next Step with the women over dinner.

"Sorta like Candid Camera?" Chandra asked, as she thumbed through an instruction manual.

"Pretty much," Mab answered, "but no one jumps out at the end and tells you you're on TV. We'll have the video cams mounted so each side of the house is covered. No one will get close without being caught on tape."

"What if we're out, like on a field trip or something?" Beth asked.

"This thing here," Mab held up something that looked like the number pad on a telephone, "is a security alarm. We'll set it with a code you punch in when you leave and punch in again when you get back home. Anybody tries to come in while we're out will be dealing with the police within minutes," she said with a self-satisfied smile. "We can set it during the day, too, while we're all in meetings, and overnight for safety."

"What if we forget the code?" Madigan asked. "We get busted?"

"We could make it something we'd all remember because it would make sense to us, but not to anyone else," Jenny suggested, "like 1 for The First, then 7-8-3-7 for S-t-e-p." That agreed upon, Shalese, Mab, and Chandra planned to meet first thing in the morning to install the new equipment.

That evening after dinner, Margot sat out back, away from the house, in a patch of grass with her back towards the setting sun. Doris watched from the porch as Margot scribbled notes on a piece of paper, turned, wrote some more, and repeated this strange ritual until she returned to her original position.

"What 'cha doin'?" Doris asked, squatting a few feet from where Margot sat.

"Hives," answered Margot, erasing something on her paper and making another note.

"Calamine lotion might work," Doris said, "or maybe Beth could whip you up something."

Margot gave her a quizzical look and then said, "Oh, no— beehives. I'm trying to figure out the best location for them. They need to face the southeast, but they need a windbreak of some kind behind them—all I have is an open hillside."

"You were serious about coming back and helping the women learn how to keep bees, then?" Doris said. Margot nodded. "How much honey do they make anyway?" Doris asked. She resettled herself close enough to glance over at the drawings on Margot's paper.

"Two hives, well-maintained, could give us fifty to one hundred pounds of honey. Retail that down at the vineyard's gift shop for $12 a jar, it would be a nice little income for the house," Margot said. She set her paper aside and looked at Doris. "So, what's your plan after graduation? You sticking around?"

"I'm thinking of moving back down to the city. Now that the old man is dead, I don't have to be looking over my shoulder all the time," Doris said, referring to the "accident" where a heavy suitcase presumably fell on her abusive husband's head, breaking his neck, not a month after she'd entered the halfway house. Somehow, Florence was connected to that, too. Doris didn't understand it, but she thanked the woman silently every day since.

"Paulina said she'd teach me to fire pottery," Doris continued. "She has some artist friends in the city who are going to help set up her studio. I kind of like the idea of learning a trade," she smiled, "considering all I have on my resume is being an ex-felon and an ex-mental patient."

"Mind if I join you?" Maren asked. She'd walked up so quietly, not wanting to disturb the conversation, neither woman had heard her, and both women jumped.

"Good God, woman," Margot said, fanning herself, "with all the crazy stuff happening around here, you don't want to be sneaking up on people."

"Sorry," Maren mumbled.

"We were talking about what we're going to do after graduation," Doris said. "I guess you'll be staying on as the cook?"

Maren nodded. "We sure could use some new pottery dinnerware," she said, smiling at Doris.

They talked until the sun sank out of view and a calm settled over the hillside. In the distance, the call of a red-tailed hawk pierced the night and the first stars twinkled dimly.

Chapter 4

The air conditioning had kicked off around eight o'clock, and Shalese raised the bedroom window. The cold night air was good for the vineyard grapes, and a welcome relief after the sweltering afternoon.

"It was amazing," Jenny said breathlessly to Shalese as they crawled under the flannel sheets and snuggled in for the night. "You can't imagine how powerful it is to be the first witness to someone coming out." She closed her eyes as if the image was just too overwhelming to look at directly.

Shalese chuckled softly next to her. "Yeah, I sort of have some idea about that," she said, remembering that just over a year ago, she witnessed Jenny's emergence into this new realm of herself. At the time, she remembered thinking it was like watching a holy event unfold, like a butterfly emerging from a chrysalis.

"Oh, yeah, huh. I kind of forgot," Jenny said, remembering now the whirlwind of emotions that had turned her life upside-down, and the incredible support without pressure that Shalese had provided.

"So, I was right? She's had a little crush on you that was making her act all prickly?" Shalese turned, scooped Jenny into her arms, and snuggled her nose into Jenny's neck. "You are downright irresistible, all right."

"You might want to watch out for Gabriella if she's in the same room with you and holding a sharp object," Jenny teased. "I told her about my struggle accepting Mab as a part of your life."

"Uh huh. You were the green-eyed monster for a little while there," Shalese murmured. "I remember for a week or so you sniped at her every chance you got. Remember the day you were so jealous you just burst into tears?"

Jenny groaned with embarrassment. "I can't even imagine life without her now," she said, smiling at Shalese. "Ready for lights out?" At the suggestive moan next to her, she reached over and clicked off the light on the nightstand.

Downstairs in the guest room, Mab unpacked her overnight bag. She felt restless, far from ready to sleep. She padded down the hall to the library hoping to find a paperback that had no redeeming message of hope and recovery. Maybe a cheap romance or one of those cozy mysteries would distract her mind from worry. She closed the library door behind her and switched on the light. *The Big Book, Codependent No More, Don't Call it Love.* She'd have to make a stop at the women's bookstore on her next trip up, flush out these shelves a little bit, she thought with a yawn.

From somewhere down the hall, there was a muffled crash and the sound of wood splintering. Was someone in the group room at the end of the hall? The women had free run of the house, but were mostly all upstairs in bed by eleven o'clock. Mab turned off the light and opened the door quietly. She paused in the darkened hallway.

She heard herself shriek as a dark-clad figure ran from the group room, through the front door, and down the steps. Mobilized, she jogged down the hall and peered out into the night only to see the figure slipping away down the path that led back to the main road.

The hall light flicked on behind her and she spun around to see eight pairs of eyes lining the stairwell and bunched up at the bottom of the stairs.

"Mab, are you all right?" Shalese worked her way through the clump of women and grabbed Mab who was shaking from the adrenaline rush. "What happened?" Jenny and several other women joined them at the entrance of the group room.

"I don't know exactly," Mab said, her voice quivering. "I was in the library, and I heard a noise. Stuck my head out of the door and saw someone running out of the house." She heaved a sigh. "They're gone now," she said looking back over her shoulder at the open door. Jenny closed the door, and put a comforting arm around Mab's shoulder.

"We should check out the group room," Mab suggested. "I heard a crash."

Like an amoeba, they shuffled hip-to-hip through the double doors into the group room and flipped on the light switch. Nothing seemed out of place at first glance—no shelves trashed, no windows broken.

"Oh!" Jenny gasped, pointing to the center of the room where the new ukulele lay smashed—wood splintered, strings snapped, unrecognizable as an instrument.

"What the . . ." Mab shook her head slowly.

"That doesn't make any sense," Chandra said. "They could have at least gotten some money if they'd stolen the damned thing. And what do they have against a ukulele, I'd like to know?"

"Well, not much we can do about it tonight. I couldn't sleep before, and I sure can't sleep now. How about I take first shift. I'll camp out here in the group room," Mab offered.

"I'll set my alarm and take the next shift," Chandra said. "Be back down about three o'clock?"

"I'm usually awake by six anyway," Doris said. "I'll relieve you then."

Shaken, but feeling the worst was probably over for the night, the women dispersed to their bedrooms.

"You sure you'll be all right?" Jenny asked Mab. "We could stay up with you," she volunteered herself and Shalese.

"Naw, but thanks, sugar. You two get some sleep. I'll see you in the morning." Mab said, checking the lock on the front door.

Back in her room, Maren pulled her journal out from under her bed, opened it, and next to the word *tire*, wrote *ukulele*.

The next morning, Mab, Shalese, and Chandra got an early start on the security system for the house.

"Am I on TV?" Madigan asked as she came in and out of the front door, waving at the eaves where the cameras were hidden.

"Born to be a star, baby," Chandra said as she folded up the ladder and headed to the back of the house.

Jenny, Maren, and Gabriella were on grocery shopping detail and passed Madigan on the front porch. "Don't forget to set the alarm when you go inside," Jenny reminded her.

"I won't forget," Madigan said. "1-s-t-e-p, right?" she stage-whispered, and with a wave to the women, and another one to the camera, she slipped back inside.

Jenny wheeled Mab's Pathfinder down the vineyard road, and drove the five miles into town.

"Feels good to be back in civilization," Gabriella commented as Jenny pulled into the Safeway parking lot.

"I love the country, but it is kinda isolated up there," Maren agreed as they crossed the lot and entered the grocery.

Gabriella grabbed a shopping cart and was headed down the aisle when she heard a man call Jenny's name. She turned to see a thin, pasty-looking man in his thirties with receding dishwater-blonde hair, scoop Jenny up, spin her around, and plant a kiss on her cheek. Maren stood next to them, wide-eyed and slack-jawed.

Jenny, flustered and crimson, wriggled to disengage herself from the embrace. "Lawrence, what on earth are you doing here?" she managed.

"I'm here for a lawyer's convention in 'Frisco. Thought I'd come up-valley and do a little wine tasting while I was on the west coast. Your mother gave me your phone number—"

"My mother gave you my phone number?" she said, grimacing. She promised herself to call Ohio that evening and give her mother a piece of her mind.

"And I was going to call, but this is so much better. Sweetheart, you look wonderful," he said stroking her hair. She shook free from his touch and backed up a couple of steps.

Gabriella joined the trio, and cleared her throat suggestively, glancing from Jenny to this overly-familiar man. "Everything all right here?" she asked.

"Oh," Jenny said, embarrassed, "Gabriella, Maren, this is Lawrence. Lawrence, these are my, uh . . ."

It occurred to Jenny that this situation had never happened to her before. Recovery programs are anonymous, so she couldn't introduce them as residents, and as close as they'd all become, she wasn't quite ready to call Gabriella a friend.

"So, how do you know our Jenny?" Gabriella interceded.

"We were going to get married," Lawrence replied. "She dumped me," he said. He shrugged and pulled a face.

·Gabriella looked hard at Jenny. "But, I thought you were a—"

"We knew each other a long time ago," Jenny interrupted her. She glanced at Maren who seemed to have been stunned silent.

"Too long," Lawrence said. "How about if I call you and we can have dinner together sometime this week?"

"This ought to be good," Gabriella said under her breath.

"I'm sorry, Lawrence, but I'm in a relationship. I'm really not free to, ah . . ." Jenny shrugged.

"Lucky guy," he said. "My loss. If you change your mind, here's my number. I believe in second chances," he smiled, and with a wink, handed her his business card. He leaned forward to kiss her goodbye, but Jenny dodged around to the other side of the shopping cart. "Nice meeting you lovely ladies," Lawrence said.

When he was out of sight, Maren said, "Smarmy little prick," then slapped her hand over her mouth. "Oh, I'm so sorry. No one asked my opinion. I mean, he *was* your fiancé, right?" She looked at Jenny.

Gabriella chuckled. "I couldn't help but notice that you didn't correct his gender slip." There was an undertone of malice that Jenny didn't like. "Does he not know?"

"My life is none of Lawrence's business," Jenny said, just a little too snippily. "Are we going to get groceries or not?" She commandeered the shopping cart and headed down the aisle.

The ride back to The Next Step was quiet in a way that gave Maren a tension headache.

"Well, I for one won't mention this to Shalese," Gabriella said. "I'm sure it would upset her to know that your old boyfriend is in the area, pursuing you."

"Shalese knows all about Lawrence, and, of course I'll tell her we ran into him."

"Hmm, ran into him. That's an interesting way to put it," Gabriella sniped. "He kissed you. He had his hands all over you, right there in the grocery."

"Look, Gabriella, don't start anything. There's nothing *to* start. I'll handle this," Jenny said as they wound their way up the road to the house.

"Oh!" Maren gasped.

Jenny slammed on the brakes at the beginning of the circular drive that led to the front porch.

"What on earth . . ." Gabriella muttered.

"It looks like someone TP'd the yard," Maren said, stepping out of the car and walking slowly up the drive. Jenny stuck her head out the window, mouth agape.

"Yes, just out of range of the video cams, too," Gabriella noticed, joining Maren. "But, it's not toilet paper, it's—"

"Rags," Maren finished her sentence. "Rags, strewn all over our yard. Why would anyone . . ."

Gabriella and Maren walked on up to the front porch as Jenny pulled the car around. Maren typed in the alarm code and opened the door while Gabriella and Jenny each grabbed two bags of groceries from the back of the Pathfinder.

157

"Shalese! Mab!" Jenny called as she walked toward the kitchen to set the bags down. Shalese stuck her head out of the office just as Mab stepped out of the kitchen and relieved Jenny of one of the bags.

"What's up?" Shalese asked, noting the alarm in Jenny's voice.

With her free hand, Jenny pointed back down the hall and towards the front lawn.

"Rags, damn it, rags," she huffed. Shalese and Mab exchanged a look, then headed down the hall and out the front door.

"I don't get it," Mab muttered, shaking her head wearily.

Gabriella and Jenny joined them on the porch and surveyed the damage. "We could call the police," Gabriella offered. "This is malicious mischief, if nothing else."

Jenny stepped out onto the porch. "What's that smell?" she said, sniffing the air.

"Smells like—" Mab said.

"Gasoline," Shalese finished for her. "Oh my God. Let's call the women out of group. We've got to get these rags picked up. One match, and the whole front yard could go up in a blaze."

Jenny and Mab went inside to round up the women. In the kitchen, Maren opened her journal, and next to *ukulele*, she wrote *rags*.

It took less than fifteen minutes for the women to gather the rags, peel them off bushes, shrubbery, unwind them from tree branches. Only a few of the rags had been soaked with gasoline. The threat might not have been fatal, but the message was clear—someone didn't want them there.

Chapter 5

Just after lunch, the women gathered in the group room for their afternoon session. The exercise was loosely based on the Ask-It Basket in the 12-step programs, infused with The Next Step spin. Madigan offered to be the drummer. She stepped outside the circle, and with her back to the women, pounded out a rhythmic beat on the newly acquired bongos as the wicker basket full of folded pieces of paper was passed from hand to hand. In the tradition of musical chairs, when Madigan stopped playing the drums, whoever held the basket was allowed to pick a piece of paper from the basket and read it aloud. This would be the next topic of discussion. Paulina was holding the basket when Madigan finished with a dramatic flurry of beats.

"Safety," she called out. The women groaned at the irony.

"Safety is an illusion," Kendra said. "We might as well be in Siberia."

"Why would you say that?" Shalese questioned.

"Imagine you're in Siberia and you're being chased by a tiger. You see this river, and you think, 'if I can swim far enough from shore, I'll be safe,'" she said, looking around the room. Blank faces stared back at her. With a sigh, she finished her analogy, "Siberian tigers, unlike normal housecats, love to swim."

Jenny's eyes danced with mirth, but she kept a straight face.

Gabriella beamed at Kendra. "That was a brilliant analogy," she said.

"How do you even know stuff like that?" Madigan asked, shaking her head.

"Are you saying, no matter what we do, how many precautions we take to keep ourselves safe here at the house, it's all just an illusion, because there *is* no safety?" Chandra clarified for herself. "Well, that just sucks."

"Let's talk about the difference between perceived threat and real threat," Jenny said, "because there *is* a difference." All eyes were on her now. "How many of you are afraid of Siberian tigers?" she asked.

Everyone shot a hand into the air. "How many of you have ever seen a Siberian tiger, outside of a zoo, that is?" The women looked around the circle. Everyone was shaking their heads.

"What's your point?" Chandra asked. "There aren't any Siberian tigers around here."

"That's my point, exactly," Jenny said. "If we were in Siberia, we'd have every reason to be afraid of tigers. If we were still in a battering relationship, we'd have every reason to fear for our lives. But we're not. There's perceived danger from the behaviors that have been happening around here lately, but nothing truly harmful has happened. No one has been harmed." There were murmurs of skepticism throughout the group.

"I think what Jenny is saying," Shalese added, "is that if we were truly in danger of being harmed, we would see to our safety. It's important to be able to discern real danger from imagined, or even potential danger, and to act accordingly."

"I guess because of our histories with violence, our tendency is to run—or fight—now, and ask questions later," Margot ventured. "It's that post-traumatic response stuff you were talking about before, right?"

"Whew, that's a lot to take in," Madigan said. "My brain is tired."

"Let's take a break to let all this sink in, then we'll meet back here in ten minutes," Shalese suggested.

Some women headed for the bathroom, some outside for a smoke, others to the kitchen for something cold to drink. Beth arrived first at the front door, her hand poised on the knob.

"I'm afraid to look outside. Who knows what they've done next," she said to Paulina, who was right behind her.

"Real or perceived?" Paulina said.

Ever so slowly, Beth turned the knob, opened the door a crack, and peered out to the front lawn. She let out her breath, and swung the door wide open. Neither woman stepped over the threshold.

"Oh for God sake, let me outta here, I gotta smoke," Chandra said, shoving through the blockade. Maren and Paulina exchanged a sheepish look and followed Chandra outside.

Shalese was busy straightening chairs in the circle. Gabriella hung around until the rest of the women had left the room. "I met your nemesis this morning," she said casually.

Shalese glanced over at her. "Sorry? I'm not following—"

"Lawrence," Gabriella said. "You know, Jenny's Lawrence? At the grocery. He seems quite smitten with her, couldn't keep his hands off her," she said lightly. Now that she had Shalese's full attention, raised eyebrows and all, she added, "Didn't Jenny tell you?" If there was a face that parodied innocence, it would have been Gabriella's at that moment.

"I haven't really had a moment . . ." Shalese's voice trailed off.

"Oh, I'm sure she meant to tell you. They were talking about dinner or something," Gabriella said.

"Lawrence? From Ohio?" Shalese said cocking her head. Just then, Jenny walked into the group room.

"Need any help setting up?" she asked, as Gabriella slipped behind her and sidled into the hallway.

"Do we need to talk?" Shalese asked pointedly.

"Sweetie, I love talking to you, but the women are due back in less than three minutes," Jenny said with a smile. Noticing Shalese wasn't returning her smile, and that her brows were furrowed, Jenny said, "Something wrong?"

"You tell me," Shalese said.

The women were filing back in, taking their seats, finishing their conversations. Jenny, taken aback at the shift of energy, took her seat across the circle from Shalese. Gabriella, who usually sat right next to Jenny and demanded her attention, had moved several seats down next to Kendra and wasn't making eye contact.

Oh, damn it! Jenny groaned inwardly.

Once again, the basket made its way around the circle, this time to the gentle rhythm Maren tapped on the bongos. After a moment, she stopped, and Jenny took a piece of paper from the basket, unfolded it and read, "Honesty." Crimson color crept slowly from her collarbone, up her neck, over her chin, and finished with a full-blown blush all over her face. Across the circle, Shalese cleared her throat loudly.

Jenny avoided looking at Shalese as each woman spoke about honesty in her life, or the absence of it up until the present. *I'm certainly not going to share today's encounter with Lawrence in the group. That doesn't mean I'm being dishonest, does it? I'll talk to Shalese privately when we go upstairs for the night.* Jenny loosened the top button on her shirt, stretched her neck, sat up straight. *I can't seem to get enough air. Why would Gabriella mention Lawrence? Just to get me in trouble?* She remembered her attempts to discredit Mab a year ago by saying she should take up fiction writing when Mab ran a theory by them about Florence's involvement in the murders. Jenny smiled. *Okay, so I was jealous of Mab and Shalese's relationship. Well, I guess that would explain it. If Gabriella thought she could break us up, she could have me all to herself. Sheesh.*

Jenny, who had been lost in thought, checked back in just in time to hear Kendra say, "Withholding is the same thing as lying—it's not telling the whole truth."

"Would you be lying then," Chandra charged, "since you still haven't come out to the group?" There was a collective gasp. All eyes were on Kendra.

"Hold on now," Shalese spoke up. "Coming out is a personal choice. It isn't anyone else's call," she said, looking pointedly at Chandra.

"No . . ." Kendra said quietly, her eyes focused on the center of the circle. "She's right. I've withheld the truth all my life because it would have gotten me killed. I've been living a lie, and I'm done with that." She raised her head and made direct eye contact with each woman in the circle, one at a time. "I've known since I was eight that I was a lesbian."

"How'd Chandra know that?" Mab asked, truly perplexed.

"You work the streets most of your life, you develop *gaydar*, along with a whole lot of other people-reading skills," Chandra said. "Sorry," she addressed Kendra, noticing the tears that now ran down Kendra's face. "I shouldn't have busted you."

Gabriella, who sat next to Kendra, reached over tentatively and patted her hand. Margot passed the tissue box.

"These are good tears," Kendra said, grabbing onto Gabriella's hand. "These are tears of relief that there's a safe place in the world for me, and people I've learned to trust," she said, wiping her eyes.

"Maybe you can even start eating now," Chandra blurted out.

"Okay, enough honesty," Kendra said, smiling. She wadded up a wet tissue and threw it at Chandra. "Yes, I'm anorexic too. I'm an anorexic lesbian. Now, will someone else please speak?" The ripple of giggles turned into hearty laughter as the women let go of the tension they each had carried for years, of lying to survive.

Later, upstairs in their room, Shalese flung herself down on the bed. "I'm exhausted," she said. "That group almost did me in." She smiled at Jenny who was brushing her hair at the dressing table. Jenny caught Shalese's reflection in the mirror—the sulk was gone, along with the edge to her voice.

"Honey, I'm sorry I didn't get a chance to tell you about Lawrence, and you had to find out from Gabriella. I had no idea he was even on the coast. He just popped out at me at the grocery. I guess he was up for the day from San Francisco. Mother gave him my number. God, it was so creepy to see him again," Jenny shivered involuntarily. She turned to face Shalese who was propped up against the headboard. "He touched me, and it felt like a dead fish—it was horrible," she said, crossing the room and climbing in bed next to Shalese.

Shalese put an arm around her and pulled her close. "Did you arrange to meet him for dinner?" she asked.

"What? No! Why would you . . ." Jenny gave a frustrated sigh. "Is that what she said? God. I wasn't this bad, was I? I mean, toward Mab?"

"Oh yeah," Shalese said with a huge smile. "Just a little bit of your own medicine come back to haunt you." She nuzzled Jenny's neck.

"What did you think of Kendra's coming out?" Jenny asked, to change the subject.

"I've gotta tell you, I didn't see that coming," Shalese admitted. "And Chandra? Whew! If she weren't so likeable, she'd be lynched by now, with that mouth of hers," Shalese chuckled.

They debriefed the day until they couldn't keep their eyes open, and fell asleep in each other's arms.

Chapter 6

Several days had gone by without incident. Shalese and Jenny sat in the office on opposite sides of the desk Saturday afternoon, rifling through a stack of applications for the next batch of residents.

"How did we become so well-known?" Jenny muttered. "We had to beg for referrals a year ago." She pulled four applications from the pile and placed them on top of the six Shalese had selected.

"The public relations, press releases, and social networking Analise has done really paid off," Shalese said. She stretched her arms over her head, her back made little popping sounds up and down her spine.

Down the hall in the group room, the graduation committee was hard at work on their day off. Analise proudly passed around the template for the official certificate of completion. "I think we should roll them up like scrolls and tie them with ribbon," she suggested.

"Oooh, then one at a time we can walk across the stage when our name's called out and be handed one of them?" Madigan said. "I saw that in a movie once." She held the template up, imagining her name printed in fancy letters. "I'm gonna frame mine," she said.

"We need food, music, and a speaker," Beth said.

"Let's ask Oprah," Madigan said. "She'd probably be proud of us."

"I'm sure she would be," Beth smiled, "but Oprah is booked years in advance. I was thinking someone more local. Maybe Shalese could ask that new woman judge to come talk to us, encourage us."

"I like that," Analise said, "and, it would be another referral resource for the house." They tossed suggestions around for a while.

"What about music? I was thinking 'Pomp and Circumstance,'" Maren offered.

"Oh, Lordy no," Madigan shook her head. "We don't want any songs about little babies losin' their weenies. That's a terrible thought, just terrible," she muttered.

"No, not circumcision," Maren said. She hummed a few bars of the popular graduation song.

"That's the song was on that movie I saw. Made me cry. Yeah, let's do that one," Madigan agreed enthusiastically. "And maybe somethin' by Stevie Wonder," she added. They compromised by choosing "We Are the World, USA for Africa," by Michael Jackson and Lionel Richie.

Paulina burst through the group room door, blanched and wide-eyed. She held something gingerly between her fingers. "Better call a meeting," she said, her voice strained. Beth and Madigan headed off to round up Jenny, Shalese, and the other residents.

When they regrouped, Paulina said, "I went for a hike down the road. It's so beautiful up here, I know I'm going to miss it when I move back to the city . . ."

Chandra made a hurry-up motion with her hand.

"On my way back up the path, I found this," she said, holding out a large orange pierced by thirteen needles for all to see.

"I don't get it. They're not like hospital needles or the kinda needles from the 'hood," Madigan said, scratching her head.

"They're just sewing needles," Beth observed. "Are you sure it wasn't there before, and maybe you just missed it?"

Paulina shook her head. "Someone put it there knowing that I'd be back, I'm sure of it."

Maren pulled her journal from her pocket and next to *rags*, wrote *needles*. She perused the growing line of words, and squinched her eyes in concentration. "I just don't see any connection," she said. "I'm pretty sure there's a clue in here somewhere—thirteen needles, thirteen women."

"What if we tried unscrambling the letters—like tar, instead of rat," Beth offered. The women stared at her with blank faces. "Just a thought," she muttered.

"Maybe the words aren't connected, but maybe the first letter of each word spells a clue," Paulina suggested, looking over Maren's shoulder at the list, "like RENT and URN."

"What kind of clue is that?" Chandra asked smacking her forehead. "If we don't pay our rent they're gonna burn us up and put our ashes in an urn? I don't think so."

"I was just trying to help," Paulina said with a pout.

"Or there's TURN and ER. No, that doesn't make any sense either," Maren said.

"Y'all are creepin' me out," Madigan said.

"I'm not liking this one little bit," Chandra said.

"These things happened one at a time, right?" Analise offered. Around the circle, heads nodded in general agreement. "What if we tried listing them in the order they happened, like from top to bottom, instead of next to each other," she suggested.

"Can't hurt," Maren said. Everyone leaned in toward the center of the circle as she rearranged the list of words, hoping she'd gotten the essence out of each clue and hadn't mis-guessed. She wrote:

Rat
Eel
Tire
Ukulele
Rags
Needles

"Oh my God!" Maren exclaimed. "The first letter of each word spells RETURN."

"Hah!" Paulina shouted, vindicated.

"Doo doo doo doo, doo doo doo doo," Doris hummed the tune from *The Twilight Zone*.

"What we suppose to return?" Madigan said. "We didn't take nothin'."

A look passed between Shalese, Jenny, and Maren so quickly no one else caught it. "Not possible," Shalese said under her breath. "I think we'd better call Mab," she said aloud, and left the room to use the phone in the office.

"Maybe someone wants us to return to the city?" Kendra guessed.

"Or wants us to return the land?" Margot added. "We've got the deed for it, though, right?"

Jenny nodded. "I have a feeling we'll get more clues," she said, "and it will become clearer. Until then, I believe we're safe."

"This seems like a strange way of communicating," Gabriella stated the obvious. "Why don't they just come right out and ask for what they want?"

The women were slow to disperse, each venturing a guess as to what the cumulative clues would spell, and whether or not they were in danger.

Mab arrived just before dinner and was ushered into the office. Maren, twitching with curiosity about what was being said on the other side of the closed door, was putting the final touches on dinner. She strained to hear the conversation between Mab, Shalese, and Jenny.

Chandra came into the kitchen, lifted the lid on a pot of baked beans and inhaled noisily, appreciatively, and was shushed by Maren.

"Why don't you just put a glass up to the door?" Chandra suggested. "What's all the secrecy about, do you suppose?" Maren squirmed. "You know something, don't you?" Chandra said, sizing her up. "Spill it."

"I don't know for sure, and I'm not at liberty to say," Maren backpedaled.

"Hey, you can tell me. I can keep a secret," Chandra said. She plastered her most trustworthy look on her face, all round-eyed innocence and slightly puckered mouth.

Maren narrowed her eyes. "You couldn't keep a secret in a locked vault," she said. Chandra chuckled.

Just then, the office door opened. Maren startled, grabbed a wooden spoon, and began stirring the beans. Chandra grabbed a cup from the sink and made a production of rinsing it out. She looked back over her shoulder to see Mab heading toward the dining room, followed by Jenny and Shalese.

Paulina, Margot, and Doris were on dinner duty. As they entered the kitchen, Maren dished up the food from the stove into serving bowls and handed each woman two bowls to carry into the dining room.

As the women were finishing their meal and talking excitedly among themselves—conversations flavored with anxiety and spiced with a touch of hysteria—Shalese tapped her glass with her spoon, drawing the attention to the head of the table.

"We've decided to forego our usual evening meeting—"

Madigan pushed her chair back from the table. "Good, I'm gonna take me a swim. It's hot in here," she said, interrupting Shalese.

Shalese raised her hand. "Hold on," she said with a grin. "We're still meeting, but we'll use the time to set up an ambush detail. We'll make a schedule and go in small groups, lining the path up to the house."

"It's about time we did something to catch these suckers," Chandra said, full of bravado. "Do we get to beat the shit out of them, if we catch them?"

"No violence!" Mab commanded.

"We're interested in finding out who is behind this harassment," Jenny said. "With the clues that Maren put together, we think we may have an idea what this is about."

"Are you going to tell us?" Doris asked.

"Yeah, we deserve to know," Beth and several others supported Doris.

"We want to wait until we have a little more information. For now, we can tell you that we suspect Florence is behind this somehow," Shalese answered.

"That crazy ol' bat?" Madigan said. "Didn't we think she'd flown the coop?"

"Not Florence herself, but someone acting on her behalf perhaps," Jenny said. "When we're finished with dinner, we'll meet in the group room." Everyone seemed to have lost their appetite and quickly carried their dishes into the kitchen like an army of ants on a mission.

Once in the group room, the women started talking over one another using words like *loose cannon, dangerous,* and *deranged.* Jenny stood at a large flip-chart with an ink marker in her hand. Mab stood and cleared her throat, and the cacophony died down. Shalese nodded her support.

"So, here's the plan," Mab said, looking around the room. The faces looking back at her were different than those who first arrived at the halfway house. These were faces of women who had learned to trust each other, to work together for the highest good of the group, and who didn't shrink back in fear, but were willing to step forward to protect what was theirs. Her eyes moistened, and her face softened.

"Here's the plan," she repeated, her voice catching. "We don't want to put anyone at risk. We don't have reason to believe this person, or these people, are armed. We merely want to see who they are, be able to identify them if we need to call on the police." She gestured to Shalese who stood up to speak.

"We want to have three people on either side of the path, just out of sight, behind the bushes starting this evening. We'll take half-hour shifts and rotate, up until midnight," Shalese said.

"Why don't we just hire a full-time watchman?" Analise asked.

"What if they don't come this evening?" Kendra wondered. "How long are we going to do this watch-thing?"

"For now, we want to keep this in-house," Jenny said. "My guess is it won't take more than a day or two. Who wants the first shift?" All hands went up, and Jenny wrote the first six names on the board. "The rest of us will be the second shift," she said.

"We're sorry to disrupt your night like this," Shalese said, "but I know we're all invested in finding out who is responsible." Everyone nodded their head.

"Remember," Mab said, "no talking, no fidgeting around. We want to be an invisible presence. If someone comes up the path, we wait until they pass the first woman on each side, then we'll jump out and surround them. One woman on each shift will have this whistle." She handed a large sports whistle to Doris. "Blow that sucker, and we'll all come running," Mab assured them. She handed flashlights with large heads to Beth and Maren. "Your job is to make sure we see their faces and can identify them."

"You're talking in plurals. That makes me nervous," Kendra said. "Maybe we should all go."

"It'll be hard enough keeping six of us at a time quiet," Mab offered. "Let's see if this works tonight. If not, we can revise it tomorrow."

"Team One, out we go," Shalese said, leading six of the residents down the hall and out into the night.

"We'll be out at eight thirty," Jenny called after them.

The sun had just set behind the vineyard as they crept down the path, staying on either side, and then faded into the bushes and trees. A muffled sneeze drew a quiet "Bless you," which in turn drew a loud "Shh." A raven called in the distance. An owl hooted from the top of a nearby redwood. There was rustling in the grass and the snap of twigs as the women settled themselves in for the next half-hour.

Back at the house, Analise said, "Madigan, come away from the window. We don't want to look obvious."

Madigan let the curtain fall back in place. "If we're supposed to be havin' a normal night, we should all be in the group room, with most of the other lights in the house off, shouldn't we?" she asked.

"That's a good idea," Jenny said. "We can keep each other company and maybe not worry so much."

They sat in a circle, filing their nails, flipping through magazines, tapping their feet, with audible sighs and restless shifting about. "Well, this isn't working," Jenny noted aloud.

"Feels like a waiting room at the dentist's office," Analise said.

"Or when you're in an elevator riding up to the top floor," Gabriella offered, "and trying to avoid eye contact."

"Or while you waitin' for your man to come off his crack run," Madigan said.

The tension broke as one by one, they created a game of *what does this feel like* using their own life experiences.

At eight thirty, Jenny, Madigan, Gabriella, Margot, Kendra, and Analise crept out of the house and down the path toward the dirt driveway to relieve the first shift. There was no moon to guide them. Shalese stepped out from the shadows and quietly called the others forward. Mab stated she was staying for the second shift, gave a quick update of the plan, and pointed the women to either side of the road. The whistle and flashlights were reassigned as the first shift slipped back up the path to the house.

After what seemed like an hour, Jenny pushed the illumination button on her watch. Twenty minutes had gone by, and the women were getting restless. She was at the end of the drive, farthest from the house. She thought she heard a noise, although muffled, from just beyond her range of night vision. She peered across the road to where Mab leaned against a boulder. At just that moment, Mab leaned slightly forward and craned her neck in the direction of the noise. The hair on Jenny's arms stood on end, and a shiver went down her back. Footsteps, definitely footsteps. Slow, cautious, not-wanting-to-be-heard footsteps, followed by a form slinking along Mab's side of the drive. As the figure came closer, Jenny could discern a cowboy hat and boots. By the size, she guessed it was a man. He stopped, tilted his head from side to side as if listening, then proceeded slowly. Jenny held her breath as he passed between her and Mab on the other side of the path.

What was the plan? Oh, no, she'd forgotten the plan. Do they holler, and rush him? Every nerve was on end. What if he was armed? Or what if he merely bolted and ran back down the hill? Her heart pounded arrhythmically in her chest. He was a few yards past her when she saw Mab step forward onto the road. Jenny followed suit. Like a well-choreographed dance, the women leaped out of the brush behind and in front of him, closing in a tight circle around him. Flashlights flooded his face, and the whistle screamed in the night. In seconds, the other women came charging down the path from the house.

"Stop right where you are," Mab boomed with authority.

The man—Lefty, the caretaker from the vineyard, wide-eyed, mouth agape in a silent holler—grabbed at his heart.

"Damnation!" He fumed when he'd caught his breath. "What are you crazy women doing out here? You about scared me to death," he said, his head swiveling from face to face.

"Question is, what are *you* doin' out here, creepin' up on our house?" Chandra shouted.

"Yeah!" cried the others.

"Mr. Lefty, you'd best come on up to the house with us. You have some explaining to do," Mab said, grabbing him firmly by one arm. Shalese, scowling, grabbed the other arm, but not before Jenny noticed the look of terror that was slowly draining out of her face.

Back in the group room, Mab rather roughly seated Lefty in a chair, and pulled another chair opposite him, knee to knee. "I suggest you start explaining yourself," she said.

Lefty, whose hands were still shaking, removed his cowboy hat, loosened the top button of his plaid shirt, and smoothed his moustache. "Ms. Montana, I apologize to you, and all you women," he stammered. "I should have phoned before I came up here, but I didn't want to alarm you."

"Well, you sure botched that one," Chandra said. "You're lucky we weren't armed."

"I was coming up to check on you women," he explained. "There's been an old beaten up pick-up truck parked just off the road, down by the turn-off to your place. Been there all day. I was pretty sure it didn't belong to any of you. Bunch of beer cans littered around it. Spells nothing but trouble, if you ask me," Lefty said, looking around at the scowling faces. "That's why I was trying to be quiet, see if I could catch someone sneaking around up here."

Shalese glanced at Mab, then at Jenny. "I guess that makes sense," she said. "But you're right, you should have phoned us first."

"Sorry, ma'am," he said again. "May I ask what you were all doing out at night, lining the driveway?" Lefty asked timidly.

"There's been some trouble up here," Shalese said. "Harassment, mostly, but it has to stop."

"We were hoping to catch whoever has been threatening our peace of mind," Jenny said.

"And give him a piece of ours," Chandra piped up.

"Sounds like a job for the sheriff. Would you like me to contact him for you? He's a personal friend of mine," Lefty offered. For the second time that night, the hair on Jenny's arms stood up and a shiver ran down her back. She wrote it off to the physical letdown after a bad scare, nerves settling, and all that.

"That won't be necessary, but thank you," Mab said. "Just to cover all the bases, you might spread the word to your vineyard workers that we're serious. This has to stop."

"If it's any of my men, I'll see to it they're held accountable," Lefty said. "You just let me know if there's any way I can help you." He took his hat from his lap, stood up, and waited for a clearing through the crowd of women so he could leave.

"What do you think?" Shalese asked. "Shall we keep watch up until midnight anyway?" It was just after nine o'clock.

"Let's push our luck and call it a night," Mab suggested. There was agreement all around. "My nerves are kind of jangled. I think I'll sit up awhile, if anyone wants to join me." Several opted to stay up and talk, others drifted upstairs.

Jenny and Shalese exchanged a look. "See you in the morning," Jenny said to Mab.

Once in the privacy of their room, Jenny shrugged out of her sweatshirt and jeans, hung them in the closet, and then sat on the edge of the bed, eyes squinting in concentration, and said, "I walked down to the road this afternoon to get the mail. I didn't see a pick-up truck."

Shalese yawned and stretched. "You probably weren't looking for one. Lefty said it was off the road a little bit, right?"

"I suppose. Something just doesn't feel right," Jenny said. She slipped her nightgown over her head and crawled under the covers.

Shalese let her clothes fall in a pile on the floor. "Well, let's see if we can find out what doesn't feel right and fix it," she said with a wicked grin as she clicked off the light.

Chapter 7

The next morning, Mab was up before dawn. She hadn't slept well—her dreams were plagued with ravens and snakes—shapeshifters, symbols of transition, if you believed in such things. She slipped out of the house and walked down the path to the main road. She walked a few yards to the left and then to the right of the mailbox, but found no pick-up. Granted, there were tire marks along the side of the road, but she couldn't tell if they were fresh or not, as the ground was dry and dusty from the summer heat. She considered the possibility that Lefty may have had the truck towed. Still . . .

Over breakfast, Mab shared her observation with Jenny and Shalese. "Something just doesn't feel right," she said. "Can't quite put my finger on it."

"See," Jenny said, elbowing Shalese. "I told you. Didn't I say that last night?"

"You certainly did," Shalese said, grinning. "But I thought we fixed it." Jenny gave her a playful thump.

At the far end of the table, Chandra interrogated Maren, whose lips were sealed like two pancakes pressed together. "You might as well give it up—I'm gonna get it out of you eventually," Chandra said. If a woman could swagger while sitting still, Chandra was doing just that. "You know something. What is it?"

"Shh. Keep your voice down," Maren admonished. "If the staff wanted us to know, they'd tell us," she said primly. Her teeth were clamped tightly around what she suspected lay underneath the clues.

"The staff knows, then?" Chandra countered.

"I'm pretty sure they do, but they haven't included me in their discussions," she said, with measured scorn. Truth be told, Maren felt slighted. If you boiled it down to the basics, The Next Step wouldn't even exist if it hadn't been for her.

"And you think they should have included you because . . ." Chandra shrugged, palms up.

"Because," Maren lowered her voice to a whisper and leaned in toward Chandra, "I'm the one who found the cookbook with the map that led to the buried treasure that funded this place."

"Buried treasure?" Chandra shouted. Conversation stopped, and all heads turned toward her. Jenny, Shalese, and Mab sat with mouths hanging open.

Maren rolled her eyes and slapped her forehead with the palm of her hand. "I didn't mean to say that," she groaned. She sent a pleading look to the far end of the table. "Really, I didn't. Please, just shoot me." Tears of humiliation stung her eyes at having broken the trust the staff had placed in her.

"You're not very good at keeping secrets," Chandra said quietly.

Everyone spoke at once. *What treasure? When was it found? How much?* Shalese stood and tapped noisily on her juice glass until she had everyone's attention.

"All right," she said, hands up in surrender, "it's time to clear the air. First of all, Maren . . ." She waited until she could make eye contact with Maren, who looked like she was facing a firing squad. "The staff owes you an apology." Maren's eyes widened. "We put you in a terrible position of having to keep a huge secret that should have been handled strictly by the staff. You've done an admirable job. Thank you." The tears that had welled up in Maren's eyes flowed freely now. Jenny and Mab smiled their appreciation.

"The reason we didn't share this with the group is that it's a lot to hold," Shalese looked at each woman in turn. "And we really need to hold this within these walls," she stressed. "Do we have agreement?" Everyone spoke or nodded their consent. Shalese motioned to Jenny, who stood and retold the story.

"This begins right after Florence took all our money and left. Remember our field trips over to one of the first places we saw, just down the road from here—that abandoned guest ranch that looked like it would be perfect in every way?" The women murmured in agreement.

"That's the one where Maren found that old moldy cookbook she drug back to the city in the limo, right?" Chandra piped up.

"Pe-e-uw!" Madigan said, "I remember that."

"That's right," Jenny said. "That cookbook had probably been there since the 1940s. What you didn't know—and what we patched together after my Dad's visit—is the cookbook belonged to Florence, who went by the name Flo back then. She and my grandmother were friends, and wrote those recipes when they'd vacation there in the summer. We did some research and found out that a wealthy politician was robbed and killed at that ranch just about the time Flo went missing. His murderer was never found. We believe Flo—Florence— may have been the murderer," Jenny said. "My dad suspects she skipped the country."

"But before she left," Shalese added, "we think she buried the money for safe-keeping—probably planned on returning for it in the future."

"The ranch—even though it was a great property—sat abandoned after that and was never sold," Mab added.

"Turns out there was a treasure map in the back of the cookbook," Maren took up the story. "Remember when the ranch was ransacked right after we started making inquiries about it? They completely tore apart that beautiful kitchen," Maren said with a pout.

"In hindsight, we think Florence, or someone connected to her, was looking for the cookbook and the treasure map before anyone else found it—there were holes dug out back that were in approximately the same place as the locations marked on the map," Jenny said.

"But I had the map," added Maren triumphantly. She looked around at the women who sat spellbound. "So Shalese, Jenny, Mab, and I went over to the ranch, dug where the X's were according to the map, and found the treasure," Maren said, breathless at the memory.

"How much money?" Analise asked.

"A hundred thousand dollars," Jenny said. Gasps and shouts filled the room, and Jenny waited for the women to quiet down.

"Why didn't you call the police?" Beth asked. "That's an awful lot of money."

"Before we could figure out what to do," Mab took over for Jenny, "the place burned down. Arson. Since I was the last one seen on the premises, I was under suspicion. After I was cleared, it seemed best to let sleeping dogs lie.

"Could we prove it was Florence who stole and buried the money? No, but the pieces were starting to add up. Since Florence left us in such a mess, it also seemed justifiable that we would use her allegedly stolen money to help us start over. Was it legal? Probably not, but we didn't know who to trust. Could have been the police were in on it. She was connected with judges, lawyers, business tycoons, bankers."

Mab stopped to wipe sweat from her brow, and took a couple of deep breaths. Was she having an anxiety attack? The room seemed to go out of focus for a moment, and she sat down. Jenny poured her a glass of orange juice and handed it to her with a look of concern.

"When we were offered the land we're on now, to build a brand new recovery house," Shalese continued, "we made a collective decision to put that money to good use. What we didn't put directly into the building, we invested to ensure the future of The Next Step. Again, was it legal? Probably not. That's why we didn't burden any of you—except Maren, who was in the thick of it—with the knowledge."

"And you could get in a lot of trouble if this ever got out," Kendra added. "Not just because you used stolen money from an alleged murderer," she shuddered, "but also because your credibility as ethical businesswomen would be called into play."

Jenny and Shalese looked at one another. Jenny had a deer-in-headlights expression on her face.

"That gives us a lot of power here," Kendra continued. Jenny shrank back in her chair. "And a lot of responsibility," she said. Shalese forced herself to breathe.

Mab squinted and cocked her head at Kendra. "What are you suggesting, Kendra?" she said, keeping her voice even.

"I'm suggesting that we remember that this place saved our lives and deserves our loyalty and support. I'm suggesting we continue to support the staff in any way we can, and to honor that you three—or four—made the best decision on our behalf that you could under some pretty trying circumstances." She looked around the room. "I'm suggesting we say thank you." The room erupted. Jenny clapped her hand over her heart and took a long, slow breath.

"Wait a minute, wait a minute," Madigan said when the room quieted down. "Do those clues mean someone wants us to return the money?"

"Girl, you missed your calling. That was a brilliant deduction," Mab said "That's our best guess. What we don't know, is who. If Florence left the country—again—one of her cohorts is acting on her behalf."

"How would they even know where we were?" Madigan asked.

"Wish I knew the answer to that," Mab said.

Chapter 8

In group the following morning, Shalese announced that there'd been a change of plans for the house. This was met with groans of resistance. "Seems there's been nothing *but* change lately," Doris complained. "We could use a little *same old, same old* for the time we have left." Murmurs of agreement rippled around the room.

"Well, this is sort of in response to all the change. We felt it might be more stabilizing for the new women to come in on a buddy system," Shalese said. "I know some of you have made plans to move on, whether it's to go back to the city or live nearby. Analise, Kendra, Chandra, Margot, and Maren have expressed an interest in staying on another six months to overlap with the new women, and lend some stability to the house."

"That means we'll be taking on five new women, and five more in February when the remainder of our original residents move on," Jenny explained.

"Oh, so you'll always have someone here who knows the ropes for a little longer than the newcomers?" Paulina asked.

"Exactly," Shalese answered. "I'm sorry there wasn't anyone ahead of you to pave the way. You are sort of our pioneers. You've helped shape this program and make it stronger. You can be very proud of yourselves."

"What about that aluminum club someone mentioned a while back?" Madigan asked.

"Alumni club," Jenny corrected. "I think that's a fantastic idea. Are any of you interested in staying in touch, maybe coming back once a month to visit, or for an open meeting? Being a safe contact in the community for women who are ready to graduate?" All hands shot up.

"I nominate Madigan as president of the alumni club," Beth said.

"Second," Paulina said.

"All in favor," Jenny said, looking around the room.

"Aye," all the women called out.

"I never been no president of anything before," Madigan beamed. "Can I be called Madam President?"

"I certainly think that's fitting," Shalese said. She reached over and shook Madigan's hand. "Congratulations, Madam President." The women clapped and hooted their approval.

"For those who will be leaving after graduation," Shalese continued when the room had quieted down, "do you want to share your plans?"

Gabriella stood and said, "I have an application for receptionist at an ophthalmology office here in town, since I have some familiarity with that profession." The others groaned. She grinned and said, "Think of it as poetic justice." Gabriella had landed a near-fatal blow to the head of her abusive former husband, a wealthy ophthalmologist in the city, rendering him blind. "It's through a bridge program that helps ex-felons find employment. And I didn't want to be too far away from Kendra," Gabriella smiled shyly at Kendra, who winked at her in response.

Madigan took the floor next. "Same bridge program is helpin' me get a job sortin' mail at the post office, back down in the East Bay. Get me a uniform—one of those cute blue things." She squared her shoulders with pride. "You have any trouble gettin' your mail, you just come see me," she said with a nod, and sat down.

Beth spoke next. "I start the alternative medicine program at the end of October. It's here in the county, so I'll be available as alumni."

Paulina stood and said, "My friends in the city have financed my new pottery studio. I'm so excited to be able to do the work I love again. And . . ." she gestured to Doris.

Doris stood next. "And I'm going to apprentice with Paulina— learn to throw pots, glaze and fire them, even sell them. I'm going to learn how to be an artisan *and* a businesswoman." She smiled broadly.

"We're so proud of all of you," Jenny said, wiping a tear from the corner of her eye.

The remainder of the morning passed talking about plans for graduation, the role of mentors, and the new women who would be interviewed to start in October. Just before they broke for lunch, Madigan said, loudly enough to draw everyone's attention, "Hey, we got through the whole night with nothing bad happenin'."

"One in a row, baby. One in a row," Mab said.

Later, down the hall in the office, Jenny, Mab, and Shalese sat around the desk, a small stack of applications waiting their decision.

"Okay, I say we take our top five, and set up interviews," Shalese said. "If they all clear, we can send letters to the others, letting them know they're being considered for our winter session in February. Does that work for you two?" Jenny nodded. Mab said, "Sounds good to me."

Jenny took the top five applications from the pile, and gave a synopsis of the first candidate.

"Okay, Mary Agnes is thirty, worked in the financial aid department at the junior college. She was jumped by a disgruntled student who didn't qualify for aid. Looks like they scuffled, he fell, cracked his head, and has permanent brain damage."

"Oh, my God, that's awful," Jenny said, cringing.

Mab who had been perusing the letter attached to the application, nudged Shalese and said, "Hey look, she's a home-girl—from Detroit. Maybe you knew her people."

"Mary Agnes? Sounds like Catholic school girl material—way out of my league," Shalese said with a chuckle. "She's been out of prison for two weeks, self-referred, has some computer skills, bookkeeping, accounting . . ."

"Let's match her up with Analise," Mab suggested after a moment of thoughtful silence. "I don't know how we're going to survive when our computer queen graduates," she grinned.

"Good idea," Shalese agreed. She pulled the next application from the pile. "Farrah, twenty-six. She's an exotic dancer," Shalese bounced her eyebrows at Mab. Jenny kicked her under the table. "Grew up in Idaho. Been here ten years. Shot the manager of her dance club when he tried to sell her to a customer. Referred by a diversion program."

Jenny grimaced. "Guess she'll be needing some new job skills," she said. "Word spreads quickly in that circuit."

"And you would know this how?" Mab said, grinning from ear to ear.

"Hey, I know stuff," Jenny shot back. "Kendra's from a small town in the Midwest, isn't she? Let's put them together." She took the next application. "Marcia, twenty-six, married since sixteen." Jenny sighed and shook her head wearily. "Why do girls get married at sixteen?"

"It's stupid, but it's not a crime," Mab said. "What did she do?"

"Stabbed her husband in his sleep after years of abuse. They tried a temporary insanity plea, but she was found sane enough to stand trial. She gets out at the end of the month. Parole officer recommended her," Jenny said, setting the application aside. "Maren for her?" she asked. "Maren's pretty grounded." Mab and Shalese nodded.

"Okay," Mab said, "next we have Cheryl, forty, owned a tanning salon. She was referred by a social worker. She tried to break off an affair with her gynecologist when he wouldn't leave his wife. He stalked her, blackmailed her, stole her dog—"

"Stole her dog? Oh, that's low," Jenny commented.

"She shot out the bedroom window of his house—apparently just wanted to scare him. His wife got hit by the bullet." Mab shook her head and chuckled. "Sounds like a real spitfire."

"Chandra might be able to handle her," Shalese suggested, and wrote Chandra's name at the top of Cheryl's application.

"Last one," Shalese said. "Holly. Hmm. Transgender, male-to-female, twenty-two."

"Twenty-two?" Mab said. "She's just a baby. What did she do?"

"Wait a minute," Jenny said. "Is she post-op? We can't have a guy living here."

"Good call," Shalese said, studying the application. "Yes, when she turned twenty-one. Found us through some political alliance group. Victim of a hate crime, fought off her attacker. The guy fell, hit his head, and died."

"Seems to be a lot of that going around," Jenny mumbled.

"Good riddance, if you ask me," Mab muttered. "That leaves Margot. Do you think that would be a good match?"

"Margot's got the patience of a saint, and she's kind-hearted," Jenny said.

"Let's hope Holly's not allergic to bees," Mab said. "Well, good job. Break out the champagne."

"May I remind you, you don't drink," Shalese said, grinning.

"A girl can dream," Mab said.

They decided Shalese would notify the new applicants, Jenny would contact the women who would be considered for February, and Mab would speak with the current residents who'd signed up to be mentors.

"We're really a great team," Jenny said, taking both Shalese's and Mab's hands and giving a squeeze.

"Yeah, whatever," Mab mumbled her embarrassment. After a year together, she still hadn't learned how to receive affection with any amount of grace.

In the group room, Maren had just finished her second lecture on nutrition and meal planning. "Huh," Madigan said, "I always thought when you ran outta food, you went to the store—if you had food stamps left, that is."

"I like the idea of *re-purposing* leftovers into a casserole," Doris said.

Gabriella spoke softly, "I never really learned to cook. We hired someone for that." She looked at Maren with a new appreciation. "Thank you," she said.

"And thank you, Beth, for telling us about how to grow our own herbs for seasoning," Maren added. The women clapped, and Beth blushed.

"We some educated women, now," Madigan said adamantly. "Well . . ." she hesitated, "some of you was already pretty educated when you came here," she said with a nod to Gabriella.

"Believe me," Gabriella said, with tears brimming, "I'm so much smarter now for having been with all of you. This is an education no amount of money could buy. I'm really . . ." Words escaped her, so she merely patted her heart. "Thank you," she said again.

Mab tapped on the group room door and stuck her head in. "Am I interrupting?" she asked.

"No," Maren said, "we just finished. C'mon in."

Mab lumbered over to the sofa and eased herself down. "We just finished selecting the next five women that will be joining us, and before you take a break, I want to tell you about who you'll be paired up with." She consulted her list and cleared her throat. "Mary Agnes is thirty, worked in financial aid, defended herself against a student's attack. Student wound up brain-damaged. She's self-referred, fresh out of prison. She has some computer skills. Analise, she's yours."

Analise nodded. "I'm not sure what I'm supposed to do as a mentor," she said.

"We'll talk more about that in our business meeting," Mab said, "but it's kind of like being a big sister."

"That should be fun—I've never had a sister," Analise smiled.

"Then we have Farrah. She's twenty-six, from Idaho. Got herself in trouble when her boss tried to sell her for sex. Kendra, we're thinking you'd know how it is coming from a small town to the big city. A girl can get mighty lost."

"I'll take good care of her," Kendra said.

"Parole officer referred Marcia, she's twenty-six," Mab read. "Stabbed her husband while he was sleeping. Seems she'd taken all she could take," Mab looked at Maren. "Think you can handle that?"

"I know about taking all you can take," Maren said, with eyes downcast.

"Next we have Cheryl. She's forty. Her doctor had an affair with her then dumped her. Messed with her head. She shot out a window at his house and hit the wife by accident." Mab eyed Chandra. "We figured you could handle this one."

"Bring her on," Chandra said.

"And finally, we have Holly, twenty-two, fought back against a hate crime, her attacker hit his head and died. Oh, and she's a transgender female," Mab added. There were gasps of surprise around the room.

"Like, 'oh, p.s., he's a she'?" Chandra said.

"I don't want to sound prejudiced," Margot said, "but do we really want someone who used to be a guy living here? I mean, it sounds like I'm going to be his, I mean *her*, buddy. I've never met anyone who was transgender before."

"You never know. Sometimes you can't tell," said Paulina. Everyone looked at Paulina and more than several eyebrows were raised in speculation. "Oh, for God sake, I'm just saying . . ."

"I think it's important that we talk about gender," Mab said, "but I want you to consider that Holly never thought of herself as male. She's post-op—"

"Means she's got no dick," Chandra interrupted. Mab shot her a look. "Just tryin' to keep it real," she said. "I mean, we're all going to be showering together, sharing rooms, dressing in front of each other."

"Oh, my god," Gabriella sputtered. "Having my own apartment is sounding better and better."

"What's the big deal anyway?" said Madigan, who'd been sitting quietly, wishing she was staying around for this mentoring thing. "So he used to be a she. We all used to be something we're not anymore."

"Easy for you to say," Margot said. "You're going to be in Oakland."

"Listen y'all," Mab leaned forward. "Just like the rest of you, Holly's had a hard life. She wound up in prison for fighting back, just like each one of you. I'm sure she's a perfectly fine woman, and I want you to make her feel at home here." She turned to Margot. "Do you think you can work with this?"

"I'll keep an open mind," Margot said evenly.

Chapter 9

It was late September and unseasonably cold. Madigan and Chandra had secured the cover over the swimming pool and were admiring their handiwork.

"Gonna miss this pool," Madigan said, her voice thick with emotion.

"Just the pool?" Chandra teased. Hands on hips, she stared at Madigan until she saw a smile take over her face. "What about me?"

"Yeah, you too, I 'spose," Madigan said. "Good thing we got that *uh-lum-nigh* club," she said, sounding out the word slowly, "so we don't lose touch—and we can take a swim in the summer."

"We'll have some good memories of the first house in the city, and this place too, won't we?" Chandra mused. "Remember your first swim in this pool?" she chuckled.

"Now *that's* something I'd like to forget," Madigan said, laughing.

"It was pretty smart of Maren to put together all those clues," Chandra said. "Kind of strange that nothing more happened after the night we about scared old Lefty to death," she reminisced.

"Still don't trust that man. He's weaselly," Madigan concluded.

Later, in the group room, the graduation committee met to put the final touches on their celebration for the following day.

"Okay," Analise said, pointing to a list on the flip chart. "Music?"

"Got it," Beth said. "The stereo will be on the porch and speakers on either side of the door. We'll play 'Pomp and . . .'" she giggled and covered her mouth. Madigan rolled her eyes.

"Sorry," Beth said. She cleared her throat, and started again. "'Pomp and Circumstance' for walking down the aisle to our seats. After we get our diplomas and return to our seats, we'll all sing along with 'We Are the World.'"

Analise passed around a copy of the program she'd created on the computer for the women to inspect, followed by a copy of the invitation to friends, family members, and people in the community.

"Got my name on it and everything," Madigan said, puffed with pride at seeing her name in print.

Analise smiled. "And we got RSVPs from the five new women coming on board, so they can see what a graduation around here looks like."

Madigan spoke next. "I got the balloons and streamers like we agreed. And," she paused dramatically as she reached into a large paper bag and extracted her surprise. "These!" Grinning broadly, she held up a beanie with a tassel she'd sewn on by hand. "Ten of 'em." The others whooped and applauded her ingenuity.

"I've got the food covered," Maren reported. "Sparkling cider, cheese, crackers, fruit, and chocolate. Oh, and spinach dip. That covers all the food groups."

"We get that judge?" Madigan asked.

"Judge Thistlewaite, yes," Analise confirmed. "She told Shalese it would be an honor to speak to us." The four women sat in companionable silence for a moment, smiling at one another.

Then Beth's smile started to waver, her lips trembled, she sniffed loudly, and blinked hard against tears that threatened to break loose. "This really is it," she summarized their time together. "I can't believe it's over."

Madigan wiped a tear from the corner of her eye, Analise took a slow, deep breath, and Maren risked saying, "I'll miss you all so much," as her throat tightened with emotion.

The air was palpably solemn that evening around the dining table. Gabriella sat back in her chair, sighed heavily, and said, "This is our last supper."

"Don't go getting all biblical on us," Chandra teased.

Gabriella gave her an indulgent smile. "I'm even going to miss *you*," she teased back.

"Yeah," Chandra said, "we should, like, do lunch one day." The visual image of that brought a ripple of laughter, and the mood lightened.

"I like the paradox that all good things must end some day— and—there is no end," Kendra said, "only continual beginnings."

Up in their bedroom later, Jenny mulled over the evening. "Continual beginnings—jeez, that sounds exhausting," she said with a yawn.

"It is exhausting," Shalese agreed. "I think next year we might take a week off between rotations—I hear Mexico is nice this time of year."

"We spend a lot of time emphasizing self-care for our residents—that one sort of slipped by us," Jenny said. "Live and learn," she said with a sigh as she reached over to turn off the lamp.

"Live and learn . . ." Shalese affirmed, "and love," she added, pulling Jenny close.

Chapter 10

"Couldn't have ordered a more perfect day," Mab said, looking up at the clear, blue, October sky. She stretched her back like a cat after a long nap, and smiled her appreciation at the vista of rolling vineyards, awash in vivid autumn colors.

Shalese stood behind her on the front porch, and looked out onto the lawn where chairs were placed in tidy rows. "Ten years ago," Shalese said, "no one could have convinced either of us that we'd be standing here graduating our first class of women in recovery." She threw an arm over Mab's ample shoulder.

"True, baby, true," Mab said, nodding her head slowly.

Streamers cordoned off ten chairs-of-honor for the graduates. Colorful balloons were tied at the end of each row, and crepe streamers rippled in the slight breeze from the top of bamboo poles planted around the lawn. Shalese checked to make sure her speech was still on the podium, turned the sound system on for a moment, and tapped the mic.

Jenny appeared with two large baskets of flowers, which she placed on either side of the porch. Doris followed with a third basket containing the diploma scrolls tied with colorful ribbons. "Looking mighty festive," she said, and placed the basket next to the podium.

Chandra burst through the door carrying two folding chairs on each arm and shooed the women out of the way. She placed the chairs to the left of the podium for the staff and the judge, walked down the steps, and turned to admire her handiwork. After a few minor adjustments, she deemed it perfect, and disappeared back inside.

With breakfast cleared away, Maren had turned the dining room into a place for feast and celebration, with balloons, flowers, platters of food beautifully arranged, and half a case of sparkling cider on ice in silver buckets borrowed from the vineyard's tasting room down the road.

At eleven o'clock, the first guests arrived. Lefty and two of the vineyard workers, hats in hand, came up the dusty path. Paulina and

Beth took up their places as official greeters at the end of the lawn. "Welcome to our first graduation," Paulina said to the three men.

"A privilege to be invited," Lefty said. The men found seats several rows from the front.

Following the vineyard workers, three women walked tentatively up the path. "Hi, I'm Mary Agnes," said a woman with long brown hair pulled to one side and fixed with a barrette sprouting a cluster of plastic daisies. She clasped Beth's hand in both of hers and smiled a Colgate smile. "But please call me Aggie. Are we at the right place for the—"

"Graduation?" Beth piped up, extricating her hand with some effort. "Yes, you sure are, and welcome. I'm Beth, and this is Paulina." Paulina gave a little wave and slipped her hand behind her back. "Go on up and find a seat. I look forward to talking with you afterward," Beth said with a big smile.

"Is she a little much or what?" Paulina whispered after the women had moved up the aisle. "The daisy thing is weird." Beth gave her a playful poke in the arm.

The next guest was a tall, older woman in a long black robe accompanied by a frail, forgettable-looking gentleman who could best be described as *beige*. She stopped just short of Paulina and said something to her companion who bent over and brushed the dust from the hem of her robe.

"*Here come the judge*," Chandra said, peeking out the front window of the house.

"You must be Judge Thistlewaite," Paulina said. "Welcome. It is so nice of you to be here for us." They shook hands. Paulina glanced at the man standing quietly behind the judge—no introductions were made. "Let me introduce you to our staff," she said turning her attention back to the judge.

"I'll find us a seat," the woman's companion said in a thin, slightly southern twang. He slipped into the row just behind Lefty and the vineyard workers as Paulina shepherded the judge up to the house.

From the window, Chandra watched the judge stop briefly on the sidewalk and exchange a glance, and an almost imperceptible nod of her head to Lefty, seated in the audience, who smiled ever-so-slightly in response. "Wonder how they know each other," she said to Margot.

"I can't imagine they hang out in the same circle," Margot said with a laugh.

Chandra yanked the curtains shut and gave a little shiver. "The last time I saw a judge, I wound up in prison," she said.

Margot gave her a reassuring squeeze. "Think of this as one of those 'corrective experiences' we hear about in group," she offered.

When all twenty chairs were occupied by guests and friends from the community, and the residents were lined up at the back, beanies carefully hair-pinned in place, tassels to one side, Shalese stood at the podium and gave a brief welcoming speech. With her little finger, she brushed at a tear that trickled down her cheek as she said, "It is now my honor and privilege to introduce to you the first graduating class of The Next Step."

Jenny pushed the button and "Pomp and Circumstance" played over the loudspeakers, as the women step-stop-step-stopped their way down the center aisle. The sparkle in their eyes and the smiles on their faces vied with the sun to light up the day.

Mab dabbed at her eyes with a handkerchief. "You may be seated," she said. She cleared her throat, and began reading her speech. "Today, history is made," she said and paused. She crumpled up the paper she was reading from and gave herself over to the moment. "Oh hell," she said, "I can't read you a speech. I've just gotta say, I'm so proud of you all, I'm ready to burst." She wiped again at her eyes, turned away from the mic, and blew her nose loudly into the hanky. Unable to regain her composure, she signaled Jenny up to the podium.

Jenny gave her a big hug, and waited until Mab was seated before continuing. "It is my distinct honor to introduce our graduation speaker, District Court Judge Margaret Thistlewaite." The audience clapped enthusiastically as the judge took the podium.

"Remember," Margot whispered to Chandra, "she's on our side."

Chandra grinned and clapped loudly. "I'm havin' me a corrective experience," she whispered back.

As the judge spoke, Shalese, Jenny, and Mab reached out to each other and held hands, making a visual united front of support and encouragement for not only their first graduates, but also for the women who would become their next group of residents.

". . . anyway I can serve you, I will be available. You are the beginning of a new day, and I honor you," the judge said in closing. The audience gave her a standing ovation.

"Okay, I can do this," Mab said, rising and crossing over to the podium. "Will our graduates please stand and approach the stage," she said, motioning to the women. Jenny took her place next to Shalese at the front of the porch. "As I call your name, please come up and receive your diploma. As you leave the stage, we have a photographer who will take your picture, so you'll never forget this day," she said.

"Fat chance of that," Chandra called out to whoops of laughter.

"Gabriella," Mab read the first name. Gabriella beamed at Jenny as Jenny handed her a ribbon-wrapped diploma. She crossed over to Shalese for a hug. Everyone clapped and hollered as she moved her tassel from the left to the right side of her beanie before posing for her picture.

"Chandra," Mab called out as Chandra basked in her moment of glory.

"Maren."

"Beth."

The women seemed transformed as they crossed the stage—proud, graceful, strong, and ready to take on life.

"Madigan," Mab called her name. As Madigan reached the middle of the stage, an older black woman stood up in the audience, braced on a cane, and hollered, "That's my baby up there!"

Madigan spun around. "Granny?" she said, slapping her hand over her heart. "That's my granny," she called out, rushing down the front steps and down the aisle into her grandmother's arms for a tearful reunion. Mab, who had found Madigan's only remaining relative and arranged to have her here, winked at Shalese and Jenny, who had both given over to tears—as had most of the audience.

With promises to catch up on their fifteen-year separation after the ceremony, Madigan hustled back up to the stage to receive her diploma and her hug. She shifted her tassel and beamed for the photographer.

When all the residents had received their diplomas and returned to their seats, Jenny stood at the podium. "Congratulations, you amazing women," she said, beaming at them. She turned to the audience and said, "The staff and our new graduates invite you to a reception inside. But first, please join us in singing our closing song, 'We Are the World.'" The crowd stood as Mab started the music.

At the chorus, everyone joined in singing, "We are the world, we are the children. We are the ones who make a brighter day, so let's start giving." The graduates, arms around each other, swayed gently, and sang through their tears. At the end of the song, ten beanies flew high in the air with whoops and hollers of joy.

Madigan worked her way through the crowd to find her grandmother, as the others made their way up the steps for the reception. "Baby girl," her grandmother said, wrapping frail arms tightly about her only granddaughter, "I wish your mamma and daddy had lived long enough to see this day. They would have been so proud of you." Madigan clung to her, her wet cheek pressed tight against the old woman's neck, and breathed in the scent of the only safety she'd known in the world, up until now.

"Granny, I didn't know where you were. I couldn't find you . . ." she sobbed. "This is the happiest day in my life."

Back up at the house, the in-coming residents found their mentors and were engaged in animated conversation. Jenny, Shalese, and Mab circulated through the crowd, dispensing hugs and well wishes.

Shalese drew up a chair and joined Analise and Aggie. Analise was explaining how she came to be the *computer queen* of the house, and how they hoped with Aggie's skills, she might take up that role when it was Analise's time to move on.

"I'm so impressed with Analise's skill," Aggie laid a splayed hand over her own heart and sighed deeply. "It would be such an honor to learn from you," she finished and again flashed a teeth-glinting smile.

"Analise maintains our website and mailing list and helps with some of the on-line banking and bill paying." Shalese turned to Analise. "I don't know what I'm going to do without you," she said, her smile tinged with sadness.

"Well, you'll have me right here as your right-hand gal," Aggie said, reaching over to pat Shalese's hand in reassurance.

"Hey, you're not getting rid of me yet," Analise cracked.

"She also does a lot of computer searches for information in the recovery field. I'm amazed at what's accessible," Shalese said with a shake of her head.

"Yes," Aggie agreed, "if you know how to search the web, nothing's sacred anymore."

A little tingle, insignificant as a feather in a chicken coop, ran up Shalese's spine.

Aggie adjusted the granny glasses on her nose and fidgeted with the plastic daisies on her hairclip. "We could be like the A-Team," she said with a titter. "Analise and Aggie, a cyber-force to be reckoned with."

Shalese smiled in spite of herself. *This girl is quirky alright*, she thought.

"Hey," Analise said, "did you know Aggie is from Detroit? You're from there, aren't you?"

"Sure am," Shalese said. "West side, lived in the projects. What school did you go to?"

"We moved to Ann Arbor when I was five. I went to St. Francis of Assisi."

Shalese chuckled. "Figured as much," she said good-naturedly.

"I know—Mary Agnes is sort of a dead giveaway, I guess. At least you didn't have to wear blue plaid uniforms," she said, wrinkling her nose. "Of course, I always found a way to bring my own personal touch," she added, patting her plastic daisies.

Shalese excused herself, crossed to the refreshment table, and ladled herself a glass of punch.

Paulina was trailing a chip through a bowl of spinach dip. "It's kind of strange meeting our replacements" she said.

"No one can ever replace you," Shalese said with a reassuring smile. "They're just add-ons."

"Thanks," Paulina said, "I needed to hear that. It's hard to leave, you know."

Across the room, Chandra leaned into Cheryl's story with rapt attention. "Then I shot out his bedroom window," Cheryl said. "Bullet wound up lodging in his old lady's leg. How's that for incredible? I wasn't even aiming for her," she said of her ex-lover's wife. "They called it attempted murder. I ask you, is that fair?" she said, with a shake of her head at the injustice of it all.

"Fare is what you pay when you ride on the bus," Chandra said.

Jenny passed Doris, Kendra, Beth, and Farrah, who were huddled in a corner talking about culture shock, coming from small town America into the big city. "If I'd stayed in Idaho," Farrah said, "I doubt very much if I'd have become an exotic dancer in a strip club," she chuckled. "More like someone's wife, with two kids, and a tractor."

"That's pretty much why I left the Midwest," Kendra shared.

"That doesn't sound so bad," Beth said. "Do you regret leaving your hometown?" she asked Farrah.

"I didn't like who I was becoming back home," Farrah said. "I like who I've become out here, I just don't like what happened to me," she said, lowering her eyes.

"What did happen?" Kendra asked. "I mean, if you don't mind my prying."

"Club owner tried to sell me to a customer. White slavery, I think it's called. So I shot him—the club owner, that is," she clarified.

"And *you're* the one that got arrested?" Doris said, huffing with indignation.

"I probably shouldn't have been carrying a gun . . ." Farrah said, "an unregistered gun," she added.

Jenny pulled a chair up to join Maren and Marcia, a petite, blue-eyed young woman with a pixie haircut.

Marcia was saying, "Prison was no picnic, but at least no one was beating on me daily," she said of her life with her husband.

"I remember those days," Maren said. "I used to stuff myself with food to numb the pain. Now I just stuff other people with food," she chuckled.

Jenny smiled and said, "Maren has become our cook here at the house. Gourmet meals on a budget is what we get."

"My old man used to hit me for being a lousy cook," Marcia said. "Maybe you could teach me?" she asked, her blue eyes boring into Maren.

"He hit you because he was a bully, not because you were a lousy cook," Maren said adamantly, speaking as much for herself as for Marcia.

Madigan and her grandmother had made themselves comfortable on the overstuffed sofa and were nibbling away at an overstuffed plate of food.

Next to them, Holly and Margot were engaged in an animated conversation about bees. Shalese joined them. "We were hoping you weren't afraid of bees when we chose Margot for your mentor," she said.

"Oh, no, I've never worried about being attacked by bees," Holly said. "People, yes. Bees, no," she chuckled. "You could actually show me how to keep them and harvest the honey?"

Margot's eyes lit up. "You bet. I don't know anyone else who's interested in bees. This is so exciting." She reached in her pocket and pulled out the sketch she'd made of where the hives would go. "Wait a minute," she said, looking at Holly. "What did you mean, 'people, yes'?"

"How I wound up in prison . . ." Holly paused, glanced off to the side, then began again. "Well, I'm post-op transgender, male-to-female. I was out with some friends—not all of them can pass as women yet. We were leaving a bar, when a bunch of guys thought they'd start a little trouble." Holly stopped, stretched her shoulders and neck, sat up straighter in her chair, cleared her throat, and resumed her story.

"One of the guys came at Bette—she still had a little five o'clock shadow problem—and started saying filthy things to her, putting his hands all over her. The rest of us jumped to her defense, but were pulled away by the other guys, who started beating on us." She wiped her forehead with the back of her hand and took a breath.

"The testosterone might be out of my body, but it's apparently not out of my brain," she chuckled mirthlessly. "I spun loose of the oaf who had me pinned against the building, grabbed him, and threw him to the ground. He sort of landed head first and was DOA at the hospital."

"Oh, my God," Margot gasped.

"I know," Holly said, "not my most ladylike moment."

The sun was setting over the vineyard when the party began to break up. The old residents, those who were leaving, would be packing their bags the next morning and loading up their possessions, as the new residents were moving in. Madigan stood, tapped her spoon on her water glass to call their attention before the crowd dispersed. "As your *uh-lum-nigh* president, I declare the first Friday of every month an open meeting here at The Next Step, so's we can all come back and see how everyone's doin'. That would be two weeks from yesterday," she declared. She glanced at Shalese, Jenny, and Mab and said, less sure of herself, "Y'all okay with that?"

"That's a wonderful idea," Shalese said.

"That was your first official act as president," Mab beamed at her. Jenny started a round of foot-stomping applause that wound up ricocheting off the walls.

Embarrassed and pleased with herself, Madigan raised her hands and said, "That's all. Y'all can go home now. I got me some packin' to do."

When the last guest had left, Chandra made sure the surveillance cameras were on and set the alarm for the night. Over dinner, the women chatted like a big, noisy family, and the festive air continued until late evening, when everyone finally drifted off to their rooms, and into a deep, happy sleep.

A little after midnight, Jenny rolled over in the bed, reached for Shalese, and came up empty-handed. She sat up, turned the nightstand lamp on, and looked around the room. Shalese's robe and slippers were missing. Jenny slipped her own robe on and tiptoed down the stairs. At the far end of the hall, the office light burned dimly through the door left ajar. She tapped lightly, so as not to startle Shalese who sat hunched over a stack of papers on the desk before her.

Shalese jerked her head toward the door. "What are you doing up?" she asked.

"Came to ask you the same thing," Jenny said. She walked around behind her and wrapped her in a hug. "Trouble sleeping? What's this?" she said, nodding at the pile of papers.

"I was just looking through the applications again," Shalese said. "What do we know about Aggie, other than she worked in financial aid and seriously wounded a student who attacked her?"

"We have her bio, right? She's local, self-referred to the program. I verified her employment and spoke to her supervisor in financial aid who very candidly told me Aggie was pretty traumatized after the incident with the student. Her references all check out—why?"

"Can't put my finger on it, exactly," Shalese said, "but something doesn't feel right—I mean, aside from the fact that she's a little strange," she said with a hint of a smile.

Shalese relayed the conversation between Analise, Aggie, and herself to Jenny. "The way she said it, about computers and 'nothing's sacred,' gave me a little shiver." Shalese stared hard at the floor as if searching there for an answer.

"You used to say that was your granny sending you some kind of message from the other side," Jenny offered. "Let's think this through," she said. "I remember you were computer-phobic when I met you. You were using that old typewriter to write your grant." Shalese stifled a smile. "Maybe you're taking this a little personally. Maybe that's all it is," Jenny suggested.

"No," Shalese said, shaking her head, "it's more than that." She gave a frustrated sigh and said, "Well, I'm obviously not going to find it rifling through a pile of papers in the dead of night. Maybe I'll ask Mab to snoop around in her background a little more, see if anything comes up. Sorry if I woke you." She followed Jenny back up the stairs and into a fitful sleep.

Chapter 11

All worries were lost in the chaos and clamor of the following morning. Pick-up trucks, moving vans, and cars packed to the brim, lined the circular drive in front of The Next Step. A steady stream of bodies carried boxes, small articles of furniture, and personal belongings to and from the house.

As many people called out *hello* and *welcome*, as called out *goodbye* and *see you next Friday*. Madigan, Paulina, and Doris made the final round for hugs.

"When me and Granny get settled in our apartment, maybe you two will come over for some supper?" Madigan addressed Paulina and Doris. "I mean, since we'll all be in the same end of the bay, and all," she added, shyly.

"I'd love to," Paulina said, with a vigorous shake of her braids.

"Me too," said Doris. "And when I get settled in, I'll check with my housemates and see if I can have you all over," Doris added, referring to the shared housing of women in recovery she'd located not far from Golden Gate Park.

"Me three," Paulina quipped, "as soon as Doris and I throw enough plates to serve a meal on."

Kendra was helping Gabriella stuff rolled-up bedding into the back of Beth's VW Bug. "See you Friday," Gabriella called over to the city-bound contingent. She turned to Kendra and whispered, "See you tomorrow," and gave her a peck on the cheek.

Beth waved from her car window as she started the engine. She had offered to drop Gabriella at her new studio in downtown Santa Rosa, before heading a few miles up the freeway to the quaint town of Healdsburg, where she would be sharing a dorm room with three other women in the Alternative Medicine Program.

Kendra waved and blew Gabriella a kiss as the two women pulled away from the curb. "Watch out for the drunks," Gabriella called, referring to Kendra's new job in the winery's tasting room just down the road.

More like the vineyard workers, Kendra thought, still convinced the last month's harassment came from them. She didn't like the way the foreman, Lefty, looked at her—like he had something on her. *You're being paranoid*, she admonished herself. She shook off the feeling, turned, and walked back up toward the house to welcome the new residents.

Chapter 12

Like so many seeds blowing in the wind, the graduates took root up and down the bay area, finding opportunities to grow themselves anew.

In the East Bay, Madigan sat in the break room with Malachi, a long-time employee at the Central Oakland branch of the post office. Her feet were propped up in a chair next to his, and she held a steaming cup of coffee between her hands.

"Epsom Salt," he said, glancing over at her toes curling and uncurling next to him. Her shoes lay akimbo on the floor.

"That's very nice of you," Madigan said. "My granny just says, 'lose 'bout two hunert pounds and yer feet'll feel fine.'" She grinned across the table at Malachi who lowered his eyes.

"I think you're fine just the way you are," Malachi said quietly. This time Madigan lowered her eyes. She could feel a blush coming on.

Paul, the office clerk, stuck his head in the break room and said, "Madigan, the boss wants to see you."

"Uh-oh," Madigan muttered. She bumped her head on the side of the table while clamoring for her shoes. "Wonder what I did wrong. Can't afford to lose this job," she said, glancing at Malachi.

"Just be yourself," he offered with a gentle smile.

Be myself. She pondered the words as she hustled down the hall. *Which self?* The old self that would blast through that door, demand to know who he thought he was to fire her after such a short time on the job? Or some version of this new self she was working on—the one that would hold her tongue until the man had a chance to speak.

"Madigan," the boss said. "Have a seat." He gestured her into a chair on the other side of his desk.

She sat, clamping her knees together so they wouldn't knock. She looked him straight in the eyes, but not with conscious intimidation, as she would have in the past. He was just a man. He wasn't going to hurt her. Who was she kidding? He was the boss and could fire her ass. She took a deep breath.

"When we signed up to be part of this bridge program, hiring and training ex-felons, I've got to tell you, I was not convinced it was a good idea," he said. He leaned forward, elbows on the desk, and looked right back at her as if he really saw her.

Here it comes, Madigan thought. *I've ruined it for everyone who might have come after me. I should 'a known this wasn't gonna work.*

"You've convinced me we made the right decision," the boss said. "I don't think we've ever had anyone come in and commit to the level of responsibility you've taken on in such a short time. You're here early, you're like some sort of mail-sorting machine—efficient and accurate—and you leave your workstation spotless at the end of your shift," he said with a grin. He leaned back in his chair and spread his hands. "You even make fresh coffee in the middle of the day."

"Then I'm not fired?" Madigan said, breathing a sigh of relief and relaxing into her chair.

"Not by a long shot," the boss said. "In fact, I'm writing a letter of commendation to the chair of the bridge program, telling her what an outstanding job you're doing. It will go in your personnel file."

Madigan knew something was called for, but she wasn't sure what. She couldn't jump up and throw her arms around the man and give him a bear hug. What would Shalese do?

"Thank you, sir," she said with a big smile. "I appreciate that." Yes sir, things were lookin' up.

As soon as Madigan got home that night, she dialed Doris's number. "I got me a letter of condemnation," she said into the answering machine. "Call me." Three days passed, but there was no return call. On the fourth night, Madigan picked up the phone by her bed but returned it to the cradle again.

"Some friend," she mumbled. "Guess they got their own life," she said quietly as she tucked herself into the second-hand bed with the squeaky springs and lumpy mattress. With a pudgy fist, she wiped away a tear that trickled towards her ear.

Across the bay, in a converted garage in the middle of a cramped neighborhood in South San Francisco, Paulina filled another shelf with fragile greenware, ready for its first firing. The pottery studio was makeshift, not what she had in mind, but would do until she started turning a profit and could move to a better location with more light. She appreciated her friends' efforts at getting her started and the free rent on the space for as long as she needed it. And she probably couldn't have been half as productive if Doris hadn't been such a hard worker. The woman was eager to learn, even though her lack of coordination proved to be a constant source of anxiety as she passed down the narrow aisles of pottery on the way to and from the kiln that was in back of the studio.

Paulina washed the clay from her hands, and pulled her copper hair into a tighter ponytail. She was ready for a break and knew Doris must be dying for a cigarette about now.

Sizzle. Pop. Boom! The explosive sound shook the studio, toppling the end pieces from the shelf. Gathering her wits, Paulina mobilized herself down the aisle, kicking aside greenware, and ran out the back door.

The first thing she saw was smoke seeping from the edges of the kiln. The second thing was a dazed Doris, sitting spread-eagle on the ground, an empty bucket lying on its side next to her, and water everywhere.

"What the . . ." Paulina mumbled. Doris broke into shoulder-shaking sobs. Paulina knelt by her side. "Are you okay?" she asked, and touched Doris's arm gingerly.

Doris jumped and curled into herself even more. "I'm sorry. I'm so sorry. I've ruined everything . . ." she gasped and hiccupped. "I'll pay you back. I don't know how, but I'll find some way—I will," she sobbed.

To Doris's surprise, Paulina fitted herself behind Doris on the wet ground, and wrapped her in a tight hug. Her ponytail, flecked with clay, hung against Doris's cheek. "What's important is you're okay," she crooned to Doris, swaying her gently. "Everything else can be fixed."

Had Doris not just spent a year in recovery, she would never have believed those words. A pang of nostalgia caught in her chest.

Two hours north, up Highway 101, in a tidy little upscale ophthalmology office in Santa Rosa's upper rent district, Gabriella settled an elderly woman into the exam chair. Mrs. Fenworthy was there for a post-op check on her cataract surgery. Gabriella noticed a fresh bruise on the older woman's arm.

"Are you still having trouble with your vision, Mrs. Fenworthy?" she asked gently. Before the surgery, Mrs. Fenworthy's poor vision had led to a series of bumps and bruises from not clearing doorways or missing steps. Thank goodness nothing had been broken.

"No, my vision is just wonderful now, dear. Why do you ask?" the woman said, smiling up at Gabriella with bright blue eyes.

Gabriella pointed to the bruise. "I thought those might be a thing of the past," she said, and watched as the elderly woman's smile crumpled and tears puddled in her eyes. A wave of nausea threatened to topple Gabriella, and she grabbed the back of the chair to steady herself. Ever-so-gently, she took the woman's hand in her own, and looked deeply into her eyes.

"I understand," she said quietly. "Truly, I do. You can talk to me about this—"

She was interrupted by a tap on the door as Dr. Bennett stepped in. "Well, Mrs. Fenworthy, how are you doing this morning?"

Quickly, the woman withdrew her hand from Gabriella's and blinked away her tears. "Coming along just fine, doctor, thank you," she said brightly.

"Well, let's just take a look," he said, releasing the chair into recline position. As Gabriella turned to leave the room, Mrs. Fenworthy shot her an unmistakable look—*leave it be*.

The reception area was empty for the moment. Gabriella sat down at her desk, grabbed the phone book, and thumbed through until she found the right listing. *Dependent and Elder Protective Services*. She dialed the number.

Tears stung her eyes as she hung up after making the report. Never again would she turn the other way when a woman was being abused. More than anything, she could use a big hug from Kendra, but since that wasn't available, her reassuring voice would have to do. She dialed The Next Step. The phone rang four times. "They must be in group," she mumbled to herself, feeling left out and alone.

The answering machine clicked on. "Hey guys," Kendra said. With a Kleenex, she dabbed at the tears running down her cheek. "I could use some support here," she sniffed. "Somebody please call me back." She left her number at work and added, "I miss you."

Just up the road from Santa Rosa was the touristy town of Healdsburg. People from all over the world came to the region for wine tasting, fine dining, and luxury spas. The nightlife there was glitz and glamour. Beth wouldn't know about that—from early morning to late evening she was in class, learning anatomy, physiology, and basic Latin.

All she had wanted to do was learn how to apply her knowledge of herbs to the field of medicinal healing. Her nights were spent studying stacks of books and articles, reading until her eyes burned. Then she'd crawl into her bed in the dorm she shared with three other girls and try to sleep among the snores, snuffles, tosses, and turns that came with group living. Really, she was too old for this. Maybe she should just find a mentor, some nice octogenarian herbalist wanting to pass along her wisdom to a young protégé before she died.

Insomnia had taken up a presence in her bed. She turned to the wall and studied the cracked stucco in the dim light from the quaint, old-fashioned streetlamp outside. Her face burned with humiliation as she recalled her morning class.

"Beth, see me after class," the instructor had said, as he handed back the exam.

Lips clamped tightly, Beth had knocked on the instructor's office door just after noon. Her hands were cold, and she couldn't seem to relax. Her shoulders had hitched themselves to her earlobes. *Breathe*, she demanded of herself, and consciously lowered her shoulders.

"Come in," Mark called from inside the office. Beth let herself in, and stood awkwardly in front of a handsome man, ten years her junior. He motioned her into a chair.

"Beth, when we did your interview, I was impressed by your knowledge and experience working with herbs. You really are what we refer to as a natural," he said with a disarming smile.

For a moment, Beth let herself take in the praise. *Okay, so maybe this wasn't going to be so bad after all*, she thought.

"This, however, is a rigorous scholastic program—one of the best in the country, if I say so myself." He regarded her over a pair of reading glasses he'd slipped on. He picked up a journal of some sort and ran his thumb down the page. He stopped, looked up again at Beth, and said, "We can't have our best students getting a D on their exams now, can we?"

Beth thought she shook her head, but it could have been that her body was tremoring beyond her control.

"I expect to see improvement on your next exam." That was it. He dismissed her. She slunk back out of his office, down the hall, and into the restroom where she locked the door behind her and threw up in the toilet.

This was life on the outside. It's what she'd spent a year working toward—and it left something missing. Beth longed to slip into the familiar world of the recovery house, pop into the kitchen where Maren would greet her warmly, pour her a cup of coffee, and hand her something mouth-wateringly fresh out of the oven to eat, and listen— really listen, to her tale of woe.

She wondered if the others marked the days until the alumni reunion meeting, when they would sit in circle once again, their joy or pain reflected in the eyes of their sisters at The Next Step.

Chapter 13

In Santa Rosa, dark clouds hung heavy in the November sky, and the day was chilly. It was Saturday, a free day for the residents to run errands, do their laundry, relax, and generally hang loose with no time-obligations for meetings or classes. Most of the women chose to stay inside. A quiet tune, played on the keyboard, drifted down the hall from the group room. A burst of giggles, subdued by the stairwell, trickled down from an upstairs bedroom.

In the office, Analise explained the computer set up to Aggie, showing her the website and mailing lists that needed to be maintained.

"Sure, I can do that," Aggie said all bright-eyed and smiling, "but you'd really be wasting a valuable resource. At the financial aid office, I reconciled statements, made deposits—you know, that kind of stuff. But hey, your wish is my command. After all," she said with an obsequious smile, "you're the queen."

"Let's see how it goes," Analise suggested. "I'll talk with Shalese and let her know your level of skill."

"Must take a lot to run a place like this," Aggie pondered aloud. "I'm sure you have your thumb on the pulse around here. What's your funding source?" she asked.

"Uh, well . . ." Analise stalled, feeling put on the spot. "There are some grants and donations—"

"I can do grant proposals," Aggie interrupted. "What are the monthly expenses here, anyway?"

"Oh, look at this," Analise said, diverting attention to the webpage they'd just pulled up. "This is our donor list."

"Impressive," Aggie murmured as she scrutinized the names and businesses. "But we can do better—much better," she said with a definitive nod of her head.

Across the hall, Jenny and Shalese sat alone in the kitchen taking a mid-afternoon coffee break.

"I'm so glad we're doing this mentor thing," Jenny said to Shalese at the end of the first week with the new residents. The two women were alone in the kitchen taking a mid-afternoon coffee break.

"It's pretty amazing, the confidence that's grown in our first batch of residents, now that they have to show others the ropes," Shalese said. "Can you believe Chandra teaching money management? How to write a check, open a bank account, scan bills for due dates . . ." Shalese shook her head in amazement.

"I know," Jenny agreed. "Quite a change from ripping off anything you can get your hands on and selling it for drug money." She chuckled good-naturedly.

"And Margot and Holly building those hives to specifications and applying for a small business license?" Shalese added.

"And Kendra showing Farrah how to put together a resume?" Jenny said.

There was a tap on the kitchen door. Analise opened it a crack and stuck her head through. "Question?" she said.

"C'mon in," Jenny motioned her into the kitchen. "What's up?"

"Aggie is really skilled on the computer—she's like some kind of whiz kid or something," Analise said. "Do you think it's too early to start her on the banking tasks? She said she did that on her last job."

Shalese glanced at Jenny, then back at Analise. "You know," she said, measuring her words, "I think I'd feel better if we waited a while."

"Okay," Analise said with a shrug, "but I won't be here forever you know."

"It's just that after what we've been through with Florence, who we knew—or thought we knew—I don't want anyone I don't know and trust near our finances," Shalese said.

"I guess I can take that as a compliment," Analise said with a lopsided grin.

"Can we check in about this in a couple of months?" Shalese said.

"Sure." Analise nodded and left the kitchen.

Jenny picked up their empty coffee cups and rinsed them out in the sink. With her back to Shalese, she said, "Is it just the Florence thing—"

"*Just* the Florence thing?" Shalese said, looking wide-eyed at Jenny.

"Sorry. Figure of speech." Jenny apologized. "Is there something else? I mean, you trusted Analise with our finances . . ." She let the question hang in the air.

"Well, not right away," Shalese hedged. "I don't know what it is, exactly," Shalese said. "Maybe just that tingle-up-my-spine thing." She walked out of the kitchen in search of Analise.

Jenny forgot to ask if Shalese had asked Mab to check into Aggie's background and had turned to follow her when she was intercepted by Maren and Marcia who were talking excitedly as they entered the kitchen. "Jenny, Maren is going to teach me how to make amused bushes for Thanksgiving," Marcia bubbled

Jenny shrugged in confusion. "Is that like some sort of holiday art project?" she asked, imagining snow-capped evergreen shrubbery with smiley faces.

"*Amuse-bouches*—" Maren said in her best French-chef accent, "tiny appetizers." She smiled at her protégé, as she handed her an apron.

"You know, Maren, there are some really top-notch culinary schools nearby. Do you have any interest in pursuing this field as a career?" Jenny asked. "I know where you could get about a zillion great references," she said.

"I've sort of been thinking about that," Maren admitted. "Do you really think I could get accepted?"

"Does the queen carry a purse?" Jenny said, grinning. "You might want to check into the application process," she urged.

Through the glass panel on the front door, Shalese saw Analise on the porch, leaning against the railing, faced toward a diffused ray of sunlight that angled through the redwoods rimming the property. It was nippy, and she had her coat snug around her.

Shalese stepped out onto the porch. "Mind if I join you?" she asked.

Analise's head jerked toward the door closing behind her. "Oh," she said, startled.

"Sorry," Shalese said.

"That's okay. I guess I was just lost in thought." Analise looked out over the vineyards. "Looks like rain," she said, noting the heavy clouds.

Shalese touched her lightly on the arm. "You're one of the senior residents now," Shalese said. Analise nodded. "I want to say this in confidence," Shalese continued, lowering her voice. Analise blinked her acceptance of being brought into the inner circle.

"I'm just not sure about Aggie yet," Shalese confided. "I'm willing to own that it might be completely my stuff or a knee-jerk reaction to the whole Florence debacle, but I feel a need to observe her awhile before allowing her too much access to our records. I'm sorry if this puts you in an awkward position, being her mentor and all."

Analise expelled a little puff of breath, and relaxed her shoulders. "I'm so glad you said that," she said to Shalese. "There's something pushy and a little controlling about her. I mean, she's nice enough— almost too nice—but I felt grilled for answers about how we got our funding, how we cover our expenses, things that seem a little premature for someone brand new to be asking, you know?" Analise searched Shalese's face for understanding.

Shalese nodded. "Let's keep this between us, and Jenny and Mab, of course. She can help on the Community Resources binder, or fliers, or something. We'll just see how things go over the next couple of months, okay? Feel free to talk to me anytime." Analise said she would.

Mab arrived in time for dinner that evening. She would stay over for the Sunday group outing, a trip to Snoopy's Home Ice Skating Rink. "I can count on one finger the number of times I've been on ice skates," she said, as she ladled rich, fragrant gravy over her mashed potatoes. "And you don't even want to know what happened when I hit the ice," she said with a good-natured chuckle. "Holy . . ." she mumbled, swallowing a forkful of potatoes. "This has to be the best damned gravy I've ever had . . ." she nodded at Maren, "and I've had me some gravy."

"Not mine," Maren deferred. "This was all Marcia's doing. My gravy doesn't hold a candle to this." Marcia beamed, blushed, and received the accolades from around the table. After a few moments of the pleasurable and appreciative sounds of eating, the conversation continued.

"I was a competition skater when I was younger," Farrah shared, "until I broke my leg in a spin."

"Geez, that's quite a loss. Can you skate now?" Jenny asked, partially out of compassion, partially wondering about liability issues.

"I can skate. I just don't do any jumps or fancy stuff. Mab, I'll have you skating backwards and doing turns by the end of the day," she promised.

"The hell, you say," Mab said, over the whoops and applause from the women.

The front doorbell rang, and the room to fell into a startled silence. Jenny and Shalese exchanged a worried glance.

"Anyone expecting company?" Mab asked. Heads shook around the table. "I'll get it, then," she said, excusing herself. At the end of the hall, she peeked through the peephole, to see the back of a cowboy hat. As she opened the door, the man turned to face her.

"Mr. Lefty," Mab said, "what can I do for you this evening?"

"Evening, ma'am. Sorry to bother you. Just wanted you to know there's been a mountain lion spotting up in the hills—one of the neighboring farmer's sheep got chewed up. Might want to make sure your gals don't go wandering alone for a day or two, until we find it." His eyes strained past Mab, down the hallway behind her.

"And what will you do when you find it?" Mab asked, already knowing the answer.

"Shoot it," Lefty said, his eyes steely-cold. He doffed his hat goodbye. It was a peculiar gesture, Mab thought, more European than cowboy. There was something oddly familiar about it.

"Thanks for the warning," Mab called after him. "Something's just wrong about that man," she muttered to herself as she reset the alarm and returned to the dining room.

"That was Lefty, from the vineyard," she reported. "Said there's a mountain lion been sighted around here, and that we shouldn't be out and about by ourselves for a couple of days. Let's use the buddy system, okay? Just for safety." This caused a stir among the women. While they were talking amongst themselves, Mab whispered, "Office, after dinner," to Jenny and Shalese.

As dinner was being cleared, the staff stepped into the office and closed the door.

"I know that man," Mab said, as they found seats around the desk. "I'm just sure of it."

"You mean even before the guest ranch down the road that we checked out?" Jenny asked.

Mab nodded. "If he's not the rich old coot that Florence was talking to in the food court, all private-like, then he's his twin brother," she said.

"I thought you said that guy was distinguished, well-dressed, cultured. Doesn't sound like the vineyard manager with his scroungey moustache, dusty, ratty old clothes, and dirty boots," Shalese said. "He is about the right age, but—"

"Clothes do not make the man," Mab said. "It's something in the way he carries himself, the tone of his voice. There's a cold, calculating arrogance that doesn't go with his position, that just gets under my skin every time I see him. It's like fingernails on a chalkboard," she said. Jenny shivered at the thought. "I think that cowboy routine is an act."

They were silent for a moment, each lost in their thoughts. "Do you know what you're suggesting?" Jenny said finally. "If he's connected to Florence, we may not have gotten this property by chance but by orchestration. He may be keeping tabs on us, maybe even connected to the harassment . . ." Mab and Shalese looked at her.

"Whoa, hold on," Shalese spoke up. "That's an awful lot of assumption and jumping to conclusions, with absolutely no proof at all."

"It could be even bigger than that," Mab said, overriding Shalese's objection. "Chandra said something about wondering how the judge knew Lefty—something about them exchanging a look at graduation. What if they're both part of those Avenging Angels Florence was mixed up with. You know, the rich and powerful that get away with murder—literally."

"Oh, no!" Shalese shouted. She slapped both hands on her cheeks. "That's it!" she said. "That's where I know her from—I'm sure of it."

"What are you talking about," Jenny asked, alarmed.

"I'm talking about Janelle Anderson, the woman from the Women's Studies department who contacted both of us about that stupid soiree? Where we were set up to meet? She was a friend of Florence's," Shalese said.

Jenny nodded. "I'm not following you," she said. "You think she's one of the Avenging Angels too?"

"Possibly. Probably—but that's not what I'm talking about. We never met her in person, right?"

"Didn't she disappear not long after Florence went missing with our bank account?" Mab asked. Shalese nodded.

"When I asked her how she got my name, she said with a computer search, and that 'nothing was sacred anymore.'" Shalese said, falling back in her chair. "Her voice, those words—that's what was familiar about Aggie—I mean, minus the English accent. Remember the other night when I said I just couldn't put my finger on what it was?" she turned to Jenny.

"You think Janelle and Aggie know each other?" Jenny asked.

"More than that," Shalese said looking down at her hands. "I think they may be the same person."

"What?" Jenny gasped.

"That does sound a little far-fetched," Mab added. "I've heard other people use that phrase, 'Is nothing sacred anymore?'"

"That's right," Jenny said, "I've used it myself. How could they possibly be the same person?"

"Have you ever heard of doctoring records? Having imposters as references? If I'm right," Shalese said, "she has access to the computer with all our personal information."

"If you're wrong," Mab countered, "we could be in some deep legal shit if we go making accusations we can't substantiate."

"That's true," Shalese said. "They may have a judge on their side."

"So what do we do?" Jenny asked.

"We wait, we watch," Mab said. "If this is some kind of set-up, they're going to have to make the next move. They don't know we're onto them, and they won't be expecting us to watch their every move from here forward."

"How could they have known to plant Aggie in a position that would put us at risk?" Jenny said, more to herself, than expecting an answer.

"She was the only one of the new residents who was self-referred. She had all the computer and accounting skills a young business would need to promote itself. What's not to want? It worked. I feel so stupid," Shalese said.

Jenny reached over and gave Shalese's hand a squeeze. "In the meantime, let's find some way to get her away from the computer, now," Jenny said.

"Without arousing suspicion," Mab suggested. "Remember, this is still just speculation we're working on."

"I've already spoken with Analise and asked her to confine Aggie's computer duties to things that are low key and don't require a password, so I don't think we're in imminent danger," Shalese said, "but we need a back-up plan in place, just in case we need to move her out of the house." The three women put their heads together.

Chapter 14

Monday morning, right after breakfast, Shalese asked Analise to step into the office. Jenny and Mab were seated already. Sensing the tension in the air, Analise sat, wide-eyed and expectant. "I feel like I've been called into the principal's office. Hope I'm not in trouble," she said with a nervous giggle, looking from woman to woman.

"This has to do with our conversation the other day, about Aggie," Shalese said. "Without putting more of a burden on you than we already have, to understand why we're doing this, we'd like you to consider an offer." Analise squinted her confusion.

"We'd like you to consider a position on the staff as our financial director," Jenny said. "You would be responsible for overseeing all things money for the recovery house."

"You mean like paid staff?" Analise said.

"Yes, paid staff," Jenny said.

"You would be the *only* person that would have access to our finances," Mab said, emphasizing the word *only*. "We believe the job is manageable without an assistant."

"Uh huh," Analise said, slowly beginning to understand the intent within the content of this unexpected offer. "In other words, I won't need to train Aggie to take over this job in the future, nor will I need her assistance to do the job as it stands. Do I have this right?" she asked. Three heads nodded in agreement.

"We were thinking we'd make the announcement of your new position on staff at the business meeting this afternoon," Shalese said.

"That is, if you're interested," Jenny added. "Do you need time to think it over?"

"Well, I didn't really have any plans for next April, when my time would be up, and I can't think of anything I'd enjoy as much as staying on here as staff. So, yes, I accept," she said. "I've heard that the JC here in town has a great business department. Do you think I could take some classes?"

"I think we can cover that expense, considering you may just be saving our butts," Mab said.

"So, no room adjustments necessary," Shalese said, checking off the next-to-last agenda item during their afternoon business meeting.

Jenny stood and pointed to the last item, *Staff*. Margot shifted uncomfortably in her chair. "Is someone leaving?" she asked. "After the mass exodus of graduates——"

"Listen to you. Did you just say *exodus*?" Chandra said with a good-humored snort.

Margot raised her eyebrows at Chandra. "As I was saying, I don't think I can handle anymore change for a while." Others murmured their agreement.

"Quite the opposite," Jenny said with a smile. "We're proud to say that we are at that place of agency stability where we can look seriously at expanding our staff to meet our needs." She gave the women a moment to digest the fact that no one was leaving.

"You all know that Analise has been assisting us in 'all things computer' for a while now," Jenny said, making little brackets with her fingers. She smiled at Analise, and continued. "We've decided to create a paid, permanent position of finance director, and have asked Analise to join our staff in that role. Fortunately for us, she accepted."

The women clapped and stomped their approval. Analise stood and took a theatrical bow to calls of congratulations. Shalese risked a glance at Aggie, who sat impassively, hands folded in her lap; the parentheses at the sides of her mouth suggested a tight little smile.

"What that will mean is no more slave labor—well, at least not at the computer. Holly, you're not off the hook for beekeeping yet," Jenny said with a chuckle. "We want to thank Aggie, who stepped right up, and was willing to learn our computer system. You're truly gifted, and we appreciate you having given Analise a hand. I now pronounce you officially off the hook," she said lightly. Again, the women clapped, and laughed, and thanked Aggie for her brief time of service.

Aggie, lips pressed together, nodded her head, accepting the accolades. Jenny glanced at Shalese, who gave her a wink, and at Mab, who mouthed, *slick, baby*.

Mab stood then and addressed the women. "I'm feeling like marshmallows—and don't y'all say anything at all about how I look," she joked. "Who wants to join me after dinner for a marshmallow roast at the fireplace?" All hands went up.

"Could we have S'mores?" Chandra asked.

"Oh, please, please, please . . ." Marcia begged, batting her big blue eyes.

Mab turned to Maren, the kitchen maven, for an answer. "We have chocolate and graham crackers, so I don't see why not," Maren said. A cheer went up as the women prepared to leave the group room.

"Seven o'clock," Mab shouted over the din, as the women filed out.

"Good distraction," Jenny whispered to Mab, squeezing her arm.

"Well, that went well," Shalese said. "Did you get a look at Aggie's face?" she asked quietly. Both women nodded. "Didn't see that coming, did she?" Shalese smiled.

After dinner, the women vied for spots in front of the fireplace in the group room, where they could wedge in their pointed sticks, plump with marshmallows. The conversation flowed easily; Analise suggested they tell ghost stories, and Kendra suggested they sing camp songs.

Aggie squatted precariously across from Shalese, her marshmallow resting high on her stick, the pointed end a glowing ember. She lost her balance and bumped against Analise to break her fall, but the pointed end of her stick jabbed wildly and wound up poking Shalese on the back of her hand.

"Ow! Damn," Shalese shouted as she reflexively withdrew her hand from the circle. A red welt from the burn was forming. The room grew quiet. Several women risked glances at each other; others merely looked at the floor.

Jenny knelt down next to her and said, "Shall I get some aloe? That looks pretty nasty."

Shalese glowered across the semi-circle of women at Aggie who had regained her balance and was blowing the flames off her marshmallow.

"Oops . . .sorry," Aggie mumbled half-heartedly. She backed away from the group and assembled her S'more.

"What the . . ." Shalese said to Jenny. Jenny shrugged.

"Whoever thought marshmallows could be dangerous?" Maren quipped, trying to lighten the mood. Several women chuckled, and the conversation, tentative at first, returned to a light banter.

Mab cast a look at Shalese and mouthed, "You okay?" Shalese nodded.

"We should do something like this, something special, next Friday when our alumni come back for the first open meeting," Kendra suggested.

Chandra turned abruptly to say, "Good idea," and bumped Marcia's arm. Marcia jerked back, knocking Chandra's marshmallow off the end of her stick. The gooey sweetness dropped into the fire and melted quickly onto the burning log.

"Oh!" Marcia shouted in dismay. "Oh, oh . . ." Frantically, she looked around her. "I'm sorry," she apologized to everyone. Her hands flew protectively to her face to ward off anticipated blows.

Instinctively, the women formed a gentle circle around her. Maren scooted forward, and with great tenderness, touched Marcia on the arm. "It's okay," she said soothingly. "It's okay, you're safe," she crooned.

Very slowly, she ran her hand up the length of Marcia's arm and clasped her hand gently. When she felt Marcia's grip, she slowly lowered Marcia's hand away from her face saying, "You're safe here, no one is going to harm you."

The others murmured their own reassurances. They had all, at one time or another, been in Marcia's shoes, where the slightest infringement would have garnered them a beating.

One at a time, the women moved forward for the ritual now known as "the layin' on of hands," coined by Madigan, and gently touched Marcia as she spent herself in tears.

Farrah retrieved Marcia's stick from the fireplace, cleaned it off, replaced the marshmallows, and composed a tantalizing, melty S'more, which she handed to Marcia with a big smile. These simple gestures of support and friendship were the healing power of the recovery house. The rest—the classes, 12-step meetings, workshops, process meetings—as Mab would say, was "icin' on the cake, baby."

Friday rolled around, and the house was abuzz with excitement over the first reunion meeting, as Madigan, Gabriella, Beth, Paulina, and Doris arrived. The staff decided to let the women catch up before trying to rein them into a meeting format. After half an hour of their animated conversation and milling about, Shalese tapped a small Tibetan bowl, and as the reverberation of the tone faded, so did the cacophony in the room.

Aggie, Farrah, Marcia, Cheryl, and Holly had created a ritual to welcome back the alumni and honor those who had remained at the house to help them transition into The Next Step. Cardboard signs saying "Big Girl Chair" were placed on ten seats around the circle. Holly composed a short song, accompanied by Chandra on the keyboard. The chorus, where all were invited to join in, was, "Holding the torch, lighting the light, guiding us home through the night."

Gabriella and Kendra sat next to one another, holding hands. "That's beautiful, Holly," Gabriella said when they'd finished singing. "Just like a sorority song."

"Yes, you do all feel like my sisters," Aggie added with a soulful look at each committee member. She reached out and took Kendra's free hand.

"Or like a favorite camp song," Kendra added, gently disengaging from Aggie's grip.

"Who's in favor of makin' this the official Next Step house song?" Madigan asked, raising her hand high. Everyone followed.

"I'll type up the lyrics and give everyone a copy," Aggie offered. Shalese, Jenny, and Mab exchanged quick glances.

"We'll do it together," Analise piped up. "There's a music program I can download so we can even print out the notes—with Holly's permission and help, that is," she said, turning to Holly.

"Oh, my gosh, you guys," Holly said, blushing. "I'm really honored." Aggie blinked several times, but her face revealed nothing.

"Wonderful," Shalese said rubbing her hands together briskly. "Now, let's get down to business. Maren, you're on," she said.

Maren, an old hand by now at presentations, started the Nutrition class, and passed around healthy snacks on individual mini-plates.

"Sure do miss this place," Madigan said. "Don't nobody bring me snacks. Granny says three meals a day are 'nuff for anyone. Anyone my size, she means," Madigan added good-naturedly.

Chandra had offered to do the life management class next. She explained to the women the difference between banks and credit unions, with a pitch for supporting your local credit union, and the difference between credit cards and debit cards. The women were mesmerized when she took a pair of scissors and cut her Chase Visa card into pieces. "If you don't have it, don't spend it," was her advice.

During the short break, Doris tapped Madigan on the arm. "I'm sorry I never got back to you," she said. "My life was sort of falling apart when your phone call came, then I just lost track. You said something about a letter of condemnation? Someone mad at you?"

"No, they wrote me a compliment letter. I just wanted to share it with someone," Madigan said. There was a new and welcome vulnerability in her voice.

"Oh, you mean a letter of commendation? Well, hey, girl, that's just wonderful," Doris said, wrapping her arms around Madigan in a big hug. "Makes me feel good that you wanted to share that with me. I promise," Doris said, pulling back a little and looking Madigan in the eyes, "I'll be better at staying in touch."

After the break, Mab facilitated the formal check-in, go-around portion.

"I sign up at the JC next week for my first business class," Analise reported proudly.

"The doc let me assist in an eye surgery," Gabriella said, her eyes glittering. "It was so cool. I got to hold the eyelid back with this sharp hooked wire thing." This was greeted with *eeuw*, and *gross*, and a variety of other not-terribly-supportive sounds.

"The hardest thing I've had to do is report suspected elder abuse of one of our patients. She didn't want me to but I did it anyway. Just about broke my heart to see the fear in her eyes." There were murmurs of sympathy around the circle. "What I've learned here is never to turn my back on abuse."

The go-around reached Holly next. She patted her throat gently, gesturing that her emotions were all backed up. Her eyes brimmed with tears as she risked speaking. "I haven't felt this safe or cared for in . . ." she looked around the room, "well, I can't even remember when I felt like this. Thank you." Everyone there could relate.

Chandra spoke next. "The Mane Design in town said I can rent a space there in April. The lead hairdresser is going out on pregnancy leave and wants to refer all her clients to me. I'll be taking a brush-up course soon. I'm really excited about this," she shared.

"Okay, I'll go next," Madigan offered, even though it was her turn. "Living with my granny is great. We look after each other. And I'm learnin' mail sortin' at the post office—gettin' pretty good at it too," she said, pleased with herself. "Got me a letter of . . ." she paused, squinted, and looked at Doris.

"Commendation," Doris supplied.

"Yup. And I have me a boyfriend now," Madigan added with a huge grin and a little bow at the clamor her announcement brought about.

Beth was next. She sat with eyes downcast until Madigan tapped her on the leg and whispered, "Your turn."

A tear trickled down her cheek, and she wiped at it with her finger. Someone passed the tissue box, and she mumbled her thanks. "Don't get me wrong," she said after a moment, "I'm so happy for all of you. You're making a great adjustment to being back in the world. It's just that . . ." She stopped to blow her nose and wipe at another stray tear. "I can't seem to remember all the information. This is a much more advanced level of medical training than I thought, and my mind just bulks at the number of books, the hours of homework. I wonder if I'm too old to go back to school . . ." She let the thought trail off.

The women squirmed with desire to comfort, reassure, advise. The group rule was no cross-talk. It forced you to sit in your discomfort, tolerate your emotions, hold responsibility for yourself.

Doris spoke up. "I know about feeling like a failure," she said. "What I don't know, is why Paulina hasn't sent me packing yet. I nearly blew up her kiln. And the pots I've been throwing are so bottom-heavy, they could stop an elephant." The women giggled around the circle. "But I do seem to have an eye for glaze, so I guess I'll keep plugging away."

After all the women had checked in, Shalese asked for a volunteer to chair the 12-step meeting. Cheryl offered to tell her story of drug and alcohol use that had led her into a series of poor choices, bad men, and even worse consequences, and her recovery journey, which eventually landed her here, where she planned to turn her life around.

They ended the meeting with a prayer for the serenity to accept the things they could not change, the courage to change the things they could, and the wisdom to know which was which. "Amen to that," Madigan added.

Five extra chairs were squeezed in around the table, and dinner was like a big, noisy, family reunion. "We did it," Mab said, leaning toward Shalese. "We wanted to create a community, and just look around this table . . ." she gestured to encompass the women engrossed in food and conversation.

"*They* did it," Shalese said with a smile.

Later that evening, hugs and waves sent the alumni on their way, with extracted promises that they would return the following month.

"I'll be back on Monday," Mab said to Shalese and Jenny, as the residents worked their way back into the house. "Got some business to tend to at the Café. Call me if you need me before that," she said, and gave them each a quick hug.

"I'm just about done-in," Jenny said with a weary smile. She sat on the edge of their bed, pulling off her boots.

Shalese scooted up behind her and kneaded her neck and shoulders. "Feels good, doesn't it?" she said.

"Mmm," Jenny groaned her appreciation.

Shalese chuckled. "Actually, I meant the day—what we've created here. I think the reunion meeting was a success, don't you? The whole program . . ." she said, not waiting for Jenny to respond, "I think we're really on the right track here."

Jenny snuggled back against Shalese. "I think you've worked out the kinks."

"We've all worked out the kinks," Shalese said.

"No, I mean in my shoulders," Jenny said. She turned and wrapped her arms around Shalese's neck, done with conversation for the night.

"Mmm." This time it was Shalese's turn to groan her appreciation. As Jenny finished undressing, Shalese reached over and set the alarm. "Chamber of Commerce breakfast in the morning," she reminded Jenny. "I shouldn't be gone long." They crawled into bed, turned out the light, and found they weren't as tired as they'd thought.

Chapter 15

Early the next morning, Analise and Aggie were hard at work downloading the music program onto the computer. A page of Holly's lyrics and notes penciled in on a hand-drawn staff of music lay on the desk, a testament to their efforts so far this morning. A pot of tea, two cups with tea dregs, and a plate where once there were muffins sat on a nearby side table.

Shalese stuck her head in the office. "Everything okay in here?" she said.

"Hi," Aggie glanced up, all smiles. "I like this Finale program," she said, having just finished the installation. "I'd never considered composing music on the computer." Aggie and Analise worked companionably, shoulder-to-shoulder, fitting the right notes into each measure.

You'd think she'd have the grace to at least be embarrassed by her behavior after the marshmallow incident, Shalese thought. "It's pretty amazing," Shalese agreed.

"She's picking it up quickly," Analise said. "It took me months to figure out," she said staring at the screen. "Put a half rest there followed by a quarter note on G," she instructed.

"See you two later," Shalese said.

"Knock 'em dead at the Chamber of Commerce," Analise called as Shalese closed the door behind her.

In the dining room, a handful of women sat around the breakfast table finishing their coffee and tea. Jenny said, "I'm driving into town to exchange that laundry detergent."

"Thank goodness," Marcia spoke up. "Every time I even go out to the laundry room, I start sneezing." Several others voiced their agreement. "Unscented is fine with me," she said.

"Anyone want to ride along?" Jenny asked.

"I'd join you, but Gabbie is coming by to pick me up for lunch," Kendra said with a huge smile and a swagger. If she were a rooster, she'd be crowing about now. "Analise said something about needing some more tampons—you might check with her," Kendra advised.

Jenny walked down the hall to the office and stuck her head in. "Going into town," she said. "Anyone need anything?"

Analise looked up and stretched. "Let me grab my bag and coat," she said. "I'd love some time in town. Oh, wait," she looked from Jenny to Aggie, "we're mid-composition here . . ."

"No biggie," Aggie said. "Now that I have the hang of it, I can keep adding the notes. If I screw it up, we can fix it when you get back," she said with a bright smile. "And I know how much you love shopping," she said with a nod to Analise.

Analise looked at Jenny and shrugged. "Shall we go?"

Overriding her own discomfort with that plan, Jenny said, "Yeah, okay, I guess. We won't be long." That left one staff person at the house—Maren—and she was baking in the kitchen. Jenny paused for a moment, considered whether to ask Maren to check in on Aggie, but couldn't come up with a good enough reason without arousing suspicion—it was just a music program—so dismissed the idea. Without a password, no damage could be done. "Whatever," she mumbled to no one in particular. "Let's go."

They left through the front door, reset the lock, and headed down the porch steps. Jenny turned to Analise and double-checked her assumption. "This is safe, right? I mean, she doesn't have the password or account information or anything, does she?"

"Absolutely not," Analise said. "Shalese was real clear about that. Come on," Analise urged, "let's go shopping." In her enthusiasm, she skipped down the last step.

As Jenny approached the road, she honked her horn just as Gabriella was turning onto the gravel path that led to the house. The women waved a greeting to each other.

"So, Gabriella and Kendra, huh?" Analise said. "Who would have figured."

"I guess when you start examining your life, you find all sorts of things about yourself you didn't know," Jenny said.

Gabriella parked in front of the house, climbed the steps, pushed 1-s-t-e-p on the keypad, and let herself in. She pushed the reset button once inside. Instinctively, she headed for the kitchen, her heels *click, click, click*-ing down the hallway. If people were around on a Saturday morning, the kitchen was a safe bet. She found Maren making fresh-baked bread smells and chatting with Margot and Cheryl.

"Hey, welcome home," Maren grinned. "You look great," she added. "Want a cup of coffee?"

"Thanks. Hi everyone," Gabriella said. "No, thanks on the coffee, Maren. Just here to pick up Kendra for lunch. Happen to know where she is?"

"Probably upstairs," Margot said, "getting all spiffed up for you," she teased.

"Good," Gabriella teased back, "I'm well worth it." She left the kitchen.

Across the hall, the office door was ajar, the light on. Gabriella decided to poke her head in and say hello to Shalese before heading upstairs to round up Kendra. The room was empty, but the computer was on.

She opened the door wider and stepped in. Aggie, who had been bent over picking up something from the floor, sat up quickly, and spun around in the desk chair. Both women gasped in surprise.

"What 'cha doin'?" Gabriella asked.

"Oh, hey," Aggie said with a grin, "good to see you. C'mon in." She slapped shut a notebook she held in her hand and turned it face-down on the desk. She clicked a button that brought the music program back on the screen. "Working on Holly's song—take a look," she said, scooting her chair aside.

"Amazing," Gabriella said, looking over Aggie's shoulder. "You think you could teach me how to do that?"

Before Aggie could answer, Kendra called out from the hallway, "Gabbie, you in there?"

Gabriella gave a little squeal and stepped into the hallway where she was engulfed in a big hug that took not only her breath away, but also any memory of the previous moment. "Hey, pookie," she purred, "you're looking mighty good." She nuzzled Kendra's neck.

"Get a room, already," Cheryl joked, as she pressed past them in the hallway.

"Good idea," Kendra cracked. "Let's go," she said, taking Gabriella's hand and leading her towards the front door.

"Have fun you two," Maren said with a wink before disappearing back into the kitchen.

"Plan to," Gabriella called back over her shoulder.

Just before noon, Maren heard Jenny's car pull into the side lot. From the kitchen window, she saw Jenny and Analise loaded with shopping bags, heading toward the back door. She swung it open for them as they struggled with their bags.

"No such thing as a little shopping trip with Jenny," Analise joked as she set her bags on the countertop.

"Maren, there was a special on salmon, so I picked some up. Did you already have plans for tonight's dinner?" Jenny asked as she slipped the fish into the refrigerator.

"I was just about to wear out my finger paging through the cookbook for something that sounded good," Maren said. "Salmon will be perfect."

"With risotto?" Analise pleaded.

"And fresh, steamed veggies?" Jenny added.

"Sheesh, you two are impossible," Maren said good-naturedly.

Shortly after one o'clock, Shalese drove up the drive and parked in the side lot next to Jenny's car. She turned at the sound of Gabriella's car as it pulled up front. After a quick smooch, Kendra got out, blew a kiss to Gabriella and waved to Shalese as she headed toward the front door. Gabriella waved from the driver's side and gave a quick honk of her horn before heading back down the gravel driveway. Shalese returned the wave with the shake of her head, remembering those carefree days of new love. What was that—about a million years ago? She chuckled to herself.

Anxious to share the result of the Chamber breakfast with Jenny, she trotted up the back steps. On the top step, she lost her footing and grabbed at the door handle to keep from toppling. The handle turned and the door swung open. With her free arm, she wind-milled herself upright and caught her breath. Miffed about the unlocked door, she vowed to bring it up over lunch. They couldn't afford to get lax, even though they hadn't been plagued by anymore incidents of harassment.

She walked down the hall toward the kitchen, where she heard Jenny engaged in lively conversation with Maren and Analise.

"Hey sweetie, pull up a chair," Jenny said in greeting. She gave Shalese a peck on the cheek.

"How'd the brunch go?" Maren asked. "Still hungry? You're just in time for lunch."

Shalese caught them up on the Chamber's offer to set up a JC scholarship and do some publicity for The Next Step. "That will make a little less work for you," she said to Analise. "They offered to create a new brochure for us," she said, excitedly. "They're sending a photographer out to take some pictures, along with fake residents, so we can maintain confidentiality," she chuckled.

Shalese changed topics. "Someone remind me to address the unlocked door at lunch. I just walked in without having to use the password."

"I haven't been out of the kitchen, but as far as I know," Maren said, "Gabriella and Kendra were the last ones to leave the house this morning. I know love can make you stupid, but we should remind them."

As the women were filing into the dining room for lunch, Shalese caught up with Kendra. "Were you and Gabriella the last ones to leave the house this morning?"

"We left around ten o'clock. Why?" Kendra asked.

"Just a general heads-up. The back door was unlocked and the alarm unarmed when I came in around one."

"I got back the same time as you, but I came in the front door. And this morning we left through the front door as well," Kendra said. " I remember setting the alarm," she added.

"Oh, okay," Shalese said, puzzled, and followed Kendra into the dining room.

"Analise, did you two finish Holly's song this morning?" Shalese asked as she took a seat next to Jenny.

"Oh, Jenny and I went shopping. Aggie was going to finish it up. We can take a look at it after lunch," Analise said.

"Where is Aggie, by the way?" Jenny asked looking around the table. Several women shrugged.

"Aggie was in there by herself?" Shalese asked, her voice registering alarm.

Analise looked first at Jenny, then Shalese. "She was just working on the music . . ."

Shalese jumped up, left the dining room, jogged down the hallway, and flung open the office door. Analise and Jenny were hot on her heels..

"Shit!" Shalese said. The computer was off, the file drawers open, papers tossed about the office, the shelves in disarray, and the lone, hand-written sheet of music sat neglected on the corner of the desk.

Analise pushed past Shalese, booted up the computer, and found the most recently opened page—the house's financial statement—which showed a recent transfer of funds, in the amount of $100,000 to an account unconnected to The Next Step.

"Holy cow," Jenny gasped. She locked wide eyes with Shalese.

"She hacked it," Analise said, shaking her head in disbelief.

Shalese smacked her forehead and sank into a nearby chair. "Can you find the account?" she asked Analise.

"No, it's not traceable," Analise said. "But it's the weekend, so I might be able to cancel the transaction on our end, even though it was electronically sent." She hovered over the keyboard, screen pages flicked on and off the screen.

"Whew!" Analise expelled her breath. "I think I caught it. I won't know for sure until Monday, when I can verify the balance activity." She leaned back hard in her chair.

"Does anyone know where Aggie might have gone?" Jenny asked, looking at the group of women huddled in the office doorway. Blank faces looked back at her.

"Better call Mab," Jenny said to Shalese.

Chapter 16

"Damn, she embezzled from us?" Mab said on the other end of the phone.

"Well, she attempted to anyway," Shalese said, and explained how Analise had tried to curb the damage. She glanced at Jenny who was mouthing something. "I think Jenny wants to know if you can come home," Shalese said, checking with Jenny, who gave an affirmative nod.

"Yeah, I guess so," Mab said. "I'm not sure what we can do until Monday, but I'd probably feel better if I was there with you all."

"I know we'd feel better," Shalese said.

"What will we do if she actually comes back? I mean, we're taking a leap of faith here . . ." Mab's voice trailed off.

"You know how lame that sounds, right?" Shalese said, and listened to the chuckle on the other end.

"See you in a while," Mab said, and hung up.

Shalese turned to Jenny and said, "She's on her way."

"Who do we even call? To whom would we report something like this?" Jenny said, her voice tense. "We have the sheriff put out an APB, and we might wind up with our house burned to the ground. I just know somehow Florence is behind this. God, I feel so unsafe," she said, and nestled into Shalese's open arms.

The doorbell rang at the far end of the hall, and one of the women answered it. Shalese and Jenny heard footsteps coming toward the office, and a moment later Cheryl tapped on the office door and stuck her head in.

"Some guy from the vineyard down the road is at the front door," she said.

"Lefty?" Jenny ventured.

"I don't know," Cheryl said, sounding confused. "He asked to talk to the owner."

Shalese and Jenny followed Cheryl back down the hallway to the door. A Hispanic man stood, dressed in overalls and a blue work shirt, hat in hand, and an expensive leather coat draped over his arm.

"I'm Shalese DuBois. What can I do for you?"

"My name is Juan Gomez," the man said, with no trace of an accent. "I am the manager of the vineyard—"

"I thought Lefty was the manager of the vineyard," Shalese interrupted.

"No, ma'am. Lefty no longer works there," Juan said. "One of our workers found this expensive-looking coat just off the road at the intersection of your drive. He thought perhaps it belonged to one of the women up here."

"Lefty is gone?" Shalese said, shaking her head in disbelief. "You know what that means, right?" she said to Jenny.

"That *is* Aggie's coat. She must've dropped it on the run," Jenny said to Shalese.

Juan looked at Shalese and then Jenny. He shrugged and held the coat out to them. "The coat?" he said.

"Oh, I'm sorry," Jenny apologized. "Thank you so much. Yes, it belongs to one of our residents, and it was so thoughtful of your worker to return it. Please thank him for us."

"Lefty's gone?" Shalese said again.

"Nice to meet you," Jenny said to Juan. She tugged Shalese backwards, and closed the door.

Shalese's eyes looked glazed. "They're in cahoots," she mumbled. "Mab knew it. She said something wasn't right about that man. I should have listened to her."

"Shalese, get a grip!" Jenny shouted, shaking her by the shoulders. "I can't have you falling apart on me now. At least wait until Mab gets here," she said. "Oh my God, that sounded so stupid," Jenny said, and burst into a fit of uncontrollable giggles, until tears streamed down her cheeks. "Like, 'just wait until your father gets home,'" she sputtered, consumed again by laughter.

It was Shalese's turn to look alarmed. Cheryl, Kendra, and Holly approached cautiously. "Everything okay here?" Kendra asked.

"It will be," Jenny said. She took a deep breath and wiped her eyes. "At least, as soon as Mab gets here." At this, she broke into another peal of giggles and snorts, as Shalese led her upstairs.

"We'll explain all this over dinner," Shalese called over her shoulder to the bewildered trio.

When Mab arrived shortly before six o'clock, she, Jenny, and Shalese met in the office for a powwow to decide how much the women needed to know. They didn't want to raise undue alarm if all this could be settled quietly on Monday. Perhaps no harm, beyond a wild breach of trust, had been done.

"Let's just lay out the facts first, then our suspicions," Mab suggested. "Then we can reassure them that whatever goes down, we've got them covered. They're safe."

"Yeah, I'm sure they'll feel reassured," Jenny said with a mirthless chuckle.

Aggie's chair was empty at dinner. Shalese waited for the women to finish eating, then stood, tapped her water glass, and cleared her throat.

"If I could have your attention," she asked redundantly, as all eyes were on her. "Almost two years ago," she began, "a friend of Florence's—our original benefactress—named Janelle, who we believed was connected to the Women's Studies department at the junior college, invited Jenny and me to a professional business women's . . . ah . . . gathering—"

"Go ahead, say the word," Mab teased, bouncing her eyebrows.

Shalese rolled her eyes, and mumbled, "Soiree. You happy?"

Mab chuckled. "Still cracks me up," she said. "You, at a soiree."

Shalese continued. "Neither Jenny nor myself met Janelle in person. I remember her saying something on the phone that unnerved me. When I asked her how she got my name, she said she was doing data collection on grant sites, and my name 'came up.'" She glanced at Jenny, who nodded encouragement. "When I expressed concern over the lack of privacy, she said, 'Oh, you know the Internet—nothing's sacred anymore.'"

Shalese stepped behind her chair, and leaned her hands on the backrest. "It wasn't just what she said," she continued, "but how she said it—sort of calloused, cold, dismissive. I remember it sent shivers up my spine." She paused a moment and adjusted her shoulders, as if those same shivers were working their way up her back right then.

"Anyway, we forgot about Janelle, until she vanished without a trace, at the same time as Florence—Florence having taken all of our money with her. We had reason to believe Janelle was connected to

Florence's above-the-law group of *elite*." Shalese gave them the *Reader's Digest* version of the story. She made a circular gesture with her hand. "Fast forward to interviewing our newest batch of residents—Aggie, in particular," she said, pacing the length of the table. The women were mesmerized and turned in their seats to follow her visually.

"Each of you brings special skills, in addition to the challenges you face, to this recovery house. These skills are what we hope to build on to help enhance your life once you leave the program. Aggie was proficient on the computer, understood finances, had done some bookkeeping, et cetera." Shalese stopped pacing, took a deep breath, and let it out slowly. She sent Jenny a pleading look. Jenny stood and continued the story. Shalese walked back to her seat and sat down heavily.

"At that time," Jenny said, "we thought Analise would be leaving. We counted on her for our computer needs," she said, smiling at Analise. "She was sort of our right-hand, our Girl Friday, and we were anticipating a big loss at graduation. I guess it was selfish of us," Jenny looked chagrinned, "but we hoped that Aggie could sort of pick up where Analise left off and save us from having to hire someone for that position." She looked at Shalese and said, "I don't remember exactly, the conversation you had with Aggie . . ."

From her chair, Shalese said, "At the graduation party we were talking about information gathering on the computer, and I said I was amazed at what is accessible. Her reply was that if you know how to search the web, 'nothing's sacred anymore.'" Shalese shook her head slowly. "Shoulda listened to Granny," she said softly. "Had the exact same effect on me as when Janelle said it. But I dismissed it," Shalese said. Her shoulders drooped, and exhaustion wore itself on her body like bad fitting clothes. "I knew something was wrong, and I dismissed it."

Mab reached a pudgy hand out to Shalese and rested it on her shoulder. "That's why we talk in group about listening to your intuition," she said, looking around the table. "Even when you're smart, and strong, and experienced," she looked at Shalese, "sometimes you forget that intuition is a survival gift." Shalese tilted her head in acknowledgement.

"So," Jenny took up the story again, "when Shalese became suspicious that Janelle and Aggie were the same person, we figured that somehow Florence was still trying to exert control over the house, and that Aggie was probably the link. If Aggie could get close to our financials, she could potentially take back the money—the one hundred thousand dollars—that Florence left behind. That's why, earlier this week, Aggie was relieved of anything financial that had to do with the computer."

"We didn't think having her download a music program would be dangerous," Analise chimed in. She'd been fidgeting in her chair, dealing with her own feelings of guilt and gullibility. "I'm sorry, you guys," she said, looking at Shalese, Jenny, and then Mab. "I should never have left her alone in there."

Jenny waved her apology aside. "Some of you saw the mess the office was in when we checked earlier today," Jenny said. "It looks like Aggie tried to transfer funds, got interrupted by Gabriella, and bolted. We won't know if she was successful until Monday, when we can check with the bank," she said in summary.

"Regardless," Shalese spoke again, "the house is safe. We have back-up funds so we can continue operating, even if something like this happened. You have nothing to worry about," she said. "You're safe."

"Except that we trusted someone here at the house who wasn't what she appeared to be," Marcia said, looking around the table. "How do we know there aren't other *plants*?" she asked.

Mab looked from Shalese to Jenny, and then said, "I suppose we should tell you that we have some concerns about Lefty—the former vineyard manager—who seems to have moved on." Several women groaned, others sighed. "Seems he may have been a comrade of Florence's as well. I saw him once, from a distance, down in the city. His good-ole-boy disguise almost fooled me, but that intuition thing we're talking about is what made me suspicious. That," she amended, "and the fact they both limped with the same foot."

"The good news is, that it seems they're on the run—again," Shalese said. "I think maybe we can breathe easy now."

"What about the judge?" Chandra asked. "Something about her I just didn't trust—talk about intuition."

"Let me call her chambers on Monday and see what happens," Mab volunteered. "Anyone else?" she asked, and scanned the circle of faces. Uneasiness filled the room like a bad smell. "All right, then.

We'll keep you up on any changes. Don't get discouraged, okay?" she said. *Yeah, right*, she thought.

Chapter 17

The next day was the Monday before Thanksgiving. Even with holiday preparations well underway, there was tension in the air. In the best of times, women who'd been abused had trouble trusting—and these were not the best of times.

Morning session had not yet begun, and several women were gathered informally in the group room. "I hope we can watch the game on Thanksgiving," Holly said.

"Once a guy, always a guy," Marcia said under her breath.

"Marcia!" Margot said, jumping to Holly's defense. "Holly is not a guy—she *used* to be a guy."

"Yeah, I like sports," Cheryl chimed in. "You gonna call me a guy, too?" she said, copping an attitude.

Holly raised her hands. "Thank you both, but I don't need anyone to defend me. I'm used to fielding insensitive, uneducated statements like that—"

"Who are you calling stupid?" Marcia said, her voice rising in pitch.

"Whoa," Shalese said as she entered the room. "Time out." She looked at the group of women, sitting there hostile and defensive, ready to pounce on each other. "What's going on here? We are not each other's enemy."

"I don't know what to believe, or who to trust," Marcia said in a small voice. She turned to Holly and said, "I mean, how can you be one thing, then just become something opposite? How do I even know that's real?" she asked.

"You mean, like you used to be a murderer, and now you're not anymore?" Cheryl said, fanning the flames. "Why should we believe that?"

"Stop!" Shalese intervened. "Let's just take a breath and use this as an opportunity to learn something." She turned to Holly and asked, "Would you be willing to share some of your process with Marcia, so she can understand a little more about your journey?"

Cheryl leaned forward. "The antidote to ignorance is education," she said, challenging Marcia with her words. Shalese's eyes narrowed in warning, and Cheryl sat back in her chair. Marcia looked abashed.

Holly turned to Marcia and asked, "Are you even interested?"

"I guess," Marcia said tentatively. "I've just never known anyone who did what you did," she said. "I don't really understand it."

"I knew when I was five years old that I wasn't like other boys. I didn't even think of myself as a boy, which really upset my father. My mother was more supportive, and even let me wear skirts to school in the second grade, after we'd moved to a new school district." Holly resettled herself on the couch, unconsciously holding a pillow in front of her, with her arms wrapped tightly around it.

"When my father found out, he beat me. It was pretty awful for a while," Holly said. She stopped and dropped her shoulders, which had been sneaking up toward her earlobes at the memory. "I was at an alternative school, and the principal actually agreed with my mother, that I appeared to be socialized more as a girl, than a boy. It didn't seem to make any difference to the kids, so I cross-dressed all the way until junior high." She glanced at Marcia, who sat transfixed.

"My father divorced my mother. This was all just too much for him. To this day, we haven't spoken." Holly paused, and gathered her thoughts. "Junior high and high school were hell. At sixteen, I tried to kill myself—I'll spare you the details.

"When I was nineteen, I started working with a therapist to prepare to make the official change, you know—to get rid of the dangling particles that had nothing to do with who I was, and replace them with what I should have had at birth. I had the corrective surgery when I turned twenty-one.

"I truly believe that if I'd been deprived of this transition, I wouldn't be alive today. I mean, imagine if you were forced to live as if you were a man for your lifetime." She looked deeply into the faces of the women that showed nothing but compassion back—even Marcia, whose eyes brimmed with tears.

"So, when someone says, 'once a guy, always a guy,' I say, no— never a guy, always a woman. It just took a while to get everything congruent."

"I'm sorry," Marcia said, and a tear slid down her cheek. "I didn't know."

"That's one of the gifts we can give each other here," Shalese said. "Knowledge."

Analise, Maren, and Chandra had quietly drifted into the room and found seats while Holly was telling her story. "And acceptance," Maren added.

"And forgiveness," Analise said.

"Sorry about that once-a-murderer crack," Cheryl said to Marcia, who smiled and nodded.

Jenny, Mab, and the remaining residents had filtered in. Mab stood, and all attention went to her.

"Let's all take a deep breath and shift gears," she suggested. "Before we start this morning's session, I want to update you. I just phoned Judge Thistlewaite's chambers to check out our suspicion that she may have been part of Florence's network, The Avenging Angels. Seems the good judge has been 'called away' on a family emergency of indefinite length. No forwarding information. They'll be replacing her soon." Mab gave a what-can-you-do shrug and sat down.

"Oh, man," Shalese groaned. Jenny just shook her head, resigned.

"Looks like we may have dodged the bullet for now—unless you have a report for us, Analise?" Mab said.

"I spoke with someone just before I came in, about the fraudulent electronic transfer of funds from our account over the weekend, and explained my attempt to retrieve and correct it. They're on it. Looks like no harm done," she said with a smile. There was a collective sigh of relief in the room.

Jenny frowned and shook her head slowly. "I'm sorry, but I'm afraid it's not that simple," she said. "These people are insidious. We may be safe for now, but they'll be back—when we least expect it."

Shalese and Mab exchanged a look, but neither could think of a response to that bit of truth.

It was with a certain amount of trepidation that they marshaled on through the day, trying for some semblance of normal. "Safe for now" wasn't quite enough to relax into the holiday spirit.

As Thursday approached, however, the mood began to shift. The graduates were expected back for the first holiday with the new residents, and everyone looked forward to another reunion. Maren chose a large turkey and bought two extra turkey legs, remembering Madigan's penchant for that part of the bird. Marcia worked with her on the menu and found recipes on-line for sweet potato soufflé, pecan and pumpkin pies, and a fruit punch.

Margot and Holly offered to decorate and spent the better part of Wednesday gathering large pinecones and making turkey place-settings from them. Holly arranged gourds, pumpkins, and some colorful leaves as a centerpiece. Margot opened a fresh stash of tapered candles and put them in star-shaped glass holders on either side of the centerpiece.

"Five stars!" Holly said with a huge grin, stepping back to appraise their work.

"Six," Maren corrected, counting the candles, three on each side of center.

"No, I meant—"

"Oh, I get it," Maren chuckled.

Music drifted from the group room as Chandra pecked out the tune to their new house song, which Holly had named *Guiding Us Home*, on the keyboard. Analise had converted it to sheet music and printed out copies for everyone.

By Thanksgiving morning, all worries from earlier in the week, all thoughts of Aggie, Florence, Lefty, and the judge, had been set on a shelf—available for retrieval, but no longer in the middle of the room to be stumbled over.

Margot lit the candles. The faces around the table glowed with a softness and vulnerability most of the women there had never before experienced. This was a family—a chosen one—and no one was going to reach across the table and slap them, or yank them out of their chair and throw them against the wall. No one was going to scream obscenities at them, or say soul-destroying things that could never be taken back. And for this, they were grateful. For this, they gave thanks, privately, internally.

Madigan stood and tapped her water glass as she had seen Shalese do and grinned hugely as all eyes came to rest on her. She cleared her throat officiously and said, "As your president of this here *alumni* club," she said effortlessly, and the women broke into applause, "I say we do a go-'round and tell everyone what we're thankful for." The women nodded their heads and murmured their agreement. "Me first," Madigan continued. "I'm thankful for whole bunches of things—"

"Make it quick. The soufflé will fall if we don't serve it soon," Maren joked, and others chuckled. Madigan made a sassy little *humph* sound.

"Mostly, I'm thankful for people who cared enough about me to teach me grown-up stuff—like I can say alumni now, without soundin' it out as I go, and my supervisor said my resume was impressive for someone who'd never worked before, and—"

"Next," Chandra shouted playfully.

"Oh, all right then," Madigan said good-naturedly.

Chandra spoke next. "I'm grateful that you guys saw more in me than I could see in myself," she said in an uncharacteristically soft voice.

"I'll go next," Gabriella said. "I'm grateful that you all helped me see myself more clearly and the ways that I'd been living life as one big compromise."

"I'm thankful that I'm accepted here for who I am, who I've always been," Holly shared. "Even by Marcia," she said with a smile and a wink in Marcia's direction.

They went full circle, ending with Maren who said, "I've never been so happy in my life, and I'm truly thankful for that. Now let's eat." She handed the carving knife to Shalese, who sliced off one turkey leg first, and called for Madigan's plate.

The women chatted amicably through dinner, their conversation sprinkled with an occasional twitter of laugher or a hearty guffaw. A few chose to take a walk after the meal, most reassembled in the group room to continue their conversations. Later, over pie and coffee, Chandra played the melody to *Guiding Us Home* on the keyboard, and they sang in makeshift harmony. Holly blushed with the pleasure of hearing her composition come alive.

On one sofa, Shalese and Jenny sat together holding hands, smiles on their faces, comfortable in their home with their new family.

Across the room, Gabriella and Kendra shared an overstuffed chair, arms entwined, whispering quietly to each other amidst the din around them.

"It's getting late," Shalese said in a low voice to Jenny. "I'm not sure how to break up this party. No one seems to want to leave," she chuckled quietly.

Madigan, who was sitting next to them and had overheard, stood up, clapped her hands, and said, "Okay, y'all. Time to go home. Get your bags, get your coats—let's go, let's go," she said, making hustling gestures with her hands.

"I don't know how we run this place without you," Jenny joked to Madigan.

"I been wonderin' that myself," Madigan said with a shake of her head.

"Happy Thanksgiving," the women called to each other as they left. "See you at Christmas."

"Christmas?" Shalese and Jenny said, looking at one another.

Chapter 18

There was no getting around it, winter had landed in northern California. Gray, foggy mornings slogged their way into gray, foggy afternoons with a backdrop of rain pelting the earth, day after day. Mud sluiced down the hills from the vineyards. The unpaved roads became brown mush, nearly impossible to navigate.

Analise was slumped in her chair behind the computer. She glanced out the window and frowned. "I don't know why I didn't just register on-line like a normal student," she complained to Shalese, who was bent over the day's mail spread across the desk.

"I think it's important for you to meet the dean of the business department, let him know who you are," she said, without looking up, "and that you're a serious student." Shalese ripped open an envelope, and separated the contents. "Besides, you'll be sort of an ambassador for The Next Step. Won't hurt that they know we have an educational fund for our residents and scholarships from the Chamber of Commerce. Might even generate some referrals," she said.

Analise cocked her head to one side and said, "You never stop, do you?"

"What do you mean?" Shalese asked.

"Hustling for the house, doing outreach," Analise said. "Do you ever take a break?"

"Can't afford to," Shalese said. She scooped a bunch of paper off the desk and into the recycle bin. "Then, while you're there," she continued their conversation, "you can go on over to the registrar's and sign up for your class."

"Easy for you to say," Analise mumbled. "It's cold and pouring down rain out there. I'm still not very comfortable with a stick-shift, and I don't know where the different buildings are on the JC campus." There was a pout in Analise's voice that caused Shalese to glance over at her.

"Analise . . ." Shalese said, waiting until they made eye contact. "You're scared, aren't you?" she said gently.

"I may look all competent and stuff," Analise said, "but I don't know how to do this. It's been years since I've been in school, and that was boarding school—my parents paid to have someone else handle the details. Yeah, I'm scared," she admitted.

Shalese leaned back in her chair, stretched her arms up over her head, and said, "You know, I'm about ready for that break you say I never take. This paperwork is driving me crazy. How about if I go with you?"

Analise broke into a smile. "You'd do that for me?"

"Only if you let me drive," Shalese said, returning a smile.

An hour later, they were sitting across an oak desk from Joshua Bordeaux, dean of the business department at the junior college.

Analise didn't think he looked like a Joshua Bordeaux, although she couldn't have told you exactly what such a person should look like—more that he looked like, perhaps, the ghost of a Joshua Bordeaux, with pale skin, watery brown eyes, and limpid blond hair, thinning at the top. Even his clothes were specter-like—a white linen shirt, pale gray slacks, a muted mauve tie, and white suede sneakers. When he'd offered his hand, she'd shaken it, reluctantly. She half expected her hand to pass right on through his. Analise glanced at Shalese, who was engaged in conversation with the dean.

"Well, that's an admirable program you women have yourselves there," Dean Bordeaux said, with a light Cajun accent—New Orleans, Analise guessed. "I'm quite impressed with the financial incentive for your residents to finish their education. In fact," he said, sitting back in his swivel chair and clasping his delicate hands over his frail midsection, "I'd like to put you in touch with the chancellor of the school. He should know about you." Dean Bordeaux nodded his head in agreement with himself.

"And you, Ms. Foxworth," he nodded at Analise, "I'm quite impressed with your desire to take charge of your life. Very good, very good," he said, nodding vigorously.

Analise resisted the urge to reach out, grab his head, and stabilize it. "Thank you, sir," she said instead, "I look forward to your program."

As soon as Shalese and Analise had cleared the building, Analise said, "Is it just me or did he—"

"Make your skin crawl?" Shalese interrupted. "Sure hope your professor has a little more—"

"Life force?" Analise finished for her.

"That's it, that's it," Shalese said in a southern drawl, nodding her head vigorously. They both chuckled as they raised their umbrellas against the rain and cut across campus to the registrar's office.

That evening, when the residents gathered for dinner, Jenny stood to make an announcement. "We want to celebrate Analise's registering for a business class at the JC today," she said, handing Analise a heavy, rectangular box wrapped in tissue paper. The women applauded as Analise stood to receive the gift.

"Oh my gosh," Analise gasped, tearing the paper off and removing the lid. "I didn't know how I was going to afford this," she said of the required textbook that ran just over one hundred dollars. "Thank you so much," she said. Her eyes brimmed with tears of appreciation.

"You're welcome," said Shalese, "but this is actually from the Chamber of Commerce. They want to make sure that if any of you want to return to school after you graduate from here, you have the means to purchase the books necessary."

"Wow, what a program," Farrah said. "Maybe I really can give up dancing when I get out of here." Each woman, in her own way, embraced the possibility for a brighter future than she'd imagined.

For Shalese and Jenny, it was daring to trust that they had put something in motion that would be sustained over time, something that would bring confidence to women who had been dealt a bad hand, and encourage them not to fold under the pressure of circumstance.

Across town, a frail-looking man in a big chair behind a large mahogany desk lifted the receiver from the phone and dialed an extended series of numbers.

"Joshua," a woman's brittle voice answered on the other end, "do you have any idea what time it is here?"

"Sorry, Flo," he replied, his voice tinged with barely suppressed excitement, "I just couldn't wait one moment longer. Your back-up plan worked. The DuBois woman brought her protégé—the one Mary Agnes said was being groomed to work with their finances—and enrolled her in the business program," Joshua reported.

"Well done," Florence said. "With the junior college scholarship fund we set up through our connection in the Chamber of Commerce, it was only a matter of time," she said, sounding quite self-satisfied.

"We'll have access to their funds soon and then I'll wire your money to your account," Joshua said.

"I am disappointed," Florence said, "that our cryptic little game of intimidation and distraction didn't buy us enough time for Mary Agnes to do her work without raising suspicion."

"Ah, well—live and learn," Joshua said. "That was fun, though, wasn't it? RETURN—brilliant, if I do say so myself. Oh," Joshua added as an afterthought, "I spoke with Sidney the other day. He intimated that we'll have no further use of the women once the money is returned. I thought I'd run that by you—"

"*Never* waste a good resource," Florence said cutting him short. Her voice, sharp and hard-edged, made Joshua wince. "But they do need to be punished for all they've put me through." Florence grabbed her strand of pearls and squeezed them, the way one would squeeze the life out of a viper. "You'll have to dream up something special for them. I'm counting on you, Joshua."

Author Bio

Jo Lauer is a psychotherapist by day. She is the published author of numerous articles, essays, and stories. Best Laid Plans is her first novel. She lives with her stuffed raven, Loudly, in Santa Rosa, CA.

You can find out more about her by visiting her website at: www.jolauer.com.

Made in the USA
Charleston, SC
13 August 2013